BLACK OPS
AMERICAN JIHAD

BLACK OPS
AMERICAN JIHAD

WILLIAM W. JOHNSTONE
WITH FRED AUSTIN

PINNACLE BOOKS
Kensington Publishing Corp.
http://www.kensingtonbooks.com

PINNACLE BOOKS are published by

Kensington Publishing Corp.
850 Third Avenue
New York, NY 10022

All Kensington Titles, Imprints, and Distributed Lines are available at special quantity discounts for bulk purchases for sales promotions, premiums, fund-raising, and educational or institutional use. Special book excerpts or customized printings can also be created to fit specific needs. For details, write or phone the office of the Kensington special sales manager: Kensington Publishing Corp., 850 Third Avenue, New York, NY 10022, attn: Special Sales Department, Phone: 1-800-221-2647.

Pinnacle and the P logo Reg. U.S. Pat. & TM Off.

First Pinnacle Books Printing: May 2006

10 9 8 7 6 5 4 3 2 1

Printed in the United States of America

PROLOGUE

Sugarloaf Ranch, Colorado, 1928

"I'm not sure I can still do this," Smoke Jensen said. "That's asking a lot for an eighty-two-year-old man."

"Mr. Jensen, you are the most fit eighty-two-year-old I've ever seen," Billy Love said. "And I think movie audiences all across the country would enjoy seeing a real gunfighter, instead of Tom Mix and the others like him."

"Oh, I enjoy a good Tom Mix movie," Smoke said as he pulled his pistol and checked the loads in the cylinder chambers. "And I enjoy a good Zane Grey novel."

"I've often wondered just how accurate those were," Love said. "I mean, if you would believe the movies, there were all these clean-living, hard-riding, fast-shooting cowboys just riding around the West to put things right."

Sally Jensen laughed. "You have just described my man," she said.

"Now, Sally, don't go building me up. I swear, you are as bad as Libbie Custer. To hear her talk, George Custer was the greatest military genius since Alexander the Great," Smoke said. He put his pistol back in his holster, pulled it out a couple of times to test it, then looked over at the newsreel producer.

"Are you ready?" Love asked.

Smoke stretched his right arm out in front of him, palm down, and put a steel washer on the back of his hand. "I'm ready," he said.

"Wait until you hear me say action," Love said. "Then make your draw." He looked over at the cameraman. "Roll camera. Speed. Slate it."

A man, holding a small blackboard on which were printed the words SMOKE JENSEN FAST DRAW, stepped in front of the camera, opened, and snapped shut an arm.

"And, action," Love said.

As soon as the words were out of his mouth, Smoke turned his hand, allowing the washer to fall. As the washer was falling, Smoke drew his pistol and shot at a tin can, sitting on a fence post. The bullet sent the can flying, at about the same time the washer landed with a clang, on a pie pan below.

There were several ranch hands gathered around to watch, and they applauded.

"Fantastic!" Love said excitedly.

"You were wonderful," Sally said, kissing her husband of over fifty years on the cheek.

"It wasn't bad for an old geezer, was it?" Smoke replied with a broad smile. "Of course, nobody was shooting back at me."

"And I imagine that's happened a few times," Love said.

"More times than I care to remember."

"Mr. Jensen, I know this is just a newsreel, but I have some friends in the movie industry. Suppose when I get back to Hollywood I talk to a few of them? I think a picture about your life . . . I mean a real picture, would be great."

"A real picture?"

"We would have to doctor it up a little for dramatic effect," Love admitted.

Smoke shook his head. "No, thanks."

"Well, if you ever change your mind, let me know, will you?"

"I will."

A slender young man came over to them. "Mr. Love, it looks like there might be some weather coming in. I'd like to take off before it gets here."

"All right, Paul," Love said. "Tell the camera crew to get their equipment aboard and I'll be right there."

"Yes, sir."

The young man walked away and said something to the cameraman. The cameraman nodded, and he and his assistant started striking the equipment and taking it to the closed-cabin monoplane that sat about fifty yards away. When the newsreel producer, Billy Love, had made arrangements to come interview and film the legendary gunfighter he learned, happily, that Smoke Jensen had a landing strip right on his ranch.

"Mr. Jensen, it has been an honor and a privilege to meet you," Love said, sticking his hand out. "This will be in theaters all across the country within three weeks. I thank you, sir."

Over at the airplane the assistant to the cameraman stuck a crank into the side of the engine cowling. He began cranking, and as he did so, Smoke could hear a high-pitched whine beginning to build up from the inertia starter.

"Clear!" the pilot called.

There was a chirp as the inertia starter was engaged, then a cough, and then a roar as the engine started. The propeller began spinning in a silver blur.

"Good-bye," Love called as he hurried to the plane and got in.

The plane turned, sending a blast of wind behind it, kicking up bits of recently mowed grass and tiny grains of sand. For a moment Sally's skirt fluttered in the prop wash as the pilot swung the plane around, nose to the wind. Smoke put his arm around her and pulled her to him as they watched.

The pilot opened the throttle to full, the plane started down the long, sod strip, gathering speed until the tail lifted from the ground. A moment later the plane was airborne. It climbed to a couple hundred feet, then made a 180-degree turn and came back over the field. Smoke and Sally waved up at it as it passed overhead, then began climbing much higher until it gradually disappeared in the West.

Later that evening, Sally sat on the sofa beside Smoke. "Happy birthday," she said.

Smoke chuckled. "I thought we agreed to quit counting them after I turned eighty."

"You can't stop time, Old Man," Sally teased. "Besides, Mildred baked a cake, just for you."

"I hope she's not going to put all the candles on it. It would be a fire hazard," Smoke said.

Sally pointed to their six-year-old grandson, who was sitting on the floor, playing with a toy airplane. "There's someone who won't have to worry about counting birthdays for a while."

"I guess not," Smoke said. "You know, I was just thinking, watching that airplane take off, getting my picture taken for a motion picture show. There have been a lot of changes in our world, Sally."

"There sure have been."

"I wonder what the world will be like when young Pearlie there is my age."

"Whatever it is, I hope he doesn't lose touch with the past. Maybe you should have taken Mr. Love up on his offer to make a picture about your life."

Smoke chuckled. "No, I don't think so."

"I was thinking of Pearlie," Sally said. "And his grandchildren," she added. "I want them to know about you. You've led a remarkable life, Smoke. Your descendants deserve to know about that."

"Yeah, well, a movie that's been 'doctored for dramatic effect' sure isn't the way to pass my legacy on."

"The cake is ready," Mildred called.

"Oh boy, cake!" Pearlie said, getting up from the floor. "Can I have some, Mama?"

"Well, you'll have to ask your grandpa about that," Mildred said. "It's his birthday cake."

"Grandpa, can I have some of your birthday cake?" Pearlie asked.

"Well, I reckon so," Smoke said. "I mean, if your grandson asked you for some of your birthday cake, wouldn't you give it to him?"

Pearlie laughed. "Grandpa, it's going to be a long time before I have a grandson."

"Trust me, Pearlie, that day will come sooner than you think," Smoke said. They were on their way to the dining room, but Smoke stopped. Sally went on a few steps beyond, until she realized that he had stopped.

"Smoke, sweetheart, are you okay?" she asked.

Smoke had a strange expression on his face, and he pointed to Pearlie. "He will, you know," he said.

"He will what? What in the world are you talking about?"

"I'm talking about Pearlie," Smoke said. "He will have a grandson someday."

"Well, yes, I suppose he will."

"That's it, Sally," Smoke said. "I know now how I will pass my legacy on."

CHAPTER
ONE

Baltimore, Maryland, the present

His name was Arthur Kirby Jensen and he was a lieutenant colonel in the United States Army. He was a direct descendant, the great-great-grandson of the old, legendary gunfighter, Kirby "Smoke" Jensen, and he was not only aware of that relationship . . . he had a distinct reason to feel a very personal connection to that particular ancestor.

Slender, and deceptively muscular, Art was just a quarter of an inch under six feet tall, with sandy hair and steel-gray eyes.

Art was having lunch with his father, and the two men were seated at a table on the patio of the Crown and Horn Restaurant. From here they could see ships, trawlers, and yachts plying the sparkling blue waters of Chesapeake Bay.

Art's father, Cal Jensen, was a retired FBI agent who still did enough consultation work with the agency to make Art wonder if he had ever actually retired at all.

"What do you hear from Grandpa?" Art asked.

Cal chuckled. "He's as happy as a pig in the sunshine. The Confederate Air Force let him fly their B-17 again. In fact, they painted his name right under the pilot's window. Captain Pearlie Jensen."

"Well, why not?" Art asked. "What's more authentic than to have their plane flown by someone who did fifty missions in a B-17 over Germany during the war? Oh, and by the way, Dad, I think it's called the Commemorative Air Force now."

"Well, whatever. The point is, your grandpa got to fly it. And speaking of flying, what time tomorrow are you leaving?"

"My flight leaves at 0900," Art answered.

"I believe you said you're going to Fort Ord?"

"Yes, to join the Seventh Infantry Division. We'll be deploying to Iraq in another month."

A waiter approached the two men.

"Gentlemen," he said. "May I recommend fried oysters? The oysters you enjoy today spent last night in Chesapeake Bay."

"Fried oysters sound good," Cal said.

"I'll have a hamburger," Art said.

The waiter looked chagrined. "A . . . ham . . . burger . . . sir?" he asked in a pained voice. "You want a hamburger?"

"Yes."

"But, sir, this is the Crown and Horn. Nobody orders a hamburger at the Crown and Horn."

"You do have hamburger, don't you?"

"We do not, sir. We are the Crown and Horn," the waiter repeated haughtily.

"So you said."

Cal looked at the menu, then pointed to one of the entrées. "What is this?" he asked.

"Why, that's a filet mignon," the waiter said.

"He'll have that."

"Very good, sir."

"Grind it up."

"I beg your pardon?"

"Grind it up into hamburger," Cal said. "My son is going to Iraq. If he wants a hamburger, then by damn I'm going to see to it that he gets a hamburger."

"But, sir, that is twenty-two dollars," the waiter replied.

"I don't care what it costs, just do it."

"Very good, sir," the waiter said.

"Damn, the FBI must pay well," Art said as the waiter walked away.

"Well, they do pay better now that I'm a consultant," Cal replied. "Are you taking your journal?"

"I never go anywhere without my journal," Art said. "You know that."

"I know. But things will be different in Iraq. There's a possibility you could lose it over there. You might want to make a copy and take that instead."

"I've got copies made," Art said. "But reading the copy isn't like reading the actual journal. I mean, the entries are in Smoke's own handwriting. There is something almost surreal about reading the words in his hand. It's like he is talking directly to me."

"I know," Cal said. "I just thought I'd mention it. By the way, how is your mother?"

"She's fine," Art said. "I had dinner with her and Lester last Sunday."

Cal sighed. "Lester is a good man," he said. "I'm glad Edna found him. Lord knows, I was no good for her."

"It wasn't you, Dad, it was your job," Art said. "That's the reason I've never married."

"Oh, Son," Cal said, "I hope you aren't staying away from marriage just because I failed with your mother."

"It's not that. I've seen too many of my friends fail at marriage just because of the stress of the military. As you know I've only been back from Afghanistan for six months and I'm getting ready to go to Iraq. Right now we're getting back-to-back assignments in Afghanistan and Iraq, and we are monitoring other hot spots around the world. It is difficult to maintain a marriage and manage a military career. If I tried to do both, I'm not sure I could do either."

"You sell yourself short," Cal said. "I've never known anyone more capable than you."

The waiter returned then, carrying a tray. He put the oysters in front of Cal, then, with a great show, removed the silver cover to display Art's meal.

"Your . . . ham . . . burger . . . sir," the waiter said. The hamburger was artfully plated with thinly sliced strips of grilled zucchini, the dark grill lines perfect diagonals against the pale green. In addition to the grilled zucchini, there were four grilled cherry tomatoes, still on the vine. A small painter's palate of mustard and ketchup completed the display.

After lunch, Art drove his father home.

"Can you come in for a few minutes?" Cal invited as they sat in front of his apartment.

"I'd better not, Dad. I've got a lot of things to do before tomorrow."

Cal nodded, then reached across the car to shake Art's hand.

"You take care over there, Son," he said. "And drop me a line now and then."

"I'll send e-mail."

Cal shook his head. "No, not e-mail. I mean, yes, send me e-mail, but I want some real mail too. This e-mail stuff isn't like real mail . . . it isn't something you can hold."

"Why, Dad, I never knew you were so old-fashioned," Art said. "All right. I'll send you snail mail and e-mail."

Fort Ord, California, one month later

Several preset charges were detonated, the explosions loud and concussive. Bullets popped and whined as they passed just inches over the heads of a group of soldiers who were crawling on their bellies through the infiltration course.

Art, who was one of the soldiers on the course, rolled over on his back to pass under the lowest strand of barbed wire at one of the hasty fortifications. As he did so, he could see the tracer rounds whizzing by just above him. A nearby explosion went off, and his face was stung with dirt and packing wad from the charge.

After negotiating the wire, Art turned back over to his stomach, then resumed his transit through the course. Although there were several men and women on the course with him, Art was more than twenty yards ahead of the next person. Passing under one more barbed-wire barrier, he wriggled on out of the course until he was well beyond the framed machine guns, which were firing a steady stream of tracer rounds over the other participants who were still engaged.

"Up here, Colonel!" the sergeant who was conducting the course shouted. He was holding a stopwatch, and he smiled broadly as he showed it to Art. "Do you realize you just set a course record?"

"Did I?" Art replied. "Well, there's nothing like machine gun fire and explosive charges to hurry a person up," he added with a self-deprecating chuckle.

"What I want to know is, why did you do it in the first place? You certainly didn't have to."

"I'll tell you why he did it, Sergeant," General McCabe said.

"General!" the sergeant said, coming to attention and saluting. "I'm sorry I didn't send someone to welcome you. I didn't know you were here."

"That's quite all right, I didn't announce my intention to come," General McCabe replied. He smiled as he returned both Art's and the sergeant's salute.

"Colonel Jensen went through the course to provide an inspiration for his men. And it is no surprise that he did as well as he did. Yesterday, he fired expert on the combat firing range, and two days ago he maxed the PT test."

"Sumbitch," the sergeant said. "I can't wait till we get you over to Iraq, Colonel. You're goin' to kick some Habib ass."

Art laughed. "I'll kick one in the tail, just for you, Sarge." Then, to General McCabe, he said, "General, did you have anything? I'm going to head back to the BOQ and take a shower."

"No, nothing in particular," General McCabe said, taking in the infiltration course with a wave of his hand. "I just thought I'd come out and watch for a few minutes. Oh, and Ann wants me to remind you not to forget that you are having dinner with us tonight. We thought we might try out that new restaurant over in Carmel-by-the-Sea."

"Sounds good, General. I won't forget," Art said.

"Oh, and, Art, you do know about Ann's penchant for matchmaking, don't you?"

Art smiled. "Yes, sir. She has made for some . . . memorable evenings."

General McCabe laughed. "You are a good sport to put up with it," he said. "Meet us at Andre's at 1900."

"Nineteen hundred," Art repeated. "Will do."

Andre's Restaurant sat high on a bluff, overlooking the Pacific Ocean. The parking lot was far enough below the restaurant that it required a set of steps to get to the restaurant level. Normally, the restaurant provided valet parking, but they were doing work to the drive so a sign stated that valet parking would not be available tonight.

That didn't bother Art, since he would not have used valet parking anyway. He found a spot at the farthest end of the parking lot. He didn't mind the extra hike up the hill, and he figured there would be other customers tonight who would need to park closer.

Art was in uniform when he was met by the maitre d' as he stepped into the restaurant.

"Would you be Colonel Jensen?" the maitre d' asked.

"Yes."

"General McCabe told me you would be arriving," the maitre d' said. "He and his party are here." He snapped his fingers, and a young woman came to him.

"This is Colonel Jensen," the maitre d' said. "Please take him to General McCabe's table."

"Right this way, Colonel," the hostess said with a pretty smile.

"Art," Ann McCabe said, coming forward to meet him as he approached the table. "So nice to see you again. This is Lisa Dunn. She is the aerobics instructor at the gym that I use."

Art smiled as he extended his hand to Lisa. Ann McCabe had a problem with unmarried officers. She didn't believe in them, and apparently had set out on a mission to single-handedly change that condition throughout the entire U.S. Army.

Sometimes, it seemed that the only criterion she looked for was that both parties be single. He had to give her credit this time, though. Lisa was a knockout. But then, she was an aerobics instructor. How could she be anything else?

"I know the colonel," Lisa said.

"You know me?" Art asked, surprised by the comment.

"Well, let's say I know of you. You broke my heart once." Lisa ameliorated her comment with a broad smile.

"Why, Colonel Jensen, I would never have suspected such a thing from you," Ann said.

"Miss Dunn, Mrs. McCabe, I don't—" Art started, but Lisa cut him off with a lilting laugh.

"It's nothing like that," she said, waving her hand. "You played football for West Point. I graduated from Wake Forrest, class of 1990, and Army beat us my senior year, fourteen to ten. I really thought we had a chance to win that game. The field announcer was calling your name all afternoon."

"I remember that game. It was a good one," Art said. "But I'm sure he called Mike Mayweather's name a lot more than he called mine."

"Did you know that Art Jensen and Mike Mayweather were the last two players at West Point to make the All American football team?" General McCabe asked.

"I'd hardly put myself in the same category as Mayweather," Art said. "He made first team All American, and finished tenth in the Heismann. I made honorable mention."

"Well, honorable mention is . . . honorable," Lisa said, and they all laughed.

"Let's enjoy our dinner, shall we?" Ann said. "Colonel, you sit there, next to Lisa."

During the dinner the conversation covered many subjects, including the fact that both Art and General McCabe would soon be leaving for Iraq. But, as often as possible, Ann brought the discussion back to Art and Lisa, trying hard to get something started between the two of them.

Art found Lisa very attractive, but was somewhat uncomfortable by Ann's persistence. After dinner, as he walked Lisa to her car, he discovered that she was just as uncomfortable. They laughed about it, and made a vague agreement to get together at least one more time before Art deployed.

Art opened the door for her, and not until she was safely behind the wheel did he start toward his own. But, less than thirty seconds later, he heard Lisa scream. Turning, he hurried back through the darkness toward her car. That's when he saw two men with her. One had his arm around her neck, the other was standing in front of her. Both of them were holding knives.

"Let her go!" Art shouted as he ran toward her.

"Say what?" one of the two men said.

"I said let her go," he repeated.

The man laughed. "And if we don't?"

"I'll hurt you," Art said easily.

"You got a gun?"

"No."

"You got a knife?"

"No."

The man laughed. "Well, soldier boy. There's two of us and only one of you. And we both got knives . . . ain't we, Leroy?"

"Yeah," the one holding Lisa said. He held his up, and the blade glinted in the gleam of a nearby parking lot lamp. "And we got this here woman."

"So, soldier boy, maybe you just better get on with your business and not try to be a hero."

Art continued to come toward them and Leroy raised his knife to Lisa's neck. "Are you blind, soldier boy? I told you, we got this woman. Now you come any closer, I'm going to cut her."

"Why are you bothering with her?" Art asked. She's not your problem, Leroy, I am."

"What you mean, she's not my problem?"

"She can't hurt you. I can."

"Man, are you crazy? You better get the hell out of here!" LeRoy said.

"No, I don't think I will." Art took another step closer and was now just a few feet from them.

"Cut him, Jason," Leroy said to his partner. "Cut this mother real good."

Jason stepped toward Art and made a low, vicious swing with his blade. Art danced to one side, avoiding the slice, then brought the knife-edge of his hand hard against Jason's Adam's apple, crushing it. Choking, Jason raised his hands to his neck and when he did so, Art grabbed the knife, then, using the butt of the handle, hit Jason hard between the eyes.

Jason went down.

"I'm warnin' you!" Leroy said, his voice now on the edge of panic. "You come any closer, I'm going to cut her."

"I told you, Leroy, she's not your problem. Hell, she's not even my problem. Right now there's just you and me, and both of us have knives."

"Yeah, but I'm holding my knife against her throat," Leroy said.

"Well, see, that's your problem. If you are holding it against her throat, that means you aren't holding it against mine. You are a slow learner, aren't you, Leroy?"

"What . . . what do you mean?"

"You haven't figured out yet that, while you are cutting her, I'll be killing you. He took another step toward them. "So, what do you say? Shall we get started?"

Leroy hesitated for another second, then, pushing Lisa away, he turned and ran through the parking lot, disappearing into the darkness.

"Are you all right?" Art asked.

"Uh, yes," Lisa said, still shaken by the event.

"What were you doing out in the parking lot? When I left, you were safely in your car."

"I left my cell phone in the restaurant and I was going back for it," Lisa said. "Would you . . ." She started, hesitated for a moment, then restarted her question. "Would you really have let him cut me?"

"I had to let him believe I would," Art said.

"Colonel, you are a very frightening man. Maybe it isn't such a good idea for us to see each other. I believe you really would have let him cut me."

"All right," Art said.

"What, no argument? No attempt to persuade me that I'm wrong?"

"You have to go with your gut feelings," Art said. "If you really are going back for your cell phone, let me walk with you. That is, if you aren't afraid of me."

"Well, right now, I'm more frightened to go back without you."

Art walked Lisa to the restaurant, then waited as she retrieved her cell phone from the maitre d'. He then walked her back to her car. Art noticed that Jason was gone.

Not one word had passed between them from the time he offered to walk her back to the restaurant until now. Then, just before she got into her car, Lisa stopped and looked up at him. The pupils of her eyes were dilated, her lips were slightly parted, and there was a strange, almost desperate expression on her face. Art had seen it before, so he wasn't surprised when she put her arms around him, pulled him to her, and put her lips against his. She opened her mouth for a tongue-tangling kiss.

Art went with the kiss, letting her take the lead, practically swallowing her tongue before sticking his own tongue down her throat. She ground her body against his, and he could feel her breasts against his chest, her pelvis pressing urgently against his groin. Finally she pulled away and looked up at him.

"Still find me frightening?" Art asked.

"Terrifying," she answered. Then she let out a sigh. "And God help me, that's what I find so exciting. Follow me home, Colonel. I'll fix breakfast for us in the morning."

CHAPTER
TWO

Near Fallujah, Iraq

"Hot damn! We've got ourselves a real juicy target here," Sergeant Baker said as he peered through the thermal sight of a Long Range Acquisition System (LRAS), mounted on a Humvee.

"What have you got, Sergeant?" Lieutenant Colonel Art Jensen asked.

"I've got five Hajs, with weapons, in a building," Sergeant Baker answered. He chuckled. "Look at the poor dumb bastards. Ole Habib thinks I can't see him. Well, he can run, but the son of a bitch can't hide."

It was 0230, pitch-black, and the Mujahedeen insurgents, called Hajs, or Habib by the Americans, were wearing black to fade into the dark interior of the building. They were shadows within shadows, unable even to see each other from no more than a few inches away. But with his thermal-imaging optics, Sergeant Baker could see them as clearly as if they were standing in the middle of the street in broad daylight.

"Give me the numbers, Sergeant," Art said.

"Yes, sir, numbers coming up," Sergeant Baker replied, punching them in.

Art looked at the numbers, then keyed the mike. "Boomer Three, this is Tango Six. I have a fire mission."

The radio call sign, Tango Six, identified Art as the commanding officer of the Third Infantry Battalion, Thirty-second Infantry Regiment, Seventh Infantry Division.

"Go ahead, Tango Six," Boomer Three responded.

"Coordinates 09089226, direction two-zero-two degrees. Range from this location is niner-fi-yive-zero meters."

Two miles outside Fallujah, Lieutenant Kirby, platoon leader of the Weapons Platoon, called out to his platoon sergeant.

"Sergeant Caviness, we have a fire mission," he shouted.

"Yes, sir," Caviness replied. "Squad leaders, ready your tubes!"

The mortar men removed the tampons from the tubes of their 81mm weapons.

"Mortar one ready!" the first squad leader called back.

"Mortar two ready!"

"Mortar three ready!"

"All weapons ready, sir," Sergeant Caviness reported to Lieutenant Kirby.

Kirby was looking at a TAD, or target acquisition device.

"Angle for mortar number one, three-zero-two degrees, three-zero minutes, one-five seconds," Kirby called.

"Two-zero-two, point-three-zero, point-one-five," the first squad leader responded.

"Angle for mortar number two, two-zero-two degrees, three-zero minutes, point-two-zero seconds."

"Two-zero-two, three-zero, point-two-two," the squad leader replied.

"Mortar number three, two-zero-two, three-zero, two-five," Kirby called.

The squad leader of the third squad responded with the numbers. "Range, two-five-zero-zero meters."

The squad leaders adjusted the angle and elevation of their tubes. Then the loaders picked up the rounds and held them just over the end of the tubes.

"Fire!" Kirby called.

The loaders dropped the rounds into the tubes.

Thunk! Thunk! Thunk! was the sound as the rounds were fired.

"Ordnance is on the way, Tango Six," Kirby said into the radio.

Art looked in the direction from which the fire mission would come, and he saw a few sparks as three mortar rounds climbed into the sky. A second later, three loud booms rattled the neighborhood as a great ball of flame erupted at the target building. The flame was followed by a huge, billowing cloud of smoke and dust.

"Tango Six, can we have a BDA?" the disembodied radio voice asked.

"Battle damage assessment?" Art repeated. He chuckled. "Nothing to assess, Boomer, you brought some heat. The building is gone. Thank you."

"We have enjoyed doing business with you, Tango Six."

"Tango Six out."

Art thought about the five insurgents who had just died. They died because they could not comprehend a technology that could find them from nearly a mile away, then unleash a deadly barrage from mortars that were over two miles away, and could fire for effect without ranging. In the current operation, scores of insurgents had died, simply because they took one curious peek over the ledge to see what was going on outside. That one brief second of exposure was all that was needed to kill them, and anyone who was with them.

* * *

The sun rose the next day on a city that was nearly deserted. The melodic call to prayer, enhanced by a loudspeaker, intoned into the morning quiet.

> *Allah u Akbar, Allah u Akbar*
> *Ashhadu all llah ill Allah*
> *Ash hadu all illha ill Allah.*
> *Ash hadu anna Muhammadan Rasululaah*
> *Ash hadu anna Muhammadan Rasululaah.*
> *Hayya lasseah, Hayya Lassaleah*
> *Hayya lalfaleah, Hayya lalfaleah*
> *Allanu Akbar, Allahu Akbar*
> *La llaha ill Allah.*

In a Baghdad suburb

The three prisoners, two men and a woman, were brought into the room. They blinked at the bank of bright lights, but they couldn't rub their eyes because their hands were handcuffed. Next to the bank of lights was a video camera, mounted on a tripod.

There were six others in the room, but all six were wearing hoods so they could not be identified by anyone who might view the videotape later. One of the hooded men stepped in front of the video camera and began reading.

"Some time has passed since the blessed attacks against the global infidelity, against America, where our glorious martyrs sent more than three thousand infidels to a fiery hell. Since that time, Americans have conducted a vicious crusade against Islam.

"It is now evident that the West in general, and Americans in particular, are doing Satan's work on earth, trying with bombs and the deaths of millions of innocents to destroy the Muslim faith.

"But we are not without our own weapons, and we stand

here before these cameras, with three pawns of the great
Satan America."

The camera panned slowly across the faces of three terrified prisoners.

"One is Italian, one is Jordanian, and the woman is Israeli.
All are collaborating with the enemy in their fight against our
people and our faith. It is for this reason that they have been
condemned to die."

The hooded terrorist folded the paper and nodded toward
the woman. Another hooded terrorist stepped up behind the
woman and, quickly, drew his knife across her throat.

The woman cried out, though her cry was quickly silenced.
The terrorist grabbed her by the hair as he continued to saw
away at her neck. Two other terrorists held her up until finally,
the head was completely severed.

"*Allah Akbar!*" the terrorist shouted, holding the woman's
severed head aloft, blood pouring from the stump of her neck.

In quick order, the heads of the other two prisoners were
also severed.

Finally, the three disembodied heads were put on a table
while the camera focused on them, remaining for an extended
period of time on each one. The eyes of the Jordanian and
Italian were closed, but the woman's eyes were still open in
horror.

The lights went dark and the camera was turned off. Not
until then were all the hoods removed.

"You took a great chance in coming here, *Al Sayyid*," one
of the men said, using a title of great respect when he spoke
to the terrorist who had read the fatwa.

"I will do what must be done to rid our region of the American infidels," the leader said.

The terrorist who was referred to as *Al Sayyid* walked over
to the table to look at the severed heads. He felt a sense of excitement, almost sexual arousal, as he looked at the heads.
Moments before they had been alive; now they were dead because of his orders. And he had not only given the order, he
had witnessed the killing.

What was it like? he wondered. Once the heads were severed from the bodies, were there a last few seconds of cognizance? Did they know, in those terrifying seconds, that their entire existence, or what was left of it, was confined to a single, bloody sphere?

"What do we do with them now?" one of the terrorists asked. He was the one who had done the actual decapitation, and he still had blood on his hands.

"Burn the bodies," the leader responded. "Burn the bodies, and take the heads out to the road so that they may be found."

"Will you be returning to your home now, *Al Sayyid*?"

"Yes," the leader replied. He reached for the videotape. "Let me have the tape," he said. "I will have a DVD made of the tape, and then we will put it on the Internet. Within twenty-four hours, nearly one billion people will witness what we did here today. The sword of Allah is terrible and swift, and all will learn that those who support the great Satan of America will be sent to hell for their sins. *Allah Akbar!*"

"*Allah Akbar!*" the others replied.

The leader left the little nondescript house where the slayings had taken place. In the street in front of the house, three children were playing. Across the street, in an open-air café, two old men sat drinking their coffee. The leader's rental car was parked in front of the café, and as he approached it, the two old men paid him no attention.

At first he was irritated by their lack of respect, but then he remembered that he was not in his own country. Of course they would not recognize him here, nor would he want them to recognize him. It would not be good to place him here where the decapitation had taken place.

He started the car, but before he could back out, a U.S. Army convoy came by. A loudspeaker on the Humvee that was leading the convoy was repeating an announcement, in Arabic.

"Civilian vehicles . . . for your own safety, do not approach the convoy. Do not interrupt the convoy integrity."

He sat in the rental car, with the engine running, as the

convoy passed by. It did not escape his notice that, as each vehicle passed, the machine guns were trained on him.

He hated Americans. How he wished that one of the infidels he had just killed had been American.

Not until after the convoy cleared the area did he pull out into the street and start toward the airport. Full passenger service had not yet resumed out of the Baghdad Airport, but that didn't make any difference to him. He would depart Iraq exactly as he had arrived, with diplomatic status on board an aircraft belonging to his government.

He glanced at his watch. He would be back home by the time news of what had just happened broke. It would reverberate all over the world, and while he was responsible for it, he could not take credit for it, even among those who would say a prayer of joy over the death of the infidels.

That was a pity, but if he labored in anonymity for such a noble cause, then surely his reward in heaven would be great. For what are the riches of this world, when compared to the splendor of paradise?

Baghdad, Iraq

The World Cable News Network had an entire floor in the Al-Rashid Hotel, and John Williams, the senior correspondent in the field, had taken a suite of rooms for his office and quarters. He was sitting at the desk, going over copy for the next feed back to the States, when Jim Leaman came in.

"Any Cokes left in the fridge over there?" Williams asked, pointing to a refrigerator. He asked the question before Jim said a word, thus preempting whatever it was that Jim had come to see him about.

"Uh, wait, I'll see," Jim said. He opened the refrigerator and looked in. "Yeah, there are three or four."

"Bring me one," Williams said. It was more an order than a request, and Jim took one out, then brought it over to his boss.

Williams popped the top, then took a long drink before he spoke again. "What have you got?"

Jim smiled broadly. "I know the army said they weren't going to let any reporters get in, but I just talked General McCabe into letting me go to Fallujah to join the current operation," he said. "You're senior here. All I need is your permission."

"Denied," Williams said.

The smile left Jim's face and he looked at Williams with an expression of shock and frustration. "What? John, what do you mean? I've been trying to get this set up since the operation began. This will be great TV. We've got to cover it."

"Oh, I agree with that," Williams said. "I didn't say we weren't going to cover it. I'm just saying you won't be covering it. I'm going to take this assignment myself."

Williams topped his announcement off with another long swallow of his Coke, staring at Jim, who continued to stand there, his expression of shock and frustration turning to one of anger.

"Do you have a problem with that?" Williams asked, after he lowered the Coke can from his lips.

Jim was silent for a long moment, fighting the anger that was building inside him.

"No," he finally said. This was too good a job to walk away from over an argument with his boss. "I don't have a problem."

"I didn't think you would," Williams said. He picked up some of the paperwork he had been doing, by that action dismissing Jim.

Jim stayed for just a moment longer, then turned and left Williams's office.

John Williams was one of the most recognized faces in cable television news. Wherever there was a newsworthy event, Williams was there, from hurricanes in the Southeast, to celebrity trials in Los Angeles, to the terrorist attacks on nine-eleven.

Williams had gotten his start at a local television station while he was still in college. When the mother of one of the basketball players died, an assistant coach bought the distraught young man a plane ticket so he could go home for the funeral. That, Williams knew, was a violation of the NCAA rules, and he broke the news on the evening newscast.

A subsequent NCAA investigation turned up several other questionable incidents in the history of the school's athletic program, some of which had occurred ten years earlier. As a result, the basketball team, which was one of the best in the country, was put on probation, the coach and his entire staff were fired, and scholarships were lost. The school and all its supporters were devastated, but John Williams received an invitation to go to work for the World Cable News Network.

Within the network, and eventually throughout the television industry, John Williams picked up the nickname "the Digger." That was because he had a particular talent for digging up the dirt behind any story. And it was said, by more than a few, that if there was no dirt there, Williams was more than willing to provide it.

Williams's aggressive style of reporting had earned high numbers for the World Cable News Network, and Williams became a particular favorite of Todd Tanner, founder and president of the network. When the war in Iraq started, Tanner called Williams into his office.

"I can't believe our government has gotten us into this war," Tanner said.

"Well, I guess we didn't have much choice," Williams replied. "After all, we were attacked on nine-eleven."

Tanner raised his eyebrows and he looked at Williams. "Do you really believe that?" he asked.

"Well, uh, that's what our government tells us," he replied.

"Yes, and Hitler told the Germans that he invaded Poland in response to a Polish raid on a German radio station," Tanner said.

Williams was an opportunist, and, very quickly, he perceived that his boss was antiwar. Until that moment, he had welcomed the war, not for any national purpose, but because he saw the war as a means of providing him with career opportunities. Well, who was to say he had to support the war for those opportunities? If Todd Tanner was opposed to the war, then he would be as well.

"I have always heard that war is the ultimate failure of international policy," Williams said.

"Precisely," Tanner replied. "Clearly, this administration has failed us. And I believe it is our responsibility to point that out to the public."

"I agree," Williams said. "I have always held journalism to be a calling, not a job."

"I'm glad that we see eye to eye on this," Tanner said. "I want you to find ways and means to undermine and embarrass this administration."

"I will be most aggressive, Mr. Tanner."

"I'm sure you will be," Tanner said.

John Williams's first job was to report on conditions at a prison in Iraq.

"The war is over," Tanner said. "I'm sure all America remembers the famous 'Mission Accomplished' banner. In every previous war there has been a release of prisoners at the war's end. Why have we not released the prisoners we are holding?"

"I don't know the answer to that question," Williams replied.

"Find out. Find out, also, what kind of prison that is. I would be interested in learning just how those prisoners are being treated."

Prison Camp Alpha, Iraq

"You have to understand, Mr. Williams, that these are not your run-of-the-mill POWs," Colonel Dell explained in answer to Williams's question. "If we released them now they would simply join the insurgents, and we would have to deal with them again."

"How do we know that?" Williams asked.

"We know because we have made a few releases, and that is exactly what happened to them," Colonel Dell said.

"Nevertheless, by continuing to hold them, we are in violation of the Geneva Convention."

"I know there are lawyers who are arguing that very point," Dell said. "But I do not believe we are in violation. Nearly all the soldiers we captured during the war have been released. We are no longer holding any Iraqi soldiers. The people we are holding now are the worst of the worst. If we are forced to release them, we will pay for it later."

"That's not the colonel's decision to make," Tanner said when Williams phoned him to report on the conversation. "It is my belief that, by continuing to hold prisoners at Camp Alpha, we are endangering our troops because it is acting as a lightning rod to intensify the hatred the other nations in that area feel toward us. Find something that we can report."

"What do you mean?"

"You are the Digger," Tanner said. "That is what they call you, isn't it? You have a unique ability to dig up dirt?"

"Well, yes, sir, but—" Williams started to reply, but Tanner interrupted him.

"And is it not true that there have been a few cases where you supplied your own dirt?"

"I . . . uh," Williams stuttered.

"Look, don't apologize for it," Tanner said. "I admire . . . and reward aggressive reporting. Do you get my meaning?"

"I think I do," Williams said.

"The more aggressive the better. Find some way we can put Camp Alpha before the court of world opinion," Tanner said. "Get it done, John. Whatever it takes, get it done."

"Yes, sir," Williams replied.

"And, John . . . if you are successful at getting this prison before the court of world opinion, then we are going to tackle the war itself. We are going to make history, John. We are going to show the world that the real power is no longer in the hands of a few government officials and bureaucrats, but is in the hands of those smart enough, and bold enough, to seize it. And WCN is unique in its position to do just that."

Two weeks of the closest scrutiny uncovered nothing that could be used to put Camp Alpha on the world stage. Then one of the guards offered to sell Williams some photographs.

"What sort of pictures?"

"The kind that could cause the camp commander, and a lot more people, a lot of trouble," the guard answered.

"I don't understand. Why would you sell out your fellow soldiers like that?"

The young man scoffed. "Huh, they aren't my fellow soldiers. Most of them are regular army. Me, I'm National Guard. All I want is to get the hell out of here and go home."

"Let me see them."

"Huh-uh," the guard replied. "Not unless you pay me."

"I'm not going to pay you unless I know they are something I can use," Williams replied. "Now let me see them."

"I'll let you see three," the guard replied. "There's a lot more, and the three I'm going to show you aren't even the best ones. But I think you'll be able to tell what they are like, just from these three."

"Okay," Williams agreed. "Let me see them."

"Wait here."

Williams waited while the guardsman left. When he returned about five minutes later, he gave Williams a white envelope.

"Here are three. I have about forty more," the guardsman said. "And, like I told you, these three aren't the best."

"All right," Williams said. He started to remove the pictures from the envelope.

"No, no, not here!" the guardsman said quickly. "You think I want to be killed?"

"Killed?"

"That's what would happen to me if news got out that I was showing these pictures around," the guardsman said.

Williams nodded, then slipped the envelope into his jacket pocket. It wasn't until later, when he was alone, that he took the envelope out to look at the photographs.

The pictures were dynamite.

The first one showed a young, American, female soldier. She was lifting her T-shirt, showing her bare breasts to a prisoner who was naked, restrained, and had a dog's leash around his neck.

The American female soldier was also pointing to the prisoner's penis.

In the second photo, the prisoner was on his hands and knees, and the American female, fully clothed, was riding him like a horse. In addition, she was waving a cowboy hat over her head.

In the third picture, the naked prisoner was blindfolded. What made the picture particularly intriguing was the blindfold being used. Williams figured that the brassiere was at least a D cup.

The photos exploded throughout the world. WCN showed them first, and was credited by every news organization that picked them up. Williams knew they would be dynamite. They were not only degrading for the prisoners, they had the added advantage of being titillating, for the American female was very attractive.

As the young National Guardsman had promised, the other pictures were even more explosive, too explosive to be shown on TV, though Williams gave a very salacious description of the poses of simulated sodomy.

As a result of the story the prison commandant, Colonel Dell, was relieved of command. PFC Abby French, the young female soldier featured in the first photographs, was brought home for court-martial, as were the five guards who showed up in the other photographs.

Camp Alpha was closed, some of the prisoners were released, while others were transferred. And, throughout the world, editorials and commentators berated America for the brutal and inhumane treatment of its prisoners.

John Williams was promoted to the position of senior reporter in the field for WCN, and, in that position, could pick and choose his own assignments.

It was that position that gave him the authority to preempt Jim Leaman, taking his place as an embedded correspondent in the Fallujah campaign.

CHAPTER THREE

Fallujah, Iraq

Art stood behind a wall looking over the city with a pair of binoculars. Behind him, Captain Chambers was staring at images on a TV monitor. The images were being projected from an Unmanned Aerial Vehicle, or UAV, circling over the city.

"Anything coming up on the monitor, Mike?" Art asked.

"No, sir," Chambers answered. "Everyone seems to have their head down this morning."

A Humvee drove up behind them and stopped. Two men got out. One was carrying a video camera, and both were wearing sleeve flashes that identified them as TV reporters.

"Is Colonel Jensen here?" one of the men asked.

Art nodded. "I'm Colonel Jensen."

"I'm John Williams with World Cable News," the one who asked the question said.

"Yes, I recognize you," Art said.

"Oh, you've seen me then?"

"Yes."

"What do you think of the coverage WCN has given the war?"

"Not much," Art said candidly.

"Oh?" Williams replied. "And may I ask why not?" The expression on the reporter's face, and the defensive timbre of his voice, showed his irritation.

"Your headquarters is where? Atlanta? The last time I checked, Atlanta was in the United States, yet your network seems determined to find anything negative you can about our effort over here."

"We are a world news organization, Colonel," Williams said. "You do understand the concept of 'world,' don't you? We are beyond the chauvinistic hubris that is so prevalent among our sister networks."

"Yes, you and Al Jazeera," Art said. "What do you need, Williams? What can I do for you?"

"I've come down from headquarters to be embedded with your battalion."

"Do I have a say in it?" Art asked.

"Not really, Colonel," Williams replied smugly. "Unless you want to butt heads with a general."

Art sighed. "All right. Just stay the hell out of the way."

"Oh, and, Colonel, if you would, please put the word out to your men that I am here to work, not to sign autographs," Williams said.

"I don't think you will have any trouble with that, Mr. Williams," Art said in a cold, flat tone of voice. "I doubt that you have that many fans among the troops here."

Art turned back toward the street and lifted his binoculars to his eyes. He swept his gaze, slowly, from side to side, looking for anything out of the ordinary.

He saw nothing.

"Colonel, the UAV has made a second pass, still no sightings," Captain Chambers said from his position at the monitor.

Art lowered his field glasses. "All right," he said. "Tell A Company to saddle up. It's time to put out some bait."

"Yes, sir," Chambers replied. He spoke into his radio.

"Goodnature Six, this is Tango Six. Get ready to move out. All other units hold your position."

A series of "Rogers" came back.

"Where will the CP be, Colonel?" Chambers asked.

"In my Humvee," Art replied. "I'm going to lead the convoy."

"Yes, sir, I'll be right behind you."

Art shook his head. "No, you take the three spot, Captain Mason will be behind me. Oh, and take them with you," he said, nodding toward Williams and his cameraman.

"Uh . . . it isn't all that necessary that we actually go out on patrol with you, Colonel," Williams said nervously. "We can get everything we need from here."

Sergeant Baker was chewing tobacco, and he spat on the ground, barely missing Williams's boot.

"So, what you are saying is, you are a pussy. Is that it?" Baker said to Williams.

"I'm not . . ." Williams started, then sighed. "I would be glad to accompany you, Colonel."

"You and your cameraman can ride with Captain Chambers and Sergeant Baker," Art said.

"That's my Humvee," Baker said. "Over there." He pointed.

The sound of a dozen or more starting engines disturbed the quiet morning air. Art walked over to his own Humvee, got into the right seat, and settled down. His machine gunner stood in the back, freed the gun to slide around on the ring, cleared the headspace, and activated the bolt.

"Let's go, Jimmy," Art said.

Nodding in compliance, Art's driver, Specialist Jimmy Winson, started forward.

"I'll tell you what I wish we could find, sir," Winson said as he maneuvered the Humvee around piles of rubble that spilled over into the street from the buildings that had been destroyed in the fighting. "I wish we could find those sons of bitches that have been beheading people."

"That would be great," Art agreed. "But they are so

cowardly that they are never photographed without wearing their hoods, so finding them is unlikely."

"Yes, sir, but that don't stop me for wishing we could find them," Winson said.

The surgical preciseness of the attacks was exemplified by the fact that, while buildings on either side of it were rubble, the Abu Hanifa Mosque, from which the call to prayer had come earlier, stood completely undamaged.

Art twisted around in his seat and saw Sergeant Taboor Tacoob getting his equipment ready. Despite his Arabic name and heritage, Tacoob was 100 percent American, and an avid fan of the Detroit Tigers basball team.

"All right, Sergeant Tacoob, do your stuff," Art invited.

Tacoob nodded, then began speaking Arabic into a microphone. His words were broadcast over a loudspeaker.

"Mujahedeen fighters, don't worry because you have tiny peckers. We Americans have medicine that can help you. Come out, let us give you the medicine that will make you into men.

"Mujahedeen fighters. Come out into the street and face us like men. Don't hide behind walls like women!

"Brave warriors of Allah. We are here to help you become martyrs. Come into the street. Tonight you can be enjoying the passion of seventy-two virgins. Oh, wait, what good will seventy-two virgins do you if you all have such tiny peckers?"

The broadcast taunting of the insurgents was in keeping with the tactics developed by the brain trust in the psy-war section. And, as it had in the past, it proved effective once again, when eight men suddenly rushed out into the street, in broad view.

Shouting curses, six of the eight men began firing AK-47s from their hip. The other two appeared to be unarmed, until a closer examination showed that each was wearing a bomb-jacket, filled with shrapnel.

Just above his head, Art's machine gunner opened up. The big .50 caliber bucked and roared as it kicked out spent shell casings. Art could see the orange balls of tracer rounds, not only from his own Humvee, but from two others, converged on the insurgents who had shown themselves. The six armed insurgents were cut down.

One of the two remaining insurgents detonated his bomb, killing himself. What he had not realized was that when he killed himself, he also killed his fellow fighter, who was cut down by the shrapnel before he could detonate his own bomb.

Art continued to lead the convoy down the street. Then from the tower of the mosque came a rapidly moving stream of smoke and fire. A rocket-propelled grenade slammed into the vehicle just behind Art.

A powerful blast ripped into the Humvee, shooting a cloud of debris high into the air. Two soldiers staggered out, one covered with blood. The Humvee's right rear door was ripped off, the surrounding metal burned black, and the gunner was sprawled facedown on the side of the road.

"Look for the shooter! Where's the shooter?" Art's gunner shouted.

Bursts of rifle fire rang out as the soldiers in the convoy opened up with rifles, firing toward the mosque. Dillard fired in the direction of the shooting with his .50-caliber machine gun.

From the Humvee trailing the one that was hit, Sergeant Baker jumped out, fired back to keep the insurgents down, and sprinted toward the disabled Humvee. Then, coming forward, he brought bad news.

"Cap'n Mason is down, sir. So's his driver," Baker said. "They're bad hurt, both of 'em."

Although armored, the RPG had entered through the windshield, then detonated inside. Machine gun fire from the mosque had followed the rocket attack.

"Get over there, we've got to get out of their angle of fire!" Art ordered, pointing toward the curb on the opposite side of the street. Winson complied quickly, followed by the other vehicles in the convoy. Behind them, unable to move, Captain Mason's Humvee continued to burn fiercely in the middle of the street. The two men who had been in the back of the Humvee were struggling to pull Captain Mason and his driver out. One of the would-be rescuers was hit by machine gun fire and he went down. The other ran to get out of the line of fire.

Art dashed out into the street toward the fallen soldier.

"Colonel!" Captain Chambers called toward Art. "Get back, you'll be killed!"

Green tracer rounds whizzed and popped by Art's head as he ran zigzagging back and forth toward the burning vehicle. It took but one look inside to see that Captain Mason and his driver were both dead.

"Mac, how bad is it?" Art asked Specialist McKay, the man on the ground. McKay, a young black soldier from Los Angeles, had been in Captain Mason's Humvee.

"I took a pretty good hit," McKay answered, straining to keep the pain from his voice. "You better get back, Colonel."

Even as McKay was speaking, bullets slammed into the burning Humvee, making clanging sounds against the armor plate.

"It's getting pretty hot out here," McKay added. "This is no place for you, Colonel!"

"If I help you, can you walk?" Art asked.

"Don't think so," McKay answered. "I think they shot off my kneecap."

"Then I'll carry you," Art said. He bent down and picked McKay up, then threw him over his shoulder.

"You'll never make it back," McKay said.

"Sure I will, Mac," Art said. "Hell, I'll just use you as a shield."

Despite the situation and his wound, McKay laughed. "Thanks a lot," he said.

"Colonel, run, run!" one of the men from the edge shouted, as Art started back.

"Damn! Look at him go! Who would've thought the colonel could run like that?"

"Well, he played football at West Point."

"Shit! He's not going to make it!"

"Come on, come on!"

With McKay draped over his shoulder, Art dashed back through the machine gun fire, once more zigzagging until he reached the street curb, cutting the angle so that the shooters from the mosque didn't have a line of sight, or a field of fire.

Two others took McKay off his back then, and laid him on the sidewalk, while the medic came over to take a look at him.

"Were you hit, Colonel?" Williams asked.

"No."

"Are you kidding, Captain?" Sergeant Baker asked. "Colonel Jensen is my main man. We call him Super Colonel. How's Habib goin' to shoot the colonel's ass? He's faster than a speeding bullet."

"Have you got them spotted, Mike?" Art asked.

"Yes, sir, they are all in the mosque. There's at least forty or fifty of them," Captain Chambers replied. "We've got to get inside."

"Let's get some tracks up here," Art said. "And get Mac back for a med evac."

Half an hour later four armored personnel carriers approached the front doors of the mosque. The doors were closed, and a sign posted on the outside read: AMERICAN SOLDIERS, THIS IS A HOLY PLACE. STAY OUT!

"Blow the doors open!" Art ordered.

"Yes, sir!" came the enthusiastic response.

The recoilless rifle on one of the vehicles fired toward the closed doors, blowing both of them off their hinges. After the doors were blown, they fired three more high-explosive rounds into the compound, followed by a spray of .50-caliber machine gun fire.

"Let's go!" Art shouted, having temporarily taken command of A Company after Captain Mason was killed.

Art led the men through the smashed doors into the open compound. Screaming in defiance, three insurgents stood up and began firing at the Americans as they came in. They were cut down in a hail of gunfire. In the next room the Americans saw several women and children, huddled together. The expressions on their faces indicated that they believed the soldiers were about to kill them.

"Tacoob," Art shouted to his interpreter.

"Yes, sir?"

Art nodded toward the women and children. "Tell them they have nothing to fear. We won't harm them."

Tacoob spoke to them, and though they weren't entirely convinced that they wouldn't be killed, his assurances eased their fears somewhat.

"Colonel," an old man said, appearing from the middle of the group. From his dress, and from the respect the others gave him, Art knew that he was a sheikh. "May I speak with you?" The sheikh's English was impeccable.

"Yes, of course."

"The dead," the sheikh said. "As a matter of respect, I ask that you gather our dead."

"All right," Art replied. "As soon as we are sure that the mosque is cleared, we'll do that."

"What do you mean, as soon as the mosque is cleared?"

"We were fired at from the top of the minaret," Art said.

"They are not there now," the sheikh said.

Art nodded. "All right. As soon as I am sure they aren't there, we'll gather the dead."

"Come with me," the sheikh said. "I will show you that the minaret is now empty."

Art and two others followed the sheikh up the spiraling staircase to the top of the prayer tower. Art kept the sheikh well in front, figuring that if anyone was still up there, the sheikh would draw the first shots.

They reached the top, and the sheikh turned toward Art.

"As you can see, it is empty," he said.

Art nodded, then stepped out onto the balcony and looked out over the city. The balcony afforded a good view of Fallujah. The city was showing scars from the battle. Art had read one report stating that nearly ten thousand of the fifty thousand buildings had been destroyed, and half the remaining buildings showed significant damage. From this vantage point, Art was ready to concede the accuracy of the report.

"All right," he said a moment later. "The tower is clear. Let's go back down."

Half an hour later, the bodies of all the insurgents had been brought together in one room.

"How many are there?" Art asked.

"I counted forty-two," Sergeant Baker said. "Damn!"

"What is it?" Art asked.

"I just saw one of them move. The son of a bitch is still alive. We'd better get a medic in here."

Art watched as Sergeant Baker went over to the wounded insurgent. He squatted down beside him, then reached out a hand to touch him. "Hold on there, partner. I'll get a medic to look at you," he said.

Suddenly there was a flash of light and a loud explosion. The insurgent was wearing a bomb, and as Sergeant Baker leaned over to tend to him, the bomb went off. Baker fell back, dead before he hit the floor.

Several others ran into the room then, drawn by the explosion. Williams and his cameraman came in as well.

"Holy shit, what happened?"

"That son of a bitch had a bomb," Art said, pointing to what was left of the insurgent. Nothing remained but a few chunks of bloody flesh.

Art heard a sound behind him and, turning, saw one of the "dead" insurgents suddenly sit up.

"Son of a bitch! He's alive!" Chambers shouted.

Art swung his weapon around and fired, hitting the insurgent right between the eyes.

"He's dead now," Art said dryly. Turning back, he saw that the video camera was pointed right at him.

Al-Rashid Hotel

John Williams looked at the footage and chortled with glee. This was better than his coverage of the prisoner abuse at Camp Alpha. Those were still photos . . . this was video, clear, sharp, and damning.

In the background, Williams heard the telephone ring.

"John," someone called. "It's for you."

Williams picked up the phone. "Williams."

"John, this is Todd Tanner."

Williams sat up more sharply. "Yes, sir, Mr. Tanner."

"I just finished looking at your Fallujah tape. It's brilliant."

"I thought you might like it."

"Go to 26.23," Tanner said.

Williams ran the tape to the point designated by Tanner.

"Play it."

"There's nothing there, it's black."

"There's audio," Tanner said.

Williams turned up the volume.

". . . shit, the son of a bitch isn't armed," a disembodied voice says.

"Oh yes, I heard that earlier," Williams said. "But without video—"

"I hate to lose that," Tanner said. "Perhaps we could lay it over some video."

"But the video stops right after the shooting," Williams said. "I'm not sure where we could put it."

"Perhaps just before the shooting," Tanner suggested.

"Mr. Tanner, if we do that it will change the whole dynamics. It will look as if Colonel Jensen knew he wasn't armed before he killed him."

"It will also guarantee this to be the most powerful piece of journalism to come from this war," Tanner said.

Williams paused for a moment before he answered. "Damn," he said. "Damn, what an idea!"

CHAPTER FOUR

Redha, Qambari Arabia

Sixteen-year-old Amber Pease knew that there were many advantages to living in Qambari Arabia. Her father, Colonel Anthony Pease, was commandant of the U.S. Marine guards for the American embassy. It was an important assignment and because of her father's position, Amber lived like a princess. They had a beautiful and very spacious home, complete with a staff of servants.

But there were many things that she missed. If she had been in the States going to a normal high school, she was sure she would be a cheerleader. But her life wasn't totally different from her counterparts' back in the States. Amber, who was a junior in the American Dependent High School in Qambari Arabia's capital city of Redha, had a boyfriend. He was Bobby Drake, a senior, and the son of the deputy ambassador. And just as she was sure she would have been a cheerleader, she knew that Bobby would be playing sports . . . football in season, then basketball.

But none of that was to be. Sometimes she allowed herself

to fantasize about what it would be like to cheer him on to victory in a big game, then go out with him after the game, to a dance, or a party. But this was the only American school in the whole Kingdom of Qambari Arabia, so there were no other schools to play. They did have dances and parties at the school, but they were always very carefully monitored. And there was absolutely no such thing as going out on a date with a boy. Such things were not done in Qambari Arabia. The Qambari teens did not do it, and protocol prohibited the young Americans from doing it.

Amber got on the school bus with the other students and took her seat next to Bobby.

"Amber's got a boyfriend, Amber's got a boyfriend," a sixth-grade boy began to chant.

"Why, Albert, the only reason he is my boyfriend is because you won't be," Amber teased. She leaned over and kissed Albert on the forehead. All the other kids in the bus laughed, and Albert's face turned red.

Amber and Bobby rode together, talking quietly and sharing the secrets of young love, until Bobby reached his stop. She waved at him from the window, as the bus continued on its way.

"Come up here and sit by me, Albert," Amber said. "We can smooch until we reach my stop."

"You're crazy," Albert said as Amber laughed out loud at her little joke.

Abdulla sat in the van and watched as the school bus stopped to let the young girl off. She was a pretty girl, blond as so many Americans were. She laughed, and shouted something back to the bus as it drove away. In her short skirt and uncovered head, her tight shirt and bare arms, he thought she looked like a whore. Didn't the Americans understand the sensitivity of the Qambaris? They knew that women in Qambari Arabia were required to wear burkas but they made no effort to comply. Well, he would see to it that this little harlot paid for her heresy.

Abdulla waited until the bus had pulled away before he started the van. Then, driving slowly, he approached the young girl.

"Miss Pease, you must come with me quickly," he called out to her, reaching over to open the door on the passenger side of the van.

Amber hesitated, then took a step back and shook her head. "I . . . I don't know you."

"I am one of the gardeners at your house," Abdulla said. "Please, come with me quickly. Your mother has been hurt."

"My mother?" Amber took a step toward the van. "What happened to my mother?"

"It is a very serious accident. Please, come quickly. There is no time."

Hesitantly, but frightened not to do it because her mother might need her, Amber got into the van.

"What happened?" she asked.

"Let me help you fasten your seat belt," Abdulla said, reaching toward her.

"I can get—" Amber started to say, but that was as far as she got. She struggled as Abdulla clamped a dampened cloth over her nose and mouth. There was a cloying smell . . . then dizziness . . . then nothing.

It was every parent's nightmare, learning that your child was missing. All the children on the bus reported seeing Amber get off the bus, and though nobody saw her getting into another car, two had noticed a white van. Both children had thought the incident was unusual enough to report it to their parents.

Bobby Drake had gotten off the bus one stop before Amber, so he saw nothing, but one of the two who did see the van was able to give a very detailed report.

"It was an old Ford van, and it had a big rusty spot above

the left taillight. The license number was 37172," Albert, the eleven-year-old son of one of the embassy staff, said.

"How do you know all that?" the military policeman asked.

"I wrote the number down in my notebook," Albert replied. "Mom and Dad said I should always report anything that looked suspicious, and that old van looked suspicious to me."

But even as the embassy was providing the Qambari police with information on the van, as well as a description of the man who had taken her, the police found Amber.

"I'm sorry, sir," Captain Hardesty, the military police captain in charge of the investigation, told Colonel Pease. "But we are going to need an official identification. You are going to have to look at the body."

Pinching the bridge of his nose, Colonel Pease nodded, indicating that he was ready. The MP took him into a room at the rear of the police morgue, then pulled back the cover. Pease looked at her, nodded, then turned away with tears streaming down his face.

"How was she found?" he asked.

"You don't really want to know, sir," Hardesty replied.

"How was she found?" Colonel Pease asked again.

"She was," Captain Hardesty started, paused, took a deep breath, then continued. "She was found nude and spread-eagled, with her panties stuffed in her mouth."

Colonel Pease was quiet.

"We'll get the son of a bitch, sir," Hardesty said. "We have two eyewitnesses. We have a make on the van and a license number. We've given the Qambari police good, solid leads. We're going to get the bastard who did this."

"Thanks," Colonel Pease replied.

"Why haven't you arrested him?" Captain Hardesty asked. The American military policeman was in the downtown office of Abdul Yusri, chief of the Redha Police Force. Abdul didn't answer. Instead he held up a coffeepot. "Would you like some coffee, Captain Hardesty?"

"No, thank you," Hardesty replied.

"You really should try our coffee. Our Quran forbids us to drink alcohol in any form, but it does allow coffee and we have made that into one of our most divine pleasures."

"I try to limit myself to no more than two cups per day," Hardesty replied.

Yusri poured a generous amount of cream into his coffee. He then added several teaspoons of sugar.

"You Americans move much too quickly," he said as he stirred the tan mixture. "You are in such a hurry to make an arrest."

"Chief Yusri, it has been my experience that in cases like this, the longer you delay, the colder the trail becomes. Now we have some very good eyewitness reports that put Abdulla Balama Shamat's vehicle at the scene of the crime. We have traced the van down, and identified him as the owner."

"Ah, that is true, my friend," Yusri said, holding up his finger. "You can put his van there. But can you put him there? Your eyewitnesses are who? Schoolchildren?"

Hardesty sighed. "We have no eyewitnesses who can testify, directly, that Shamat was there."

"Well then, you can see our dilemma, can't you?" Yursi asked as he took a drink of his coffee.

"But it is a dilemma easily solved," Hardesty said. "We have taken DNA samples from the young girl's body. All it requires is a DNA matchup with Shamat."

"I see," Yusri said. "And exactly what is this DNA sample?"

"Semen," Hardesty said.

"Semen. By that, you mean a man's, uh, sexual excretion?"

"Believe me, Mr. Yusri, semen has proven to be a very reliable means of acquiring DNA."

"And how, exactly, do you propose that we would make use of this . . . unclean thing?"

Hardesty looked puzzled for a moment. "Simple," he said. "All that is necessary is to acquire a DNA sample from the suspect and compare it to the DNA from the semen."

"You do not understand," Yusri said. "Semen is unclean. It is against the law of Qambari Arabia for anyone to touch semen."

Hardesty laughed. "Well, you don't have to worry about that," he said. "Our laboratory has already isolated the DNA. Your people will have nothing to touch."

"The DNA? It is extracted from the semen, yes?"

"Well, yes, but . . ."

Yusri held up his hand and shook his head. "It makes no difference. If it is extracted from the semen, it is a part of the semen. Our lab technicians cannot touch it."

"You don't have to. We'll provide you with the charted data. All you have to do is make the comparisons."

"That won't work, either. You are asking that we convict one of our own, on evidence that is not provided by our government. We cannot do that. Especially since the evidence you would be supplying comes from a source that we cannot deal with in the first place."

"I don't understand," Hardesty said. "You are willing to let the monster who murdered Amber Pease go free, simply because your lab technicians are too squeamish to work with DNA?"

"I would not expect you to understand," Yusri said. He took another swallow of his coffee, then smiled over the rim of the cup. "But then, you are in our country, aren't you? So, you have no choice but to comply by our laws."

Hardesty clenched and unclenched his hands several times to prevent getting any angrier over the situation. Finally he let out a long sigh.

"Very well," he said. "We'll . . . uh . . . pursue other means."

"I think that would be best," Yusri said.

It took another week before the U.S. was able to get some DNA from Abdulla Balama Shamat. They got it by the simple expedient of paying someone to get a sample of Shamat's blood. One of the Qambaris who worked for Colonel Pease, one who felt the horror and shame of having such a beautiful young girl slaughtered in his country, volunteered to undertake the mission. Under the observation of two American military police, Omar Sarid brushed against Shamat in an open-air shopping mart. He was carrying a serrated piece of metal, and he managed to get both skin and blood.

"Watch where you are going!" Shamat said angrily after the encounter.

"A thousand pardons, sir," Omar replied. "I was not paying attention. I am shamed by my clumsiness."

Shamat glared at him, then walked on through the crowd, rubbing at his scratch irritably.

Omar brought the sample back to the car where the two American Military Police had observed the entire incident.

"It is very necessary, so we can establish a train of evidence," Captain Hardesty explained to them when they brought the blood and skin tissue to him.

"It's a match," the chief lab technician told Hardesty after the lab work was completed. "The DNA found on Amber Pease matches the DNA taken from Abdulla Balama Shamat."

The next day, Ambassador Paul Tobin went to see the sultan, Jmal Nagib Qambar.

"Your Excellency, we have irrefutable evidence that one of your subjects, Abdulla Balama Shamat, raped and murdered young Amber Pease. And we ask that you arrest him and deal with him," Tobin said.

"I see," Qambar said, fitting a cigarette into a long jade holder. "And just what is this evidence?" he asked, snapping a gold lighter under the tip of the cigarette.

Tobin showed him the DNA reports.

"Yes," Qambar said, exhaling a long stream of tobacco smoke. "I was told of this. From semen, I believe?"

"Yes," Tobin said.

Qambar took a few more puffs of tobacco and looked at the reports before he spoke again. Then he shook his head.

"I'm sorry," he said. "You have to understand that my people are a simple people, tied to ancient customs and strong beliefs. They would never stand for the conviction of someone, based upon DNA, which they cannot understand, taken from semen, which they can understand. Allow my police to investigate in our own way. We have a long history of dealing with criminals. And remember, just as your sophisticated DNA is not available to us . . . we have ways and means of extracting information that is not available to you."

CHAPTER FIVE

The Kingdom of Qambari Arabia

The Mercedes sports car raced through the streets of the capital city of Redha, sending pedestrians scattering and frightening a horse that was pulling a cart, laden with vegetables. The cart overturned and the farmer watched in dismay as his produce was scattered through the street, much of it ruined as it was run over by traffic.

A policeman, seeing the speeding car, recognized the driver as Prince Azeer Lal Qambar, so he breathed a quick prayer that no one would be injured, and he did nothing. It was not healthy to run afoul of the family that ruled Qambari Arabia.

Azeer Lal Qambar was forced to slow down, and then come to a stop. There was a wreck a few blocks ahead, and all traffic had come to a standstill.

Azeer honked his horn a few times, more in anger and frustration than any real belief that the traffic would become unsnarled. When the traffic remained at a standstill, Azeer became impatient, and he left the road and began driving down the sidewalk.

Some sidewalk merchants had spent several minutes earlier in the day, very carefully displaying their wares on colorful rugs. They watched in helpless and frustrated dismay as the royal prince drove over their merchandise, destroying much of their inventory.

When Azeer reached the location of the wreck, he left the sidewalk and drove between the wrecked cars and the green crescent-marked ambulance that was there for the injured. Two EMTs were carrying an injured man on a stretcher, but when Azeer roared through they had to drop the stretcher in order to get out of the way. Azeer skirted just around the dropped stretcher as he honked his horn impatiently, then sped away, leaving the traffic congestion behind him.

When Azeer reached the palace, he was greeted by his father, the sultan, Jmal Nagib Qambar.

"Azeer, I see that you are back from your vacation. I trust it was enjoyable?"

"Yes, Father, it was very enjoyable," Azeer replied.

"I am glad you are here," the sultan said. "I want you to meet with the American ambassador. He is here to talk about your trip to America."

"Father, why do we not tell the Americans to leave Qambari Arabia?"

"My dear son, without the Americans' appetite for our oil, we would be nothing but another wandering tribe, trying to survive in the desert. We need the Americans, and they need us. It is like the lowly tickbird and the majestic camel. Neither likes the other, but neither can survive without the other."

"Which are we, Father? The tickbird, or the camel?" Azeer asked.

Excusing himself, Azeer went into the office of foreign trade. He was the head of foreign trade, a position he occupied by appointment from his father. In truth, it was merely a position created for him. He knew nothing about foreign trade, didn't understand such things as tariffs, or money exchange, or the balance of trade. He did know that, because of the oil, America bought a lot more from Qambari Arabia than the QA bought from the U.S.

It was an attempt, on the part of the U.S. government, to narrow the gap in trade that was the purpose of this meeting. The American ambassador was here to extend the formal invitation from his government.

"Prince Azeer, how delightful to see you," Ambassador Tobin said, standing to greet Azeer as he entered. "You have been on vacation, I hear."

"Yes," Azeer said without elaboration.

"I trust you had a good time?"

"I had a very good time."

"Good, good," Ambassador Tobin said. He removed a folder from his briefcase. "Here is the official invitation from my government, for you to make a fact-finding visit with regard to trading agreements. There are letters of introduction to everyone you might need to see, as well as preclearance for customs and that sort of thing."

"You are most kind," Azeer said.

Ambassador Tobin grinned obsequiously. "In our fight against terror, we have had no better friend in the region than Qambari Arabia," he said. "This is just a means of expressing our gratitude toward you and the royal family."

"You are too kind," Azeer said.

"Prince Azeer, I wonder if you have any news to report on the investigation into the rape and murder of young Amber Pease."

"Nothing to report yet," Azeer said. "You of course have our deepest regrets that such a thing happened. Come, Ambassador, I will walk you to the door."

It was a dismissive comment and Ambassador Tobin picked up on it at once. He started toward the door. "Please feel free to contact me if you have any questions about anything."

"I will," Azeer replied. "As you said, the friendship between our two countries must be nourished."

As Tobin started to leave, he saw a newspaper lying on the table by the door. Although the paper was printed in Arabic, the photo on the front page, above the fold, told the story. It showed the terrified face of a prisoner who was about to be beheaded. There were five hooded terrorists standing around him. Four were holding AK-47s, the fifth, behind him, was holding a knife.

"That is a picture of Bernie Gelb," Tobin said.

"Yes."

"I haven't seen this news release. Would you read the caption to me?"

"Of course," Azeer replied. Picking up the paper, he began reading. "Bernie Gelb of Miami, Florida, an employee of Energy Resources, was beheaded yesterday by the Jihad of Allah. In a statement released by Jihad of Allah, it was stated that 'the Jew was executed for crimes against Islam, the heresy of Zionism, and violating the people of Iraq by aiding the American invaders.'"

"Invading? He was helping to restore electricity for the people of Iraq, for crying out loud," the ambassador said.

"Yes, but not all understand the benevolence of America," Azeer replied, putting the paper back down.

"A ghastly thing, to behead someone."

"Indeed," Azeer replied. "Much evil has been done by both sides in this war."

"You will continue the investigation into the Amber Pease case?"

"Yes."

"I know you cannot use the DNA, but we have turned up some other leads that you may find helpful. A witness who said he saw Amber getting into the van, and who was able to pick the driver out from photographs."

"Yes, we appreciate your help," Azeer said. "But it will be necessary for our police to develop their case. I'm sure you know how it is."

"Yes," Tobin replied, suppressing his frustration. "I know exactly how it is."

Ambassador Tobin left the meeting nearly boiling over with rage. There was no doubt in the mind of any reasonable person that Abdulla Balama Shamat had killed Amber. He knew it, and he knew that officials of the Qambari Arabian government knew it. But they had done nothing about it. And that was as far as he could go. He knew the relationship of the United States with Qambari Arabia was a delicate one. It was his understanding of just how delicate it was that had earned him this appointment.

Redha, Qambari Arabia

The markings on the side of the yellow bus read, in both English and Arabic: AMERICAN DEPENDENT SCHOOL.

There were eleven students on the bus, ranging in age from six to sixteen. All were children of the American employees and servicemen attached to the embassy. Amber Pease had been a part of the group until six weeks ago, when she was kidnapped, raped, and murdered.

Amber had not been taken from the bus, but as a precaution, a U.S. Marine now rode the bus with the students from the embassy quarters to their school in the morning, and from the school to their quarters in the late afternoon.

It was late afternoon now, and the children were all returning from the school, laughing and teasing with each other, looking forward to the weekend that was coming up. An embassy party was planned, not only for the adults, but also for the kids, and the party was the subject of speculation and conversation.

"We're supposed to have a surprise," eleven-year-old Tamara Gooding said. Tamara's father was an attaché to the embassy. "I wonder what it will be."

"I know," Terry Goodpasture said. "It's the new Harry Potter movie."

"No way! It hasn't even come out yet!"

"Way! We're getting it early."

* * *

Two blocks away a man sat at a sidewalk café drinking a cup of coffee. When he saw the school bus approaching, he opened his cell phone, dialed a number, and pushed SEND. He had done this many times before, in order to be able to time when the signal would get through to the phone he was calling.

He heard the other number ring, one short ring, just as the bus passed a kiosk. At that instant, a huge ball of fire erupted from the kiosk. The blast ripped into the side of the bus. By the time the sound of the blast reached him, and the others at the sidewalk café, the bus had overturned. Fire and oily smoke roiled up from the wreckage.

Smiling, he closed the telephone and walked away.

The three men rose as a sign of great respect when their host entered the room.

"*Al Sayyid*," they said, bowing.

"Sit, sit." He sighed. "You have been very careless. The Americans have identified all three of you."

"But the Americans have no jurisdiction over us," one of the men said.

"You. Your van was identified. You did not even bother to remove the license plate. And you left your DNA."

"I did not think that—"

"That's just it. You did not think. And you. When you cut off the head of the Jewish American, did you not know that one in your own camp would betray you?"

"I did not know. Tell me who it is and I will see to it that he never betrays another."

"He has been punished for his sin. But now the Americans have turned your name in to our police, asking that we arrest you."

The third man looked at the first two. "You should have been more careful," he said, chastising them.

The honored one looked at the third man. "The Americans

have traced the number on the cell phone you used to trigger the bomb. That has led them directly to you."

"But the Americans can do nothing."

"It will be better for all if you leave our country."

"But, *Al Sayyid*, where will we go?"

The honored one smiled. "The Prophet has told us that one hides best in the bosom of the enemy. You are all three going to America," he said.

CHAPTER
SIX

Atlanta, Georgia

Although he was born and raised in Atlanta, Georgia, and his vast television empire was headquartered there, Todd Tanner, founder and owner of World Cable News, considered himself more a citizen of the world than of America.

Publicly, he had spoken out against the war in Iraq, stating that it was a war of American aggression. But privately, he relished the war. Until the war his numbers had been sagging, but since the war, his audience share was at an all-time high. And because he was taking an openly hostile attitude toward the war, he had ordered that all his reporters look for stories that would put the United States in general, and the current administration in particular, in the worst possible light.

Because of the anti-American slant he gave all his stories, his reports were picked up by the foreign networks at a rate of five to one over the reports of any another American network.

Tanner had cut his teeth in political expression during the Vietnam War. At the time he owned one small, local TV station, left to him by his father. It was not only an independent station, it was the lowest-rated station in the Atlanta market. As a result, he had very little public influence. But he learned that by making himself very visible in the antiwar campaign, he could often garner coverage from other TV sources.

Todd Tanner gained national recognition when he married Joan Fanta, a movie actress whose most memorable screen roll was in the sexploitation film *Maryella*.

Joan had been an active war-protester for some time, showing up at antiwar rallies, encouraging young men to burn their draft cards, and throwing buckets of ketchup, representing blood, at soldiers who were departing or returning from duty in Vietnam.

But Joan really burst onto the scene when she made a trip to Hanoi. While in Hanoi, she stood by the gun crew of an antiaircraft gun as they fired at attacking American airplanes. When one of the American planes was hit, exploding in a large ball of fire, Joan clapped her hands happily and squealed with delight, "Oh! We got one of them! We got one of them!"

Tanner's marriage to Joan elevated his own status as the two of them became very active protesters throughout the rest of the war. Then, after the war, Tanner hit upon the idea of transmitting the signal of his small Atlanta station, via satellite, to cable systems all across the country. Not long after that, he started a twenty-four-hour news network. The experts laughed at him, deriding him for thinking that he could make a network pay off when it had only news shows for its fare. But pay off it did, and now WCN was recognized around the world.

Now, with the war, his network was growing even bigger than before. And he was actually beginning to wield some personal power. The exposure of the prison abuses at Camp Alpha, the resultant relief of command of Colonel Dell, and the court-martial and conviction of Private French proved that.

But his latest coup, catching on video an American colonel shooting a prisoner, was his greatest accomplishment so far. The colonel was going to be tried in what was sure to be a very high-profile trial. And WCN would profit handsomely from it.

Last week, Todd Tanner was honored by the University of California at Berkley.

"I am an American as I am a Georgian," he told the audience gathered there. "But those are merely means of classification. They are not expressions of citizenship, for I consider myself a citizen of the world.

"To that end, I long ago issued orders that my reporters and commentators were never to use the word *foreign* in any of their reports.

"We are the eyes, ears, and conscience of the world. No place on earth is foreign to us."

Tanner checked the time on the wall clock, then left his office and walked into the control room to watch, live, the evening report.

Jim Leyland, the anchor of *World Evening Report*, his hair perfectly coiffed, his whitened, straightened, and capped teeth prominent, stared into the camera smiling warmly.

"Coming back to you on camera two in five seconds, Jim," the director said. "Three, two, one."

The red light came on camera two, and the teleprompter box just beneath the lens displayed the copy.

"In Iraq, the United States is conducting a sweep operation of Fallujah, but at a terrible cost," Leyland began reading. "Some say that the cost is too high, as at least four Americans have lost their lives in the last twenty-four hours.

"Despite that personal tragedy, however, many experts say that America is suffering its greatest damage in the increasing animosity its operations are causing throughout the world community. Recently an incident happened in Fallujah that illustrates the mistakes we have made from the very beginning of this war.

"A high-ranking American officer shot and killed a wounded prisoner. And if that wasn't enough, this happened inside the Abu Hanifa Mosque, one of the holiest places in all of Islam.

"John Williams is our reporter in the field, and he files this report."

The anchor, comfortably ensconced in his Atlanta studio, was replaced by a man in camouflage BDUs, flak jacket, and helmet. He was holding a microphone as he stared earnestly into the camera. Behind him was the rubble of what was left of the several buildings that had been leveled by military action over the previous hours.

"Jim, as you can see by the rubble around me, the fighting here has been quite intense, and the destruction, wrought by the American forces' indiscriminate use of bombs and artillery, has been significant," John Williams began. "And while there have been a few acts of heroism committed by American soldiers in this battle, there have apparently been many more acts of despicable conduct in violation of all that our nation stands for. Yesterday, just such an act occurred, and our cameras were there. I caution you, this is very graphic."

A video of the action began playing on-screen as several armed soldiers were seen standing in a room of some sort.

"This is a room in the Abu Hanifa Mosque," Williams's voice-over said. "It is a holy place for Muslims, and here the wounded Mujahedeen have been brought for processing and interrogation. But Americans were killed in the fighting leading up to this point, and tempers were running high. As you are about to see, the rules of the Geneva Convention are not always followed."

"Son of a"—*bleep*—"he's alive!" someone shouted, though it wasn't obvious who shouted it.

Bleep—"the son of a bitch isn't armed," another disembodied voice said.

The camera moved in on one man who swung his weapon around and fired. A little spray of blood and detritus sprayed from the back of the Mujhedeen's head, as he fell back, his arms flopping out to either side.

"The bastard isn't alive now," the shooter replied.

The shooter turned toward the camera, which then moved in for a very close picture of his face. It held for a moment, and then the screen went black. When it came up again, it was, once more, John Williams.

"As you can clearly see, the prisoner was unarmed and posed no threat to the American soldiers. And what makes this particular incident so disturbing, Jim," Williams said in his well-modulated, TV newsman voice, "is the fact that the soldier you just saw, the soldier who shot and killed the unarmed, wounded man, was not just any soldier."

Once again, Art's picture was on the screen.

"He was Lieutenant Colonel Arthur Kirby Jensen, the commanding officer of the battalion."

The broadcast went to split screen, John Williams in Iraq and Jim Leyland in Atlanta.

"John, was there any provocation for the colonel shooting the wounded prisoner?" Leyland asked.

Williams shook his head. "No provocation whatever," he replied.

"But, to establish some standard here, was there a reasonable expectation on the part of the colonel to think that either he or his men were in danger?" the anchor in Atlanta asked.

"For an ordinary citizen, perhaps," John Williams replied. "But Colonel Jensen is not an ordinary citizen. One would not think that an officer of his experience and proven capability would panic. That leaves only one conclusion. He shot the unarmed Iraqi, not out of fear for his own life, but out of a sense of revenge for his own men he had lost in the operation. But, as I'm sure you can understand, that kind of example set by the higher ups does not bode well with the men. Can there be any questions as to why our younger and somewhat more impressionable soldiers find themselves caught up in such things as prisoner abuse and desecration of the Quran and religious sensitivities?"

"You are there, on the scene, John. What kind of effect is this having on the Iraqi nationals?" Leyland asked.

"As you can imagine, the murder of a Muslim in a mosque has had a devastating effect," Williams replied. "And remember, these are the very people we are trying to win over."

"Have you spoken to the colonel in question?"

"I have spoken to him, Jim, but he refuses to grant an interview."

"Is he facing any type of disciplinary action?" Williams asked.

Williams shook his head. "I can't answer that question," he said. "As you know, there is a camaraderie among these men. I doubt that any of the soldiers involved would file a report on what just happened. I'm sure that seeing this report will be the first information any of the higher ups have on Colonel Jensen's behavior."

"Then your report is doubly important, John," Leyland said from his studio in Atlanta. "For not only have you brought the news of this, yet another American atrocity, to the attention of the world, you have also alerted the American command so that justice might be done. Good job, thank you."

"Thank you, Jim."

The screen returned to a one-shot, full screen, of Jim Leyland.

"That was John Williams, embedded with the Seventh Infantry Division, and coming to you from the contested streets of Fallujah, Iraq. When we come back, we will have as our guest Senator Harriet Clayton of New Jersey. Senator Clayton recently introduced a bill demanding that the United States withdraw all troops from Iraq and issue a formal apology to the Islamic world for going to war against their religion. It will be interesting to get her take on this incident, the latest in a long string of American atrocities."

*Camp Casey, headquarters of the Seventh ID,
just outside Baghdad, Iraq*

"Colonel, if you don't mind, I'm going to run over to the PX and get some things for the men," Specialist Winson said. "I mean, figurin' you're going to be tied up with the general for a while."

"Sure, go ahead," Jensen said. "But I don't have any idea how long this is going to take. I have no idea what the general wants with me."

"Well, hell, Colonel, excuse me for bein' blunt, but if you don't know, you just ain't thinkin' straight. He's goin' to give you a medal for what went down in Fallujah."

"I doubt that. It was just another operation."

"No, sir, it wasn't just another operation. Everybody saw you shootin' Hajs here, savin' Americans there, givin' commands, keepin' order. You ought to at least get the Silver Star out of all this."

"We'll see," Art said. "Oh, here." He took some money from his billfold. Get some goodies for the men from me."

"Yes, sir," Winson answered.

Seventh ID headquarters was set up in a villa that had once belonged to one of Saddam's sons. It was a large, sprawling, and beautiful house, though the various rooms had been turned into offices and quarters for the officers and men of the headquarters staff.

"Colonel Jensen," the adjutant said, standing as Art went into the spacious foyer, now serving as the reception room. "Have a seat, sir. I'll tell the general that you are here."

"All right," Art said. He looked around the foyer. "Pretty good digs," he said.

"We struggle, but we get by," the adjutant said. He picked up the phone. "General McCabe, Colonel Jensen is here. Yes, sir." He hung up, then looked over at Art. "Go right in."

General McCabe was standing in front of his desk when Art went into his office. McCabe pointed to a large leather sofa.

"Have a seat, Art," he said.

Nodding, Art took the seat, and General McCabe sat in a chair across from him. McCabe put his hands together, almost in a prayerlike attitude, sighed deeply, then leaned forward. Art didn't know what this was about, but the body language wasn't good.

"How have things been going for you for the last few weeks?"

"They're going well," Art replied.

"Are you getting all the supplies you need when you need them? Fuel? Ammo? Food? Water?"

"Yes, sir, I have no complaints."

"That's good," McCabe said. "That's good," he repeated absently. It was obvious to Art that the general was very detached from this part of the conversation.

"General, is something wrong?" Art asked.

General McCabe sighed again. "Art, do you recall the incident in the mosque in Fallujah a few weeks ago when you shot a terrorist who had been pretending to be dead?"

"Yes, sir, of course."

"I believe you said that the incident was filmed by a television crew."

"Yes, sir, John Williams from WCN."

"That was absolutely the wrong person in the wrong place at the wrong time," General McCabe said.

"I beg your pardon?"

General McCabe reached over to the table beside his chair and picked up a file folder. "I want you to know, Colonel, that I had nothing to do with this. I had submitted your name for a Silver Star. But what I got back was this." He removed a paper from the folder and handed it to Art.

For Immediate Delivery to: *CG 7th Infantry Division*

**DEPARTMENT OF THE ARMY
HEADQUARTERS, JUDGE ADVOCATE
GENERAL'S OFFICE
WASHINGTON, D.C.**
SPECIAL ORDERS
NUMBER 341
EXTRACT

Action: LTC JENSEN, ARTHUR K. 488-51-2278 3rd Infantry Battalion, 32nd Infantry Regiment, 7th Infantry Division, is hereby relieved of command

and ordered to report to Fort Leslie J. McNair, Washington, D.C., NLT thirty (30) days from receipt of these orders.

Upon reporting to Fort Leslie J. McNair, officer will surrender himself to Commanding Officer of the Judge Advocate Corps for purposes of a Court-Martial under Articles 118 and 119 of the UCMJ. FOR THE COMMANDER:

> M.F. PIERCE
> Major, AGC
> Adjutant

OFFICIAL
Leonard B. Collins
CW3, USA
Asst Adjutant
Distribution
1 – Rec Set
1 – Ref Set
40 – LTC Jensen
5 – 201 File
5 – HHC, 7th ID
5 – 32nd Inf. Rgt
5 – 1st Bn
5 – Msg Ctr

Art read the orders, then read them again to make certain he wasn't mistaking them. He looked up at General McCabe, who had been unable to look at Art while he was reading.

"Looks like I'm going home," Art said.

"I'm sorry, Art," General McCabe said. "Goddamnit, you are my best officer, and I said that very thing to the dumb asses back at DA."

"Articles 118 and 119?" Art said. "What are those articles?"

"Murder and manslaughter," General McCabe said.

"What?" Art asked explosively. "Holy shit! They are charging me with murder?"

"It all has to do with the video Williams took of you in the mosque."

"Damn."

"You made a mistake, Art."

"General, I—" Art started, but McCabe held his hand up to stop Art in midsentence.

"You made a mistake," he repeated. "You shot the wrong man. You should have shot that son of a bitchin' reporter."

Art chuckled. "Maybe I should have."

"You've got thirty days before you have to leave. You can stay here as long as you want, or leave as soon as you want. It's your call."

"If it's all the same to you, General, I think I'd like to get out of here as soon as possible," Art replied. "I'm going to have to make some plans for my defense."

"I'll have you on a plane tomorrow," McCabe replied. He stuck his hand out. "Good luck."

CHAPTER
SEVEN

Washington, D.C., the Senate floor

Senator Todd Canady, Democrat from Massachusetts, rose to address the senators assembled.

"Mr. President, I rise in support of SR-137 as introduced by our esteemed colleague, the senator from New Jersey, Senator Harriet Clayton, and I thank Senator Blackman of California for yielding the rest of her time. I also reserve the right to revise and amend my comments."

Canady, who had occupied his seat for forty-five years, cleared his throat as he shuffled a few papers around. Though once he'd been considered to be presidential material, Canady's problem with liquor and a drunk-driving accident that resulted in the death of a young campaign worker dimmed any chance he may have had of winning the White House.

Canady looked toward the C-SPAN camera, knowing that people all across America were watching him now.

"Mr. President, my esteemed colleagues, the U.S. military presence in Iraq has become part of the problem, not part of the solution," he began. "If the other nations of the Middle East do not fall into line with our aggressive policies, then rather than condemn them, we should respect them for their independence of thought, and their courage of action.

"Let's face it. The war in Iraq is not a war against terror, it has nothing at all to do with terror. Instead, it has become a war in Iraq for the independence of Iraq. Do not be fooled by this administration's insistence that we are fighting terror, or that it has anything to do with what happened on nine-eleven. We are facing Freedom Fighters doing battle against the American occupation.

"The sad truth is, the brutal murder of a defenseless prisoner of war by Lieutenant Colonel Art Jensen is not an anomaly. Instead, it has become all too common an occurrence among our men and women serving in Iraq. And now, as our storm troopers march through Iraq leaving a trail of death and destruction, they are undoing in a matter of three years the goodwill generated by six generations of Americans.

"Our administration tells us that we are there to bring freedom to the Iraqi citizen. But it is not freedom the Iraqi citizen yearns for. Unfortunately freedom has to take a backseat to a more fundamental need. What the average Iraqi citizen wants is a country that is not a permanent battlefield. He also wants a future that is free from permanent occupation.

"I am ashamed to say that Saddam's torture chambers have been reopened under new management—U.S. management.

"We have but one recourse now, and that is to start, as soon as possible, to repair the damage we have done. Even now it may be too late, but we have no other choice. And the most visible evidence that we are serious in trying to recoup our goodwill would be for the swift trial, and extreme punishment, of Lieutenant Colonel Arthur Kirby Jensen."

There was absolutely no chance that the Senate Resolution to withdraw all soldiers from Iraq was going to pass. Clayton knew it would not pass, Canady knew it would not pass, and the few dozen senators who voted for it knew that it would not pass. It was introduced for one reason only: to send a message that they were the only hope for the extreme left wing of the party.

Television wasn't the only media covering Art's adventure in Iraq. He was also on the cover of *Newstime* magazine.

Art was shown in full battle dress, standing near a Humvee, studying a map that was spread open on the hood. It was obviously not a posed photograph. Splashed under the photo was the blurb: FROM THE HOT SANDS TO THE HOT SEAT.

Inside, the lead story was about Art.

Lieutenant Colonel Arthur Kirby Jensen is the kind of poster soldier the army likes. He stands six feet tall, weighs 185 pounds, has closely cut, light brown hair, gunmetal gray eyes, a square jaw, and a strong chin. "He is," one of his contemporaries stated recently, "the kind of man women turn to look at when he walks into a room, though he is totally unaware of his body except as a means of accomplishing his mission."

Jensen is a West Point graduate whose military career has apparently precluded marriage. He has been a brilliant soldier, making lieutenant colonel as he made all previous ranks, on the "five percent" list . . . which means he was promoted ahead of his contemporaries. By all accounts, Jensen is a brilliant tactician, an accomplished commander, and a warrior who is skilled with every weapon.

But even before he entered the military, he had gained some national prominence as an All American starting linebacker on the football team while at West Point. The cadet captain, Jensen graduated at the top of his class at the academy, number one in his classes in Airborne training, Special Forces Operations, and languages.

Arthur Kirby Jensen is the great-great-grandson of one of the legends of the American West. Like Wyatt Earp, Wild Bill Hickock, Temple Houston, Frank

Morgan, and Falcon MacCallister, Kirby "Smoke" Jensen was a gunfighter about whom books were written and songs were sung.

It is, perhaps, this "shoot first and ask questions later" syndrome in Colonel Jensen's family background that has caused him his latest difficulty. Colonel Jensen was caught, on camera, killing an unarmed and wounded Iraqi prisoner. The video, which has been shown around the world, has made even deeper the distrust the rest of the world now has of America.

"The damage Colonel Jensen has done to the United States is practically incalculable," Senator Harriet Clayton said in a recent interview. "The best we can do now is hope that, by rigorous prosecution, we can prove to the rest of the world that the United States will not allow such uncivilized behavior by its citizens to go unpunished."

For Colonel Jensen the punishment has already started. He was immediately relieved of his command and returned to the United States where he faces courtmartial for violation of several Articles of the Universal Code of Military Justice. The UCMJ is the code of laws by which all members of the military are bound. Although Colonel Jensen could face the death penalty if he is found guilty, most military legal experts believe that his penalty will be a lengthy imprisonment.

*Office of the secretary of the army,
the Pentagon, Washington, D.C.*

The Honorable Jordan T. Giles, secretary of the army, sat at his desk, studying the report that was in front of him. Like former Congressman J.C. Watts and Supreme Court Justice Clarence Thomas, Giles was an African-American who espoused a conservative philosophy. However, Giles preferred to think of himself as an American who happened to be black, rather than the more politically correct African-American.

A decorated veteran of the Vietnam War, Giles was proud of his military background, and he felt a special kinship with the army. His no-nonsense approach to his job and his willingness to go to bat for his soldiers made him extremely popular with the officers and enlisted personnel who served under him.

One wall in Giles's office was a veritable picture gallery. There were signed portraits of Reagan, Ford, and Nixon, as well as both Bushes. In addition to the presidents, Giles had a section dedicated to his own personal heroes: Generals George Patton, Douglas MacArthur, Benjamin O. Davis Sr., the nation's first black general, and Colin Powell, the nation's first black chairman of the Joint Chiefs of Staff and secretary of state.

When the phone buzzed, Giles picked it up.

"Mr. Secretary, there is a Colonel Nighthorse from the Judge Advocate General's office to see you."

"Yes, I've been expecting him. Send him in, Betty."

Giles got up from his desk and walked halfway to the door to meet Colonel Nighthorse. It was something he often did when he wanted to put his visitors at ease. Also, if he took them to the small seating area he had in the corner of his office it seemed to create a more relaxed atmosphere than when they talked with the desk between them.

Lieutenant Colonel Temple Houston Nighthorse was wearing the summer casual uniform of dark green trousers with the officer's stripe down the side of the pants, and a lighter green, short-sleeve shirt with no tunic. The shirt had silver leaves on the shoulder epaulets. There was a splash of color from the ribbons and badges over his left breast pocket.

Giles put out his hand in greeting. "Colonel Nighthorse, thank you for coming by to see me."

"I consider it an honor, sir," Colonel Nighthorse replied.

Giles steered him toward the seating area, then pointed to the leather sofa. "Please, have a seat. Would you like something to drink? Coffee, tea? A soft drink, perhaps?"

"No, thank you, sir," Nighthorse said, sitting on the end of the sofa. Giles sat in the leather chair, separated from Nighthorse and the couch by a small coffee table.

Giles pointed to the Combat Infantryman's Badge just above the three rows of ribbons over Nighthorse's left pocket.

"The CIB," Giles said. "I'm impressed. You didn't get that with JAG."

"No, sir. I was an infantry officer before I went back to law school. I was with the 101st during the first Gulf War."

"That's quite an interesting background for a lawyer. And perhaps, under the circumstances, a background that will be very useful to you. Do you know why you are here?"

"General Moran didn't say, sir. He just said I should come see you."

Giles got up then, and when Colonel Nighthorse started to rise as well, Giles held his hand out. "No, stay here."

Giles walked over to his desk, picked up the report he had been reading earlier, then brought it back with him.

"I am sure you have heard of the incident with Colonel Jensen and the killing of an, allegedly, unarmed and wounded prisoner?" Giles asked.

"Yes, sir, it's sort of hard to miss. It's been on TV and in all the papers."

"Lieutenant Colonel Jensen is a brilliant officer who was, no doubt, destined for stars," Giles said, lightly tapping the file folder with the index finger of his right hand. "Until . . . this," he added, holding up the report. He handed the folder to Nighthorse. "It's all yours, Colonel."

"Good," Nighthorse said. "I think Jensen is being used as a scapegoat. I would like the opportunity to defend him."

Secretary Giles shook his head. "Sorry, Colonel, you won't be defending him. I want you to prosecute. I asked General Moran to give me his best lawyer, and you're the one he sent me. You should be honored."

"Honored? Believe me, sir, it is no honor to pillory an officer like Art Jensen. To tell the truth, I believe I would have done the same thing in his situation. This is one cup I'd as soon let pass."

"Wouldn't we all?" Giles replied.

Colonel Nighthorse opened the folder and glanced inside for a moment, then looked up in surprise. "Article 118? Mr. Secretary, we are charging Colonel Jensen with murder?"

"Read this," Giles said, handing Nighthorse a paper. "It is a statement of official military policy."

Nighthorse started to read.

"Read it aloud, please," Giles said.

Nighthorse cleared his throat and began to read.

"Basic U.S. policy underlying the treatment accorded enemy prisoners of war and all other enemy personnel captured, interned, or otherwise held in U.S. Army custody during the course of a conflict requires and directs that all such personnel be accorded humanitarian care and treatment from the moment of custody until final release or repatriation. The observance of this policy is fully and equally binding upon U.S. personnel, whether capturing troops, custodial personnel, or in whatever other capacity they may be serving. This policy is equally applicable for the protection of all detained or interned personnel, whether their status is that of prisoner of war, civilian internee, or any other category. It is applicable whether they are known to have, or are suspected of having, committed serious offenses which could be characterized as a war crime. The punishment of such persons is administered by due process of law and under the legally constituted authority. The administration of inhumane treatment, even if committed under stress of combat and with deep provocation, is a serious and punishable violation under national law, international law, and the Uniform Code of Military Justice."

"Now, to answer your question, Colonel, yes, we are charging Jensen with murder. With all of the negative press we've been getting lately on everything, from putting women's underwear on prisoners' heads, to mishandling the Quran . . . we cannot afford to be perceived as whitewashing this incident."

"Mr. Secretary, we'll never make the case for murder," Nighthorse said.

"I know," Giles replied. "That's why we are also charging him with Article 119, manslaughter."

"Even that is going to be a difficult case to make."

"Colonel, I haven't been misinformed about you, have I?" Giles asked pointedly.

Nighthorse sighed, and looked for another long moment at the folder.

"I'm sure there is more video footage than has been shown on television," he finally said. "Will I be able to get it?"

"Yes. WCN has offered to make the tape available."

"I'm sure they will," Nighthorse said. "They do seem to thrive on news that is negative toward the military."

"Well, if it is any comfort, they don't limit their prejudice to the military," Giles said. "They seem to be anti-American in general."

"Is there any chance for a settlement of some sort? Maybe if we offer to let him plea out 119?"

"There is always a chance, even after the trial begins, to come to some settlement. At this point, though, Colonel Jensen doesn't seem all that interested in a settlement. He is convinced that he was in the right, and he plans to fight it."

"I can't say that I blame him," Nighthorse said. "Who is defending him?"

"I don't think his defense attorney has been assigned."

"Get the best, Mr. Secretary," Nighthorse said. "I mean this with all sincerity. Get the best."

"I'll see to it," Giles replied. "In the meantime, whatever you need, if my office can provide it, let me know." He took a picture of Jensen from the file folder and looked at it for a moment before putting it back. "Go for the conviction, Colonel, because if you lose, I want it well understood that there was no whitewash here. I want everyone to know that the trial was real."

"Mr. Secretary, the only problem with that is, even if he

wins this case, Colonel Jensen will not come away unscarred."

"I know," Giles said. "It is a terrible situation, no matter how you look at it."

The phone buzzed, and Giles picked it up.

"Yes, thank you, Betty," he said. Giles put the phone down and stood. Colonel Nighthorse stood as well.

"I'm sorry to rush you but I have a meeting with the president," Giles said, walking his guest toward the door.

"It's quite all right, sir," Nighthorse answered. "I guess I'd better start preparing my case."

"Good luck, Colonel."

"Thank you, Mr. Secretary. I'm going to need it."

Temple Houston Nighthorse was the great-great-grandson of Night Horse, a Lakota Sioux subchief who took part in the Battle of Greasy Grass. The Battle of Greasy Grass was better known as Custer's Last Stand.

Night Horse got his name when he was fifteen years old, stealing twenty horses from a camp of Crow, who were encroaching on Lakota territory. The name was subsequently run together to form the family name of Nighthorse. The name remained the last existing vestige of Temple Houston Nighthorse's connection with his Indian past.

Nighthorse's grandfather, Russell Nighthorse, was raised on the Indian reservation at Pine Ridge, but he joined the army when he was eighteen years old. Russell was at Fort Shafter, Hawaii, when the Japanese bombed Pearl Harbor, and he fought in the Pacific, throughout the war, earning the Silver Star.

Russell's son, Dennis, who was Temple's father, was born at Fort Benning, Georgia, in 1947. Russell retired from the army in 1960, as a master sergeant. Dennis was the first in his family to complete high school, graduating in 1965. He had planned to go to college, but he married his high school sweetheart, then went to Vietnam instead. He left behind a pregnant wife.

Temple Houston Nighthorse was born in February of 1967.

Dennis never saw his son. He was killed in Vietnam, ironically serving with the Seventh Cavalry.

Temple's mother was Irene Dunnigan, an Irish girl who never remarried, but worked hard all of her life to make a home for her son. It was Irene's plan for Temple to go to college, and he agreed with her, but argued that by joining the army, he would be able to pay his own way.

Irene was against it, given what had happened to Temple's father, but Russell helped Temple convince his mother that it was a good idea. With her reluctant blessing, Temple joined the army, went to Kuwait and then into Iraq for the first Gulf War, then came back to serve out the rest of his time at Fort Benning. Taking his discharge, Temple went to college as he had promised, studied law, got his degree, then, to the surprise of nearly everyone, went back into the army where he joined the JAG Corps.

Temple had excelled as a lawyer with the JAG. In a very high-profile case, he defended a colonel who had fired his pistol close by the head of a prisoner, extracting from him information that disclosed the location of an Improvised Explosive Device. That information saved several of the colonel's men, but it was a violation of UCMJ. Temple's defense got the colonel acquitted.

There were several other cases that he tried as well, not as high in profile, but very important, dealing with such things as defense contracts, etc. Because of that, Temple was noticed by more than a dozen high-powered law firms, all of whom tried to recruit him.

He could have made a lot more money with any of the firms, but he chose to stay in the army. As he told his grandfather, "It isn't a matter of money. It is a matter of honor."

The old master sergeant nodded at his grandson. "I am glad you understand honor," he said. "That tells me that you know the meaning of the circle. The blood of my grandfather, Night Horse, is your blood. The heart of my grandfather is your heart."

CHAPTER
EIGHT

Burning Tree Golf Course

Asa Kinnamon was just getting into the golf cart when his cell phone rang.

"Kinnamon," he said.

"Asa, this is Cal Jensen."

"Hello, Cal," Asa said. "I thought you might call."

"Yes, well, Art doesn't know anything about it yet. But I wanted to call, just to see what would be the possibility of you defending him."

"I've been reading about it," Cal said. "And of course, it's been on all the news. Seems like celebrity trials are all the rage now. Ever since the O.J. Simpson trial."

"Celebrity trial?" Cal said. He chuckled. "I hardly think that Art qualifies as a celebrity."

"Neither was Scott Peterson before his trial. Believe me, your son is a celebrity."

"What about it, Asa? Will you defend him?"

"Yes, of course I will."

"About your fee—" Cal started, but Asa cut him off.

"Don't worry about that."

"I don't expect you to defend him for nothing. I know you are a high-dollar lawyer. I mean, at least you are famous. I see you on TV all the time, commenting on trials and such."

"It won't cost you or Art anything," Asa said. "But it is going to cost a great deal of money in order to take my billing away from the firm. So, if you don't mind, I'm going to have our people construct a Web site, soliciting funds for Art's defense."

"What will we have to do?" Cal asked.

"Nothing," Asa said. "I'll take care of everything at my end. You are going to have to take care of things at your end."

"What do you mean?"

"Didn't you say that Art didn't know you were going to contact me?"

"That's right, he doesn't know."

"You are going to have to convince him to let me defend him. And I don't think it's going to be that easy."

Cal sighed. "I know," he said. "If you and I didn't go back a long way, I don't think I would stand a chance in hell of convincing him. But, given our connection, I think I can."

"All right," Asa said. "You get started at your end, and I'll get started at mine."

Asa finished the game, then went home. A note from his wife told him that she was attending a flower and garden club meeting.

I assume you ate at the club, the note said. *If not, I'm sure you can find something.*

Asa took a shower, then looked around for something for his supper. Opening the pantry, he found a can of pork and beans. In the refrigerator, he found a package of wieners. He chopped up a wiener in a bowl, mixed it with the beans, then went into the study.

There are some things, smells, sights, and sounds, that bring on instant recall. Asa had just such a moment when he took the first bite of his supper.

Near Parrot's Beak, Vietnam, 1967

"Damn, Kinnamon, I'd sure like to go to Las Vegas with you sometime. You're the luckiest sumbitch I know. Your last four meals have been beans and franks," PFC Morris said. "How do you do that?"

"You've got to run your hand over the box before you choose," Kinnamon replied as he dipped a spoonful of beans and franks from the olive drab can.

"What do you mean? What do you do that for?"

"Beans and franks give off a special vibration," Kinnamon said.

"Ha! You're as full of shit as a Christmas goose."

"Oh yeah? Well, I'm eating beans and franks, what are you eating? Ham and scrambled eggs?"

"Is that what it is?" Morris asked as he stared at the pale gray congealed mess in his can. "I thought it was dog puke."

"Here comes the LT," one of the other men said.

First Lieutenant Cal Jensen came up to join the others in his platoon.

"Where are the Cs?" he asked.

"There's a whole case of them over there," Morris said. "But Kinnamon's already got the beans and franks."

Cal picked up a box, opened it, and examined the contents.

"Hey, no fair, LT. You can't peek," Morris said.

"Sure I can," Cal teased. "I'm an officer. We've got special privileges."

Using the little P-38 hand-operated can opener that hung from his dog tag chain, Cal opened a can of ham and lima beans. He fished a spoon from his shirt pocket and began eating before he spoke.

"Be ready to go in half an hour," he said, almost casually.

"Go? Go where?"

"Up there," Cal said, pointing to a nearby hill. "We're going into a blocking position."

"Holy shit. Did you piss off General Westmoreland or something, Lieutenant Jensen?" Morris asked. "I mean, has he got it written down somewhere? Any time there is a shit detail, give it to the good ole third herd. They'll handle it."

Cal nodded. "That's right, but how'd you figure that out, Morris? That's supposed to be a military secret."

They were taken up in three Hueys and put out along the trail, just before nightfall.

"Kinnamon, you and Morris set up a listening post just down the trail," Cal said.

"How far?"

"Don't go any more than fifty yards," Cal said. "I don't want you so far that you can't get back."

"I like the way you think, LT," Kinnamon said. "Come on, Morris, let's go."

Cal watched the two men go down the trail; then he checked all the other men, getting them in position. After that, he set up his platoon CP, and the waiting began.

It was after midnight when Cal heard a whisper over his radio.

"Papa Three, Papa Three, there are people coming down the trail," Kinnamon called.

"I'll send up a flare," Cal replied. He put in the call, and a moment later a large flare, launched by a distant 105 howitzer, popped overhead. It floated down slowly, under a parachute, bathing the area below in a very bright, very harsh light.

"Holy shit! There's hundreds of 'em!" This time Kinnamon's voice wasn't a whisper, but a frightened shout.

Almost immediately thereafter, the gunfire started. It continued after the flare had burned out, the orange-red tracer rounds of the American weapons mixing with the green tracer rounds of the North Vietnamese troops.

The firing continued unabated for several moments.

"Kinnamon, Morris, if you can, get back here with the rest of us," Cal said.

"Morris is dead," Kinnamon's voice came back. "And I'm hit pretty bad. I'll hold my own down here."

"The hell you will. I'm coming for you," Cal said.

"Don't try it, LT. You'll never make it."

Back in his study, Kinnamon set the now-empty bowl of beans and wieners down. Pulling up his pants leg, he examined the scars in his leg. There were four purple puffy marks where the bullets had gone in. Two of them had severed his shinbone and he walked with a limp, until this day.

Cal Jensen had made it. He braved the enemy fire and came down the trail to Kinnamon, then, picking him up, threw him over his shoulder and carried him back to relative safety. The platoon was relieved the next morning, when an entire company was inserted by helicopter. Dust-off came in with the insertion helicopters and Kinnamon and Cal, who was also wounded, were medically evacuated.

The two had gone to Third Field Hospital back in Saigon where they were assigned to adjacent beds. That was the beginning of a friendship that had lasted until this day.

After the war, Kinnamon went to college, then law school. His flamboyant style and his natural ability combined to make his career take off. Now viewers of *Court TV* knew him very well. In his most recent case he had defended the son of a United States senator. The young man was being charged with vehicular manslaughter. Kinnamon got his client off by so discrediting the administration of the sobriety test that it became inadmissible. What made that a particularly stunning victory was the fact that the senator's son was so drunk at the scene of the accident that he could barely stand.

Ironically, had he not been drunk, the wreck would have been the fault of the driver who was killed. Tire marks indicated that the head-on collision had happened in Kinnamon's client's lane, meaning that the driver of the other car had crossed over the center line. Those same tire marks also indicated that Kinnamon's client was the only one to apply his brakes. Clearly, the other man was asleep at the time of the accident, but the law is such that being drunk is a worse offense than being asleep.

Fort Meyers, Virginia

"It's not exactly the Waldorf, is it?" Cal asked as he examined the transient BOQ room Art was occupying. The room had one single bed, a brown chest of drawers, a table with two hard-back chairs, a small, green, cloth-covered sofa, and a matching chair.

Cal had come out to Fort Meyers to visit Art. Art had bought a pizza, and the box and a few rims of crust were all that remained.

"It could be worse," Art replied. He poured a cup of coffee, then handed it across the table to his father. "I'm not in jail and I don't have guards posted outside my room. I am released to my own recognizance. It's just that I must occupy quarters on the post."

"Yes, I guess so," Cal said, taking a drink of his coffee. "So, who is your lawyer? Has he been assigned yet?"

"Lieutenant Colonel Clayton Barnes," Art replied.

"Have you met him?"

"Yes. He's a good man. A graduate of Duke. Very intelligent."

"Has he ever seen combat?"

Art shook his head. "Not many JAG officers have seen combat."

"Colonel Nighthorse has."

"Colonel Nighthorse is an anomaly."

"He's also a damn good lawyer," Cal said. "The army is coming at you with their best, son. You need to meet them with the best."

Art chuckled. "I don't have a lot to say about it," he said.

"Sure you do. The UCMJ allows you to hire a civilian lawyer."

"What civilian could I get who could do battle with Colonel Nighthorse?"

"Asa Kinnamon."

"Sure," Art said. "Like Asa Kinnamon is going to defend me. What's wrong? Are there no Hollywood stars, or football players, or congressmen in trouble right now?"

"Don't worry about that. He will defend you. I've already spoken to him."

Art was silent for a moment. "Dad, you didn't call on your friendship with him, did you?"

"Yes, I did," Cal admitted unashamedly.

"Well, even if he would agree to defend me, I can't afford him."

"You don't have to pay him."

"You can only take friendship so far, Dad. I'm sure he's not going to do it pro bono?"

"Something like that."

"What do you mean, 'something like that'?"

"Asa has already raised three million dollars for your defense fund."

"What?" Art gasped. "How the hell did he do that?"

"He did it by using the Internet. You would be surprised at how many people support you in this."

Art shook his head. "No," he said. "No, I refuse to be a poster boy for some political agenda. I'll go with Colonel Barnes."

"You can keep Colonel Barnes," Cal said. "In fact, I'm sure that Asa would want you to keep him. But, Art, you are in a battle for your life. Not to fight with every tool at your disposal would be foolish. It's your call, but I urge you . . . no, I'm begging you, let Asa defend you."

Outside, there was a rumble of thunder, and Art got up from the small table and walked over to separate the blinds so he could look through the window. In the parking lot he could see his dad's Ford Explorer SUV sitting next to his own three-year-old Lexus.

"Looks like it's going to rain," Art said. "Will you be all right going home?"

"I'll be fine," Cal said.

Cal's unanswered question hung between them like another presence in the room.

"All right," Art finally said after another long moment of silence. "Call your friend. Tell him . . . tell him I am grateful for his help."

Fort Leslie J. McNair, Washington, D.C.

One of the oldest military installations in the United States, Fort McNair was, for many years, called the Washington Arsenal. It was renamed Fort Leslie J. McNair after the lieutenant general who was the highest-ranking American officer to be killed during World War II.

Ironically, General McNair was killed by friendly fire when American bombers, off-target because of bad weather, dropped bombs on his location.

As Asa Kinnamon's Jaguar rolled toward the gate at Fort Leslie J. McNair, he saw a military policeman hold up his hand to stop him. Kinnamon lowered the window.

"What is it, Sergeant?" he asked, as the MP approached him. "Did I not signal my turn or something?"

"You have no military registration," the MP explained patiently. "I'll have to give you a visitor's pass."

"Oh, right, I forgot about that."

The MP recorded Kinnamon's name and purpose of visit on a clipboard, then handed Kinnamon a card that said VISITOR, with instructions to put it on the lower right-hand corner of his windshield.

"Thanks," Kinnamon said. "Oh, where is the Headquarters Building?"

"Straight ahead, Sir. You can't miss it," the MP said, pointing.

For all his notoriety, even Kinnamon's fiercest fans would have trouble recognizing the man who exited the Jaguar in front of the Headquarters Building. Normally Kinnamon let his long, gray-blond hair hang loose. Today it was pulled back and tied behind his head. On his TV appearances, his favorite mode of dress was a fringed buckskin jacket, a black turtleneck shirt, and black trousers. He generally accented his outfit with several ropes of gold chain. Now he was wearing a dark gray suit, white shirt, and maroon tie.

Kinnamon started toward the big redbrick building, but stopped when someone got out of a nearby Lexus and called to him.

"Mr. Kinnamon?"

The man who accosted him was in the class-A green uniform, complete with tunic. There was almost insufficient room to display all the ribbons above his left breast pocket. Shining, silver oak leafs were on each epaulet.

"Colonel Jensen," Kinnamon greeted, starting toward him with his hand extended. "How are you doing today?"

"I have to confess that I'm a little nervous," Art admitted. "I mean, I am not unaware of the results of the most historic trial ever to take place here."

"Oh? What trial was that?"

"The trial of the conspirators in the Lincoln assassination. They were tried here . . . and executed here."

"Whoa," Kinnamon replied with a little chuckle. "That's a disturbing thought."

"So, how does it look?" Art asked.

"I won't lie to you, Colonel, it doesn't look good. But I don't think you'll be joining the Lincoln conspirators hanging from a gallows," Kinnamon said.

"I'm still a little hesitant about using—" Art started, then stopped.

"About using a civilian lawyer?" Kinnamon asked, finishing the comment for him.

Art nodded. "Yes. No offense meant, but I am in the army, after all. It seems, somehow, dishonorable for me to use civilian counsel."

Kinnamon laughed out loud. "No offense taken. You are a

hoot, Colonel," he said. "Here you are, on trial for your life, and you are concerned about the army's sensitivities."

"I guess you're right," Art said. "After all, my father did recommend you."

"Your father and I go back a long way, Colonel. We were in Vietnam together," Kinnamon said. "Only I was a private then and your father was a lieutenant. I am happy to report, though, that he wasn't a pain-in-the-ass lieutenant. And, truth to tell, I probably wouldn't even be here if it weren't for Cal Jensen."

Art was already aware of the relationship between the two men. He knew that his father had gotten a Distinguished Service Cross for his action on the night in which he and Kinnamon were both wounded.

Their relationship had not ended with the war. Cal left the army and became an FBI agent and Asa Kinnamon went to law school. Over the last thirty-five years the two had worked together on several cases. It seemed only natural that Cal would go to his old friend when he needed a lawyer for his son.

CHAPTER
NINE

The General Court-Martial convened with a board of five male and two female officers. The two female officers and two of the male officers were lieutenant colonels. There were also two full colonels, and a major general who was acting as the board president.

These officers would serve as the jury, so it was not necessary for any of them to be members of the bar. As a matter of principle, the convening authorities tried to make the ranks of the members equal, or superior, to that of the charged, though the regulations required only that when a commissioned officer was being tried, all the members of the board would be commissioned officers.

The last to enter was the law officer, Colonel Nelson Brisbane. Unlike the members of the board, the law officer, or military judge, did have to be a member of the bar of the highest court of a state. The military judge would have no vote in the final outcome.

At the defense table sat the defendant and his defense attorneys, the civilian, Asa Kinnamon, and the JAG officer who had been assigned to the case, Lieutenant Colonel Clayton Barnes. Lieutenant Colonel Temple Houston Nighthorse was the prosecutor, and he and Barnes greeted each other with a silent nod. Nighthorse did not look at Art.

"By whom will the accused be defended?" Colonel Brisbane asked.

Colonel Barnes got to his feet. "Please the court," he responded, "the accused has retained civilian counsel, Mr. Asa Kinnamon. The accused has further asked that I continue as military counsel to provide Mr. Kinnamon with any assistance as may be needed, with regard to the peculiarities of military law."

"Very well," Brisbane replied. "Mr. Kinnamon, would you state your qualifications before the bar?"

The civilian lawyer, who was tall and ruddy-faced, stood. He made the slightest nod toward the military judge.

"I am Asa Kinnamon of Kinnamon, Turner, Goodson and Watts, with offices in New York, Philadelphia, Baltimore, and Norfolk. I work out of Baltimore and have been admitted to practice before the state bars of Maryland, Virginia, New York, Pennsylvania, Delaware, Missouri, Texas, and California. I am also admitted to the bar of the United States, the Supreme Court of the United States, and the International Court of Justice in The Hague, as well as the International Admiralty Courts."

"Thank you," Brisbane said. "Trial Counsel?"

"I am Lieutenant Colonel Temple Houston Nighthorse, duly qualified before the bar, assigned to the Judge Advocate General's Corps for the Fort Myer Military District. This covers Fort Myer, Fort McNair, and Washington, D.C."

"It would appear," the military judge said, "that counsel for both sides have the requisite qualifications. The court will now be sworn."

With a scrape of chairs and a few throat clearings, the seven officers behind the bench-barrier stood. They were arranged according to rank, with the senior officer in the center. They raised their right hands.

"Do you," Colonel Brisbane began, then read the name of each of the officers appointed from a copy of the general order convening the court, "swear or affirm that you will faithfully perform all the duties incumbent upon you as a member of this court, that you will faithfully and impartially try, according to the evidence, your conscience, and the laws and regulations provided for trials by courts-martial, the case of the accused now before this court?"

"I do," they all mumbled as one.

When they were finished, Colonel Brisbane looked toward Nighthorse. "Trial counsel may make his opening statement."

Nighthorse stood up and looked at the board of officers. "The task we have before us is not a pleasant one. We are going to have to decide upon the fate of an officer who, until the incident in question, has had a brilliant military career. I know that many in the country might think killing the Iraqi prisoner was justified. Some might even think it was heroic.

"But Colonel Jensen is not being tried in the court of public opinion. You are trying him. This is a unique case, but you are uniquely qualified to hear it. Like Colonel Jensen, you are army officers all, professional military men and women, representatives of the United States. And let's face it, ladies and gentlemen, in the kind of war we are waging against terrorists, any one of us could find ourselves in the same situation.

"The question is, will we allow ourselves to descend to the level of the evil we are fighting? Or, will we conduct ourselves as Americans, and as soldiers, subject to the UCMJ? In the final analysis, this issue is not as difficult to understand as it might appear. It boils down to whether Colonel Jensen killed the Iraqi prisoner or not. Clearly, he did, for we have it on tape. And killing a detained enemy, even if done under stress of combat and with deep provocation, is a serious and punishable violation under national law, international law, and the Uniform Code of Military Justice."

Not until then did Nighthorse look toward the defendant.

He was surprised to see that Jensen met his gaze squarely, not belligerently, not self-consciously, but openly, and with confidence and self-assurance.

It was Nighthorse who broke eye contact before he sat down.

Asa Kinnamon stood then, and began reading from a paper.

"Oh ye who believe, what is the matter with you, that when ye are asked to go forth and sacrifice your life in the cause of Allah, ye cling so heavily to the earth? Do ye prefer the life of this world to the hereafter?

"In the name of Allah, I call upon you to kill Americans by whatever means, by force of arms and by suicide bombs." Kinnamon looked up from the paper then, and stared into the face of each member of the court-martial board before he added, "And by deceit. Do not worry about the Americans." He punctuated the comment by holding his finger up. "They will punish their own soldiers for carrying on the fight against us!" He paused for a long moment before he continued. "And they will be the means of their own defeat. The Americans are weak in body, mind, and spirit, for even now the American press clamors for the head of Colonel Jensen."

Asa put the paper on the table, then looked up at the court. "Your Honor, the fatwa I just read to the court was issued within the last twenty-four hours. I suggest that the terrorists will be following this trial with great interest. I hope we do not provide them with even more incentive to put our men and women in harm's way."

After the first day of the trial ended, Art stopped by a fast food place to have a hamburger. He was trying to get ice for his drink when a very pretty woman smiled and took his cup from him.

"This one is tricky, Colonel," she said. "Let me do it for you."

She held the cup under the ice dispenser standing so close

to him that she was actually pressing her hip against him. He could feel the heat of her body through her dress.

The ice tumbled into the cup.

"There you go," she said. As she handed the cup to him, she put her other hand on his. "Is there anything else I can do for you?"

The touch of her hand, the timbre of her voice, and the glint in her eye indicated that her question was a double entendre.

"Thank you, you've been very helpful," Art said.

"You're sure?"

"It's been a hard day," Art said. "Trust me, I would not be very good company."

"Too bad," she said as she walked away, swaying her hips perhaps just a bit more than was necessary.

Because there were no quarters on Fort McNair, Art was staying at a transient BOQ at Fort Myer, Virginia, which was only a ten-minute drive away. Although the room would be depressing to most, to Art it was as homey as the proverbial rose-covered cottage with a white picket fence. His uniforms were hung neatly in the closet and two pairs of shoes sat glistening on the floor under his bunk.

Art saw his AWOL bag on the shelf above his closet, and he took it down, opened it, and removed an old, hard-bound journal. The cover of the journal was green, and it was of the type that had served merchants for many years . . . long before the advent of computers, as a means of keeping records of their transactions. Such a book could also work as a personal journal, and that was exactly the purpose this one served.

Art held it for a moment, thinking of the man who had kept this journal, marveling at the fact that the journal was written specifically for him, even though it was started several years before Art was born.

Art opened the cover and read the very first page. He didn't have to read it. He knew it by heart.

June 2, 1928

Dear Art,

I am your great-great-grandfather, and though my name is Kirby Jensen, I am known to friends and family alike as Smoke Jensen. At the risk of being immodest, I will tell you that in my day, I was a man of some renown. I owned, and still own, Sugarloaf, one of the finest ranches in the state of Colorado. Whatever its fate is by the time you read these words is beyond me, but I intend to keep it until the day I draw my last breath.

I was also rather good with a gun, an ability that saved my life more than a few times. I like to think that I never abused that talent, but in fact used it to protect the rights and the lives of others.

As I write these words, I am full from a cake my daughter-in-law has baked me for my eighty-second birthday. My six-year-old grandson, Pearlie, who will someday be your grandfather, has helped me celebrate the occasion. I am leaving instructions for this journal to be passed down to Pearlie's first grandson.

That would be you.

I am further leaving instructions that his first grandson be named Art, and I have every faith and confidence that that will be the case. It is for that reason that I will address you by that name as I write this journal.

I want you to know something about your namesake. Art is the name of the man who took me in and raised me as if I were his own son. I never knew his last name, and sometimes think that perhaps he didn't know it himself, or had forgotten it, or long ago decided he had no wish to remember it.

Most folks called him Preacher, and he was one of the finest men ever to roam the mountains of this great country. It is strange to think that Preacher fought in

*the Battle of New Orleans, while I have lived to see
such modern marvels as the radio and airplanes. I can
only imagine what wonders you will see in your life-
time.*

*I intend, Art, with what time I have remaining, to
speak to you through this book. I will share some of my
experiences with you in the hope that it might help you
in your own journey through life. Because, despite all
the wonders clever scientists are developing, in the end,
everyone's life comes down to one thing.*

Character.

*Be of good character, Art. No matter what trouble
you may encounter, if you are of good character, it will
serve you well.*

Art closed the book. He knew much of the history of his
family because it had been passed down by word of mouth. He
knew, for example, that his grandfather, Pearlie, was named
after Smoke's very good friend. Grandfather Pearlie had
served in World War II as a B-17 pilot. During the war Pearlie
met and married an English girl and brought her back to the
States. In 1948, Art's father, Cal, was born. Cal was an infantry
officer in the Vietnam War, but left the military after his tour
was completed. He came home to become an FBI agent. He
married his college sweetheart and Art was born in 1972.

When Art was eighteen years old, his grandfather asked
him to stop by for a visit. During that visit, Pearlie pulled out
an intricately carved box, opened it, and removed the journal.

"This is from my grandfather," Pearlie said, holding up the
book. "He left it to you."

Art laughed. "That would be my great-great grandfather,"
he said. "He was dead long before I was born. What do you
mean he left it to me?"

"Look what it says, right here," Pearlie said, opening the
cover.

*I wrote this journal for, and I leave it to, my great-great-
grandson, Art.*

Art looked up in surprise. "How . . . how did he know my name?"

"Because he named you," Pearlie answered.

That ledger became Art's proudest possession, and, long ago, he stopped being amazed at how so many of the entries seemed aimed specifically at him. He felt that he was in direct contact with the old mountain man, and, in a very real sense, he was.

From the journal of Smoke Jensen

I was building a ranch and working hard to fulfill a dream. I had just come through a bad winter and cattle losses to weather, wolves, and rustlers were so high that there was a question as to whether or not I would even be able to keep my ranch. In order to help out, I took a job with the Sulfur Springs Express Company, working as a shotgun guard. That earned enough to keep me going, but not enough to recoup what I had lost during the winter.

The local bank was carrying my note and when I applied for an extension they turned me down. In fact, they informed me that I had a one-thousand-dollar note due in two days, and if I didn't make the payment, I would lose Sugarloaf.

Then Sally, my wife, and your great-great-grand-mother, came up with an idea. She suggested that we lease our land for one year to one of the big eastern cattle combines. The lease money would pay off the loan. We would sell what was left of our herd to the combine and at the end of the year we could start all over again with a new herd on land that we owned free and clear.

I confess to you, Art, I didn't much like the idea of letting someone else run cattle on our land, but I had to admit that this was probably the only option open to us. So I agreed, and I started into town to send a few telegrams and make all the arrangements.

As it turned out the telegraph lines into Big Rock were down, so I had to ride to Etna, which was one hundred miles away and a town I had never visited before. I sent word back to Sally that I would be gone for a few days, then started out on what I thought would be an uneventful ride.

I'd been riding for two days and was about four miles outside of Etna when my horse threw a shoe and I had to stop. I had just lifted the left foreleg of my horse to look at the foot, when I looked up and saw three men riding hard, toward me. I didn't pay that much attention to them, my biggest concern being the shoe. As it turned out, though, I should've paid a lot more attention to them.

The horses made an obvious turn so that they were riding directly toward me. I had no idea what they wanted, so I kept an eye on them as I started filing the horse's hoof.

The riders came right up to me and reined to an abrupt halt.

"Howdy," I said.

"Havin' some trouble?" one of the riders . . . a man with a long, pockmarked face and a drooping eyelid . . . asked, swinging down from his horse. The other two riders dismounted as well.

There was something peculiar about the riders, about the way they stared at me, and how they let one man do all the talking. Two of the riders were wearing identical plaid shirts and as I looked at them more closely, they looked enough alike that I realized that they must be brothers. There was something about them that was a little peculiar, though, and I decided that the quicker they left, the better it would be.

"It's nothing I can't handle," I answered.

"What are you trying to do, mister? Put a shoe on a split hoof?" one of the men asked.

I should have known better than to fall for an old trick like that, but, out of concern for the horse, I looked at his foot. That was when the pockmarked and drooping-eyed rider slammed the butt of his pistol down on my head. After that, everything went black.

I don't know how long I was out before I heard someone tell me to get up.

Opening my eyes, I discovered that I was lying face-down in the dirt. I had no idea where I was or why I was lying on the ground, though I sensed that there were several people standing around me, looking down at me.

My head throbbed and my brain seemed unable to work. Who were these people and why were they here? For that matter, why was I here?

I tried to get up, but everything started spinning so badly that I nearly passed out again. I was conscious of a terrible pain on the top of my head, and when I reached up and touched the spot gingerly, my fingers came away sticky with blood. Holding my fingers in front of my eyes, I stared at them in surprise. I was also surprised to see that I was not wearing the blue shirt I had put on that morning, but was wearing a plaid shirt.

"What happened?" I asked, my tongue thick, as though I had been drinking too much.

"I'll tell you what happened, mister. Looks to me like there was a fallin'-out among thieves," a gruff voice said. "The other boys turned on you, did they? Then they knocked you out and took the money for themselves."

I shook my head slowly, trying to make sense of things. I wasn't sure what he was suggesting, so I just hesitated.

"That is right, ain't it?" the man asked. "The other two turned agin' you?"

"I'm not sure I know what you are talking about," I said.

"Lyin' ain't goin' to do you no good, mister," the man said. "Too many people seen you in that shirt you are wearing. And just because you wound up without any of the money, it don't make you no less guilty. You're going to hang, fella. I don't know which one of you killed Mr. Clark back there in Etna when you held up the bank, but it doesn't matter who pulled the trigger. Everyone is just as guilty. Now, are you going to get up, or am I going to have to tie a rope round your feet and drag you all the way back into town?"

"I'll get up, I'll get up," I said.

I was right in sensing that there were several people around me, because now that I looked around, I could see six more men glaring at me and brandishing an arsenal of weapons, ranging from revolvers to rifles to shotguns . . . all of which were pointing at me.

"The name is Turnball. I'm the town marshal back in Etna," the burly man said, holding open his jacket to expose the tin star pinned to his shirt. "And these men are my deputies. I reckon you and your friends figured you could rob our bank 'cause Etna is so small, but you got yourselves another thing coming. All right, now you can get up."

I got up, and the marshal pointed to my shirt. "Anyone who would wear a plaid shirt while robbing a bank is just too damn dumb to be an outlaw," he said. "Hell, half the town of Etna described you."

"They may have described this shirt, they didn't describe me," I said.

"Same thing."

"No, it isn't the same thing. This isn't my shirt."

The marshal laughed. "Oh, you mean you stole the shirt before you stole the money from the bank?"

"No. I mean whoever attacked me took my shirt and put this one on me."

"Now that's the dumbest thing I've ever heard. Why would anyone do that?"

"To throw the suspicion on me," I explained.

The marshal shook his head. "Save your breath, I know what happened. You boys got into a little fight, and they lit out on you. I'm arresting you for the murder and bank robbing you and the others done in my town," Turnball said.

A couple of the other riders grabbed me roughly, twisted my hands behind my back, then shackled them together.

"Help him on his horse," the marshal ordered. "And pick up them empty bank bags. Like as not, we'll be needing them as evidence."

"Marshal Turnball, you're making a big mistake," I said, as I was put, roughly, onto my horse. "I did not hold up any bank. I've never even been in Etna."

"You want to explain these empty bank bags here?" Turnball asked, holding one of them out for me to examine. Clearly printed on the side of the bag were the words Bank of Etna.

"They must've been left here by the men who jumped me. They're the ones you are looking for. Not me."

"Jumped you, you say?"

"Yes, they knocked me out. That's when took my shirt and left this one. That's also when they left the bank bags lying around. They set me up."

"You got any witnesses to that?"

"Well, no," I answered. "Certainly no one who would testify, as they would be testifying against themselves."

"Too bad you got no witnesses, mister, 'cause I do have witnesses. I've got at least half a dozen of 'em. And they'll ever' one of 'em swear they seen you and the other robbers ridin' out of town."

"Your witnesses are wrong, Marshal. They are either mistaken, or they are lying."

"Mister, I am one of them witnesses," Turnball said.

*"And I don't cotton to being called a liar by anybody,
and least of all, not by you. So, don't you go tellin' me
what I did and what I did not see."* He pointed at my
chest, adding, *"I remember them plaid shirts you and
one of the other robbers was wearin' like as if there was
a picture of 'em drawn on my eyeballs."*

"I told you, this isn't my shirt," I said again.

"You are making a huge mistake."

"No, friend," the lawman responded. *"The only ones
who made any mistakes around here were you and your
friends. And you boys made three of 'em."* Ticking them
off on his fingers, he enumerated: *"Your first mistake
was in pickin' a bank in my town to rob. Your second
was in havin' a fallout with the other thieves, and your
third was in getting yourself caught. Now, let's go."*

Art Jensen felt himself growing sleepy, so he closed the
journal and put it on the table beside his bed.

"Well, Grandpa Smoke," he said under his breath, "looks
like we're both in trouble for something we didn't do."

Turning off the lamp, Art lay there in the darkened BOQ
room, thinking of the coincidence. He was reading about a
trial his great-great-grandfather had faced in his own life, and
now here he was, over one hundred years later, facing a trial
of his own.

It was as if his great-great-grandfather was here in the
room with him now.

"Remember, Son," Smoke seemed to be saying. "In the
end, it all boils down to one thing. Character."

CHAPTER
TEN

The BOQ at Fort Myer, Virginia

Art stepped out of the shower the next morning to the tune of "The Army Goes Rolling Along." He grabbed his cell phone, which was the source of the music.

"Colonel Jensen," he said.

"How did your first day go? Did Kinnamon give 'em hell?" The caller was Art's father, Cal Jensen.

"Hi, Dad," Art replied. "I suppose he did, but you have to hand it to Colonel Nighthorse. He gave about as well as he took."

"Yes," Cal said. "I've heard he is pretty good."

"Oh, he's better than pretty good," Art said. "He's damn good."

Cal chuckled. "I guess, as far as qualitative analyses go, 'damn' good is better than 'pretty' good."

A graduate of the University of Alabama, Cal Jensen had played football for the legendary Bear Bryant, on the same team as Joe Namath. Namath went on to the New York Jets, Super Bowl III, and football fame. Cal went to Vietnam where he won the Distinguished Service Cross, the Silver Star, the Bronze Star with a "V" device, and two Purple Hearts.

The same tenacity and physical courage that had made him an outstanding football player and an exemplary army officer served him well during his career with the FBI. When the daughter of a U.S. congressman was kidnapped and buried alive in a ventilated coffin while her kidnappers tried to extort money, Cal Jensen single-handedly broke the case. He killed all three kidnappers in a shoot-out, then found the young girl and rescued her.

Cal was retired now, but he still maintained close contacts with the FBI, and had been called upon for advice by more than one of the bureau's directors.

"Are you coming to the court today?" Art asked.

"I hadn't planned to," Cal replied. "But I will if you want me to."

"No need. I was just curious."

There was a moment of silence before Cal responded. "You'll be all right, Son," he said. "No matter what happens, no matter what the verdict is, you'll be all right."

"You think so?"

"I know so," Cal said. "Because it all boils down to one thing."

"What's that?"

"Character," Cal said.

Art chuckled.

"What's funny?"

"You sound like you've been reading Smoke's journal. That's what he says, too."

"You pay attention to Smoke," Cal said. "He knows what he is talking about."

The courtroom

The members and participants of the court sat very quietly as they watched a drama play out on the TV screen. They saw half a dozen soldiers in a darkened room, carrying their weapons at the ready, while they looked down upon what appeared to be dozens of bodies, lying on the floor.

"Son of a bitch! He's alive!" someone shouted. You could hear the voice, but you could not see who was speaking.

". . . shit, the son of a bitch isn't armed," a disembodied voice said.

One of the soldiers swung his weapon around and fired. The flame pattern of his muzzle flash, and the pop of the round was followed by a mist of blood and detritus exploding from the back of the head of an insurgent who had suddenly sat up.

"He's dead now," the shooter said dryly. As he turned toward the camera, it was clear to the viewing audience that the soldier who shot the insurgent was Colonel Art Jensen.

Art held his hand up toward the camera lens, blocking it off, and shortly thereafter the screen went black.

The TV was switched off and Nighthorse turned his attention toward his witness, John Williams.

"Mr. Williams, this is extraordinarily graphic footage. Did you take it?" Nighthorse asked.

"Actually, my cameraman took it," Williams said.

"But you were present?"

"I was present, yes."

"There appeared to be several bodies on the floor. Who were they, and what were they doing there?"

"They were Hajs and—"

"They were what?" the law officer asked, interrupting the interrogation.

"Hajs," Williams said. "Uh, it's what the men call the insurgents. All the dead insurgents were brought into this room and laid out on the floor."

"But not all of the insurgents were dead, were they?" Nighthorse asked.

"No. As you saw in the video, one of them was still alive." Williams paused for a moment. "That is, he was alive until he was killed by Colonel Jensen," he added.

"No further questions."

Kinnamon stood up.

"Mr. Williams, is this the same footage shown on national TV here in America, and all over the world?"

"It is not," Williams replied. He looked at the board of officers. "As I am sure you can appreciate, it was necessary that we tone down the footage we broadcast. There are one billion Muslims. If they were to see this scene, as graphically presented as it is here, it could cause an even greater outpouring of hatred for America than exists now. And of course, we bleeped out some of the language when it was broadcast."

"And so, out of a sense of patriotism, you withheld the most graphic footage. Is that it?" Kinnamon asked. The tone of his voice suggested that the question was sarcastic and Nighthorse picked up on it right away.

"Objection. Your Honor, that question was purely rhetorical and asked in a sarcastic tone of voice," Nighthorse said.

"Withdraw the rhetorical question," Kinnamon said, quickly, before the law officer could respond. He turned his attention back to Williams. "What do you mean when you say that he was still alive?"

Williams looked confused. "I don't understand your question, counselor," he said. "It was obvious on the tape that he was still alive."

"For you to say that he was *still* alive suggests that he had been badly wounded. However, an autopsy disclosed that the only wound he suffered was the fatal wound inflicted by Colonel Jensen. Isn't that right?"

"I suppose," Williams said.

"You did see the autopsy, didn't you, Mr. Williams? You knew that he had no previous wound?"

"Yes, I knew."

"Yet, you said he was 'still alive' as if there was some question to it. These were experienced combat veterans, Mr. Williams. Do you think they could not tell if a man was dead or alive?"

"I suppose they could tell. I really don't know where you

are going with these questions. I don't know where you are going with them."

"You did say that the Americans were the ones who laid out the dead insurgents in this room, did you not?"

"Yes."

"But this one was alive?"

"Yes."

"Since, according to the autopsy report, he had no previous wound, how do you suppose he wound up with the other insurgents?"

"Objection," Nighthorse said. "That calls for speculation."

"Sustained."

"Do you really believe that the American soldiers brought him into this room thinking he was alive?"

"Objection. Again, the question calls for speculation."

"Sustained."

"Actually, there were two of them alive, weren't there?"

"I saw only one alive," Williams replied.

"In the video, I noticed a pall of smoke hanging in the room. What was that from?"

"There was smoke everywhere," Williams replied. "It was just after a battle."

"You know where that pall of smoke came from, Mr. Williams," Kinnamon said loudly. "Are you trying to slant your testimony?"

"Objection," Nighthorse said. "He's badgering the witness."

"Sustained. A calmer approach if you please, Mr. Kinnamon," Colonel Brisbane said.

"Very good, sir," Kinnamon said. Then, to Williams, "You are aware, are you not, that but a moment before these pictures were taken, one of the supposedly dead insurgents set off a bomb? And that bomb killed Sergeant Baker?"

"I can testify only to what I witnessed," Williams replied. "I did not witness the explosion."

"Did you hear it?"

"I heard an explosion," Williams said.

"You heard an explosion, you step into the room immediately afterward, you see smoke hanging in the air and chunks of bodies lying around on the floor, but you cannot testify to the fact that there was a bomb?"

"As I said, I did not witness the explosion. I can testify only as to what I saw." Again, Williams looked toward Art. "And what I saw, and recorded, was Colonel Jensen killing an unarmed man."

"No further questions at this time, but I reserve the right to recall," Kinnamon said.

"Prosecution may call the next witness," Colonel Brisbane said.

"Prosecution calls Captain Michael G. Chambers," Nighthorse said.

Captain Chambers was brought into the courtroom and sworn in.

"Captain Chambers, did you participate in an operational sweep of Fallujah on April eleventh of this year?"

"Yes, sir."

"And during that operational sweep, did you have cause to find yourself inside the Abu Hanifa Mosque?"

"Yes, sir."

"Did you, on that occasion, witness Lieutenant Colonel Jensen kill an unarmed prisoner?"

"He wasn't a prisoner," Chambers answered.

"What do you mean, he wasn't a prisoner?"

"We were keeping the prisoners in another area," Chambers said. "So, technically, this man was not a prisoner."

"If he wasn't a prisoner, what was he?"

"He was dead."

"I beg your pardon?" Nighthorse said, reacting to the answer.

"This room was where we brought the dead. We had no prisoners there."

"But he was not dead, was he?"

"No, sir."

"How long after you surrender before you are classified as a prisoner?"

"I don't understand the question."

"Captain Chambers, don't play games with the court," Nighthorse said.

"Sorry, sir, it's just that I don't think it's right, what's being done to Colonel Jensen."

"Would the court instruct the witness to answer the questions honestly and without equivocation?"

"Captain, you will answer the questions, or you will face charges," Colonel Brisbane said admonishingly.

"Yes, sir."

"Now, Captain, I ask you again. If a soldier surrenders to the enemy, how long after he surrenders does it take for him to become a prisoner?"

"As far as I know, it is instantaneous," Chambers replied.

"Then this insurgent, by surrendering, was a prisoner the moment he surrendered. Am I correct?"

"We don't know that he was surrendering," Chambers replied.

"We don't know that he wasn't either, do we?"

Chambers was quiet for a long moment.

"Did you find a weapon of any kind on the body?" Nighthorse asked.

"No, sir," Chambers said very quietly, mumbling the words.

"Louder, please. Did you find a weapon of any kind on the body?"

"No, sir."

"Then, if he was unarmed, and making his presence known, isn't it reasonable to assume that he was surrendering?"

"I suppose so, yes, sir."

"And in fact, do we not hear a voice on the video saying, 'shit, the son of a bitch isn't armed'? We did hear that, didn't we?"

"Yes."

"And were those words spoken before Colonel Jensen shot the insurgent?"

"I don't know."

"You don't know? Captain, you just watched the video and heard it, just as the rest of us did."

"Yes," Chambers said. "I know what we just saw. But I'm telling you that I was there . . . and I don't remember hearing it."

"Did Colonel Jensen give the prisoner an opportunity to surrender?"

"No, sir."

"On the videotape, someone is heard shouting, and I quote, 'Son of a bitch! He's alive!' Who was that?"

"That was me, sir."

"Did the insurgent shoot at anyone?"

"No, sir."

"Did you see a gun in the insurgent's hand? A grenade? A bomb? Any kind of weapon?"

"No, sir."

"What happened next?"

Chambers was quiet for a long moment.

"Captain Chambers, what happened next?"

"He was shot."

"Who shot him?"

"Colonel Jensen."

"Did the insurgent shoot at anyone?"

"No, sir."

"Did he make any threatening moves?"

"Well, yes, sir, sort of."

"Sort of? What do you mean, sort of?"

"He sat up."

There was a nervous tittering of laughter in the court, though it stilled instantly at a stern glance from Colonel Brisbane."

"He sat up?" Nighthorse asked. "Is that what you are calling a threatening move?"

"You had to be there, sir," Chambers said. "You know how sometimes you can be startled? It was like that."

"So, you are saying that, because you were startled, Colonel Jensen shot him?"

"Yes, sir. I mean, no, sir. I mean . . ." Chambers let his response trail off.

"No further questions," Nighthorse said.

Asa stood up, but he didn't leave his table. "Captain Chambers, do you recognize the voice of the man who said, 'shit, the son of a bitch isn't armed'?"

"Yes, sir."

"Who was it?"

"It was Private Bostick."

"And where is Bostick now?"

"He's dead. He was killed by an IED about a week after this."

"Did you hear him say that before Colonel Jensen shot the insurgent?"

"No, sir. That is, yes, sir, I did hear it, but I don't think he said it before the shooting."

"If I told you that this same tape had been played for seven others who were in the mosque that day, and that all seven have testified that they do not think these words were spoken before the shooting, would you be surprised?"

Chambers shook his head. "No, sir, I wouldn't be surprised at all," he replied. "But I am surprised to hear that it was before the shooting."

"Captain Chambers, how did the insurgent get into that room?"

"I don't know, sir."

"You testified that only the dead were brought into that room. Do you think one of your men may have brought the insurgent in thinking he was dead? Or do you think the insurgent sneaked into the room in order to commit an act of terror?"

"Objection. Again, this calls for speculation on the part of the witness."

"Sustained."

"In fact, Captain Chambers, the insurgent that Colonel

Jensen shot was not the only insurgent in the room who was still alive, was he?"

"No, sir, there was another one."

"What happened to him?"

"He blew himself up."

"And, in the act of blowing himself up, was anyone else injured?"

"Sergeant Baker was killed," Chambers said.

"And how long after the first suicide bomber killed himself was it before the second insurgent showed himself?"

"Objection, Your Honor," Nighthorse said.

"What are you objecting to?"

"Counsel referred to the suicide bomber as the 'first' suicide bomber, implying that the second insurgent was also a suicide bomber. We know now, of course, that that was not the case. There were no weapons found on the second man."

"Objection sustained."

"How long was it after the suicide bomber killed himself, before the second live insurgent showed himself?"

"Oh, it was very soon, sir. Just a matter of seconds," Chambers said.

"And you said that he suddenly sat up?"

"Yes, sir."

"If Colonel Jensen assumed that everyone in there was already dead . . . and one had shown himself not to be dead, but had, in fact, detonated a suicide bomb, isn't it reasonable to assume that when the second sat up very quickly, Jensen considered him a threat?"

"Objection! Again, this calls for speculation," Nighthorse said.

"Your Honor, this witness is a professional military officer who is trained to speculate under certain situations," Kinnamon said. "Indeed, the fate of our nation hangs on the ability of such men as Captain Chambers and Colonel Jensen to be able to make immediate decisions. I think it is reasonable to ask Captain Chambers . . . as an expert witness . . . if he believes it was reasonable for Colonel Jensen to perceive a threat."

"Colonel Nighthorse?" Colonel Brisbane said, offering Nighthorse an opportunity to respond.

"This has nothing to do with military professionalism, and everything to do with Captain Chambers being able to testify as to what was going through Colonel Jensen's mind. We train our officers to react to specific situations, not to read other people's minds," Nighthorse said.

Brisbane thought for a moment, stroking his chin as he did so. Finally, he nodded. "Objection is sustained," the law officer said.

"Your Honor, if we cannot use trained army officers as expert witnesses in matters of military tactics, who can we use?" Kinnamon asked in frustration.

"The objection is sustained. Please proceed, Mr. Kinnamon," Brisbane said.

With an audible sigh to show his dissent, Kinnamon continued his questioning.

"Captain Chambers, you were there when the first insurgent set off the bomb that killed Sergeant Baker, were you not?" Kinnamon asked.

"Yes, sir, I was."

"And you saw the second insurgent sit up very suddenly?"

"Yes, sir."

"Did you perceive that as a threat?"

"Objection, Your Honor. We've already been through all this. It calls for a conclusion."

"In this case the conclusion is valid, as it goes to the witness's own experiences," Colonel Brisbane replied. "You may answer the question, Captain Chambers."

"Let me ask it again."

"I remember the—"

Kinnamon held up his hand to stop Captain Chambers. He knew what he was doing. He was replanting the question in the minds of the board of officers who were hearing the case.

"When the second insurgent sat up, did you feel that you were in danger?"

"Yes, sir."

"What did you do about it?"

"I was bringing my own weapon to bear," Chambers said. "And if Colonel Jensen had not beaten me to it, I would have killed him."

"You would have killed him?"

"Yes, sir."

"You realize that if you had killed him, it would be you on trial here, today, instead of Colonel Jensen?"

"Yes, sir."

"Knowing that now, if you had it to do over again, do you still say you would have killed him?"

"Objection, again, this calls for speculation."

"Overruled," Brisbane said. "You may answer the question."

"Yes," Captain Chambers said. "Even knowing what I know now, if I had it to do over, I would have killed the son of a bitch."

There was a tittering of laughter from the room.

"Strike the appellation from the record," Colonel Brisbane ordered.

"Thank you, Captain, I have no further questions. Your witness, counselor."

Before Nighthorse stood up for his redirect, Colonel Brisbane rapped his gavel against the desk. "Gentlemen, I'm going to ask that we adjourn for the day. This court will reconvene in the morning."

The court stood at attention as Colonel Brisbane and the board of officers filed out of the room. Kinnamon began gathering up his papers.

"How do you think it's going?" Art asked.

"Hard to say," Kinnamon said. He glanced over at Nighthorse. "He's good. He's damn good."

Art laughed.

"What's so funny?"

"That is exactly the qualitative analysis of his skills that I gave my father," Art said.

* * *

Colonel Nighthorse held the cell phone until his party came on the line.

"This is Gordon."

"Gordon, this in Nighthorse. You made the DVD that we are using in the Jensen trial, didn't you?"

"Yes."

"Is there any chance it could have been doctored?"

"Doctored? In what way?"

"There is one line of audio just before Jensen shoots the insurgent. The line says, 'shit, the son of a bitch isn't armed.' Is it possible that line could have been dubbed in there?"

"I suppose it's possible," Gordon said.

"Is there any way to check it?"

"I'd have to go to the original tape to find out," Gordon said.

"Do that for me, would you?"

"Sure, no problem."

CHAPTER
ELEVEN

Kennedy Airport, New York City

The 767 was guided into its parking place by a wand-wielding ground-guide. The Arabic markings, in green on the side of the airplane, were duplicated in English.

Royal Fleet of the Kingdom of Qambari Arabia.

When the engines were shut down a Jetway was extended to the plane's cabin door. The Jetway led to a private debarkation area, for this was not a commercial plane, but the private aircraft of the royal family of the Kingdom of Qambari Arabia.

Prince Azeer Lal Qambar stepped out into the VIP lounge where he was met by representatives of the Qambari Arabia consulate.

Imad Alla Hamdi bowed very low and remained in that position until Prince Azeer told him he could rise.

"You have cleared me through customs?"

"Yes, *Al Sayyid*. There was no difficulty."

"What about the three I sent earlier, as members of our trade council?"

"They were all admitted without difficulty," Hamdi said. "Abdulla Balama Shamat is in Dallas, Balli Daftar Taleb is in Missouri, and Azoon Jabri Shadloo is in Alabama."

"Alabama," Azeer said with a scoffing laugh. "It is easy to ask someone to become a martyr for Allah. But to ask someone to live in Alabama requires much faith and loyalty."

"Even though their names are on the list of suspected terrorists, no one questioned them. There was no difficulty in getting them visas."

"I didn't think there would be. The stupid Americans will do anything to win our favor. They grovel for our oil the way a beggar pleads for crumbs to eat. They are decadent infidels whose lives have no value. Where is the car?"

"It is just outside the door, *Al Sayyid*. With diplomatic plates it was not difficult to bring it here," Hamdi replied.

Ostensibly allies of the United States and vital to the U.S. because of its oil, Qambari Arabia was anything but friendly. The tiny country was ruled by the dictatorial family that gave the country its name. They controlled their people by allowing, and even planting, hatred and distrust for America, all the while making public pronouncements of friendship with the United States.

In addition to being a prince of the family, Azeer Lal Qambar was a member of a Qambari Arabia Trade Council in the U.S. This gave him access to all levels of U.S. government and business, a position that he was about to use to his advantage.

As Azeer rode in the back of the limousine to the elegant consulate quarters on Fifth Avenue, he turned on the TV in the back of the car.

". . . another example of the American military shooting itself in the foot," one of the talking heads was saying.

"But, Ted, Colonel Jensen was acting alone. And but a moment earlier, one of the others, who had only been pretending to be dead, set off a bomb that killed one of the colonel's men. Surely you can see that he thought he was justified."

"Thinking he was justified and actually being justified are two different things," Ted replied. "And, as a high-ranking officer, in fact, as the officer in command, Colonel Jensen had the responsibility to set aside such things as fear and uncertainty. He is charged with making decisions, and we can only but hope and pray that he makes the right ones."

Azeer followed the news until the car pulled through the gates of the consulate. One of the staff met the car, opened the door, and bowed lowly as Azeer exited.

"Hamdi, I sent a list of people that I wanted to meet with. Have you made contact with all of them?"

"I have, *Al Sayyid.*"

Azeer smiled. "The Americans weep over what happened to them on nine-eleven. When I am through with them, nine-eleven will pale into insignificance."

"Generations of Muslims will give praise to the name Azeer Lal Qambar, in recognition of your service to Allah," Hamdi said. "*Allah akbar.*"

"What? Oh yes," Azeer replied. "Allah is great," he added, almost as an afterthought.

Naji, Osman, and Dawud were shown into the reception room of the Royal Suite of the Qambari Arabia consulate quarters. They were told they were going to meet someone important, but they had no idea who it would be. When they learned it was to be Prince Azeer, they were surprised and honored by the prospect.

The three men stood in front of Azeer, who did not offer to let them sit, nor did he make any offer of food or drink. He was drinking coffee, liberally laced with alcohol . . . an open defiance of his religion, though he considered himself above any religious law.

"You have come to serve me?" he asked.

"Yes, *Al Sayyid,*" Naji replied. "And to serve Allah."

"We will become human bombs," Dawud said.

"We will gladly martyr ourselves for Allah," Osman added.

Lifting his hand, Azeer waved the comment aside. "The time may come when I will ask you to do that," he said. "But not yet. I have another task for you."

"Your wish is our command," Naji replied.

Azeer picked up a copy of *Newstime* magazine with Colonel Art Jensen's picture on the cover.

"Do you know of this man?" he asked.

"Yes," Naji replied. "The Americans are trying him for killing a prisoner."

"I believe they will find him guilty," Dawud said.

"And they may execute him," Osman added.

"We cannot let that happen," Azeer said.

The three men looked confused.

"Pardon me, *Al Sayyid*, but why is it not a good thing for the murderer of one of our own to be punished?" Naji asked.

"Oh, he should be punished," Azeer said. "But not by the Americans. They are doing that to curry favor with the Muslim world. They want to show that they will punish those who do wrong to Muslims. But I say it is for us to try him, and for us to punish him. We must show our own people that we are the true defenders of Islam, not the Americans."

"I see," Naji said. "But how are we to do this?"

"You must take Colonel Jensen prisoner," Azeer said. "Bring him to me. We will try him, then we will behead him. And we will post video of the trial and the beheading on the Internet for all the world to see."

Transient BOQ at Fort Myer, Virginia

Lieutenant Colonel Art Jensen lay on his bunk and read from the journal of his great-great-grandfather. As always, it was exactly as if Smoke Jensen was in the room with him, talking directly to him.

From Smoke Jensen's journal

"All rise!"

At the shout of Marshal Turnball, who was acting as the bailiff, everyone in the courtroom stood.

I joined them.

Since the small town of Etna didn't have a courthouse, my trial was being held in a schoolroom, and I studied the alphabet, which had been neatly written by the schoolteacher at the top of the blackboard.

The judge came in then, a large man that some might even say was fat. He was bald, except for little puffs of white hair that stuck out over each of his ears. He sat down, cleared his throat, and picked up the gavel and banged it a few times on the bench, then looked over toward the jury.

"Has the jury reached a verdict?" he asked.

I looked hard at the jury. It hadn't been much of a trial. The court assigned me a lawyer, and when I suggested I might be happier with a lawyer of my own pleasing, I was informed that, other than the prosecutor, I had the only lawyer in town.

I don't know much about lawyers and all the palavering they do, but I do believe I could have done a better job defending me than Mr. Asa Jackson did.

At first, Mr. Jackson tried to make the case that I didn't do it. But the more he talked, the deeper he dug me into a hole. I asked the judge to postpone the trial until I could get another lawyer, but he refused, and now I was standing here with the others, waiting to see what verdict the jury would return. And I must confess that I had some more interest in what the jury would have to say than anyone else in the courtroom.

"Has the jury reached a verdict?" the judge asked.

The jury foreman leaned over to spit a wad of tobacco into a spittoon before he answered. He wiped his mouth with the back of his hand.

"We've reached a verdict, Your Honor," he said.

"Would you publish the verdict, please?"

"We, the jury, find this here feller," and he pointed at me, "guilty of murder and bank robbin'."

I must confess to you, Art, that I wasn't surprised by their verdict. They had four witnesses who swore that they saw me in the bank. All four identified me by the plaid shirt I was wearing when the sheriff arrested me. Of course, it wasn't my shirt, but that argument didn't carry any weight with them.

"Thank you, Mr. Foreman," the judge said. "Marshal, bring your prisoner before the bench to hear his sentencing."

Marshal Turnball came over to me and demanded that I hold my hands out to be handcuffed. I did so, and he clamped the manacles on my wrists before he led me up to stand before the judge.

"Mr. Jensen," the judge said, looking at me with an evil expression on his face.

"Three days from now, the sun will rise on this fair land of ours. A gentle breeze will send the sweet smell of flowers to all who take the time to appreciate them. Birds will fly and creatures in the forest will run free. Fish will swim and jump in sparkling silver waters, and children will laugh and play as children do. Honest working men will sweat to feed their families, and good women will toil at their daily labor.

"But you will see none of this, Mr. Jensen, because on Thursday next, when the first ray of sunlight peeps over the eastern horizon, a lever will be thrown, a trapdoor will fall from under your feet, and you will be hurled into eternity. I sentence you to hang by your neck until you are dead . . . dead . . . dead.

"And may God have mercy on your evil, vile, and worthless soul, sir, because I have none."

The judge ended his pronouncement with the banging of his gavel, and Marshal Turnball and one of his deputies led me out of the court and down to the jail.

It was looking very bad for your great-great-grandfather.

Nighthorse's apartment, Alexandria, Virginia

Nighthorse was looking over documents when his phone rang.

"Nighthorse," he answered.

"Colonel, this is Kyle Gordon. You asked me to check if the DVD had been doctored?"

"Yes, what did you find out?"

"Nothing," Gordon said.

"You mean it wasn't doctored?"

"No, I mean I didn't find out anything. And I'm not going to find out anything. The original tape has been reused."

Nighthorse was silent for a moment. "That's suspicious, isn't it?"

"No, not really. They do it all the time. Especially once it has been edited and transferred to broadcast tape or DVD."

"I see," Nighthorse said, as he drummed his fingers on the table.

"Sorry I couldn't find out any more for you."

"Let me ask you something. Is it possible that one line of dialogue could have been accidentally moved?"

"You ever been typing on your computer, highlighted something, then dropped it in where you didn't intend to?"

"Yes."

"It's that easy," Gordon said.

"All right, thanks."

CHAPTER TWELVE

Transient BOQ at Fort Meyer, Virginia

When Art left his quarters the next morning, he saw two men wearing coveralls. One of the men appeared to be raking the lawn, though as there was nothing to be raked, Art became immediately suspicious. Because he was unarmed, he started to go back inside, but just as he did so, the two men turned toward him. Both were armed, and both were pointing their weapons directly at him.

"What is this?" Art asked.

"Come with us, Colonel," one of the men said. His features were Mideastern, and he spoke with a slight accent.

"Why would I want to do that?" Art asked.

"Because if you don't, we will kill you right here."

Art thought for a moment, then nodded. "Seems like a reasonable enough request," he said.

At that moment a van drove up and stopped. The two men waved their pistols toward the van, indicating that Art should get inside. Art had no choice but to comply.

JAG Court Building, Fort Leslie J. McNair, D.C.

In the room where the trial was being held, the nine officers of the jury were in place, as were the counselors, clerks, and those who had been approved to make up the gallery.

Conspicuously absent was the defendant.

The law officer looked up at the clock, which now read 9:32.

"Mr. Kinnamon," Colonel Brisbane said, "your client was aware that court would resume at 0900 hours this morning, was he not?"

"Yes, Your Honor, he was aware."

"Where is he?"

"I don't know, Your Honor. It isn't like him to be late."

"Have you tried to contact him?"

"Several times, Your Honor. He isn't answering his cell phone."

"He is staying at the transient BOQ at Fort Myer?" the judge asked.

"He is, Your Honor."

Brisbane looked over at the prosecutor's desk. "Colonel Nighthorse," he said.

"Yes, sir?"

"Send two MPs to the BOQ. Have them bring Colonel Jensen to this court, under guard."

"Yes, sir," Nighthorse answered.

"This court will stand in recess until 1300 hours," Brisbane said. He looked at Kinnamon. "At which time, your client had better be present, or when we do find him, he will be kept in confinement for the duration of this trial."

The judge and board of officers exited the room. Kinnamon, who was still at the defense table, took his cell phone from the briefcase and turned it on. Once more, he dialed Art's cell number, and, as before, he got no answer.

Frustrated by his inability to contact Art, Kinnamon dialed Art's father.

"Cal Jensen."

"Cal, Asa here."

"Asa, how is the trial going?"

"It isn't."

"I beg your pardon?"

"Art didn't show up this morning."

"What? Why not? Where is he?"

"I was hoping you could tell me that."

"No, I don't have any idea," Cal said. "I haven't heard from him."

"Cal, he wouldn't . . . uh . . . what I mean is, Art isn't the kind who would . . ." He let the question hang.

"Run away?" Cal replied. "Come on, Asa, you know him better than that. There has been no suggestion that he is AWOL, has there?"

"He *is* AWOL," Kinnamon replied. "The only thing left to decide is whether he is purposely absent, or if he is absent for reasons beyond his control."

"I don't like the sound of this," Cal said.

"No, neither do I," Kinnamon said.

Kinnamon had just clicked off the phone when Nighthorse came back inside.

"You weren't talking to Colonel Jensen, were you?" Nighthorse asked, nodding toward Kinnamon's cell phone.

"No, I was talking to his father."

"Does he know where Colonel Jensen is?"

"No. Look, I'm sure there's nothing to it. He probably just overslept."

"Colonel Jensen, oversleeping?" Nighthorse replied. He shook his head. "I don't think so."

Nighthorse's phone rang then, and he answered it.

"Colonel Nighthorse."

Kinnamon could hear the voice on the other end, but he couldn't hear it well enough to understand what Nighthorse's caller was saying.

"Very well," Nighthorse said. "Come on back."

"Was that the MPs?" Kinnamon asked.

"Yes."

"Did they find him?"

"No."

"I don't mind telling you, Colonel, I'm a little worried about this."

"You should be," Nighthorse answered. "If Colonel Jensen has taken off, he is just making the situation much worse."

"I'm not worried about that," Kinnamon said. "I know he hasn't run away, and I think you know it too. And if he didn't run away, that means that he is absent by reasons beyond his control."

Nighthorse sighed. "Yes," he agreed. "I've considered that possibility as well. Colonel Jensen has been very much in the spotlight lately. I would think he might be a tempting target for some terrorist operation."

Royal quarters at the Qambari Arabia consulate,
New York City

Azeer viewed the videotape of the captured American colonel. It showed hooded and armed men standing on either side of the prisoner. The prisoner sat on a chair, staring at the camera. Something about the way the prisoner was staring at the camera disturbed Azeer. Then he realized what it was. For Azeer's purposes, the prisoner needed to be frightened, and that fear needed to be obvious.

But the expression on the prisoner's face was not one of fear. It was one of defiance.

"Colonel, do you have anything to say?" an off-camera voice asked.

"Yeah, I've got something to say. Do any of you assholes ever take a bath? You smell like shit."

Another figure stepped into the picture then, and slapped the prisoner in the face.

The third figure stepped back and the camera zoomed in on the prisoner, showing the red mark from the blow just administered.

"Ask your government to pull its troops out of Iraq and, perhaps, we will spare your life," the off-camera voice asked.

"Go to hell," the prisoner said.

Again, the prisoner was slapped hard, in the face. This time his left eye began to swell shut, and a little trickle of blood started from his nose.

"Surely, Colonel Jensen, you have something to say to the American people."

"Yes," Art said.

"Ahh, that's more like it. I thought we could make you come around. What do you have to say to your fellow countrymen?"

"Put your money on the St. Louis Cardinals. They are going all the way this year."

"I do not understand."

"You wouldn't."

The video ended with the last exchange.

Azeer looked at Hamdi. "What does he mean when he says put your money on the St. Louis Cardinals? What is that?"

"I believe that is a baseball team, *Al Sayyid*," Hamdi said. "You know how the Americans are with their childish games."

For a moment, Azeer was confused as to how mention of a baseball team would turn up on the videotape, but then he realized what the prisoner was doing. He was making certain that the videotape could not be used as a propaganda tool.

"He is mocking us," Azeer said.

"Yes, I believe he is," Hamdi agreed.

"He is a most unusual man."

"What sort of man would mock his own death?" Hamdi asked.

"A very brave man," Azeer replied. "Foolish, but brave. Such a man could be dangerous to us. We must kill him. I want video of his head being severed, and I want the video posted on the Internet for all to see."

"I will inform Naji," Hamdi said.

As Hamdi started toward the telephone, Azeer happened to

see a copy of today's newspaper. The headline glared boldly from the top of the page. HIGH-PROFILE DEFENDANT IS AWOL.

Azeer picked up the paper and began reading.

> *Authorities did not want to believe that a soldier with Lieutenant Colonel Art Jensen's record would actually go AWOL.*
>
> *"Out of deference to his rank and service, we did not keep him in custody," the JAG officer from Fort McNair said. "But in retrospect, we should have."*
>
> *Jensen, who is being tried for murder of an Iraqi prisoner, failed to show up for a court appearance on the second day of his court-martial. "By his absence," Colonel Brisbane said, "he has brought discredit to himself, the U.S. Army, and the effort of the coalition forces in the war against terror."*
>
> *Colonel Brisbane is the law officer of the army's case against Jensen. In a court-martial the law officer is the same as the judge in civil courts.*

"Hamdi, wait!" Azeer called.

"Yes, *Al Sayyid?*"

"Tell them not to kill the colonel," Azeer said, as he continued to read the paper.

"I beg your pardon, *Al Sayyid*. You do not want Jensen killed?" Hamdi asked.

"No. If we kill him, we will have a martyr. If we keep him alive, we will have a man whom the authorities believe is running away from his obligations." He tapped the newspaper. "According to this story, Colonel Jensen, alive and absent, is a humiliation for America. Let's keep him alive for a while longer. Better for us that he is a live coward than a dead hero."

"Very good, *Al Sayyid*," Hamdi said.

"The American press is a wonderful thing for us, Hamdi," Azeer said, smiling at the article he had just read. "They take great delight in reporting stories that makes their country look bad."

"Yes, I have noticed that," Hamdi replied. "But I've never been able to understand why."

"Controversy, my dear Hamdi. Controversy," Azeer said. "Controversy sells newspapers. Patriotism does not."

Somewhere in Washington, D.C.

"We are to keep him alive," Dawud said, hanging up the phone.

"Alive? I thought we were to behead him."

"We were, but apparently he has become an embarrassment to the Americans. They do not know that we have captured him. They believe he has run away to avoid the trial."

"They think he is a coward?"

"Yes. That is why the prince wants him kept alive."

"Silence, you fool!" Naji said, cutting a glance toward the other room of the two-room apartment they were occupying. "You know better than to refer to him in that way."

"The door is closed. I do not think he can hear us," Dawud said. "Anyway, even if we keep him alive, he will never be free to tell anyone about Prince Azeer."

"You had better pray to Allah that he does not," Naji said. "Otherwise, you may find your own head severed."

"I'm not worried," Dawud said.

Naji looked at his watch. "What is keeping Osman? He should have been here with the food before now."

"And the beer. He is bringing beer too, is he not?" Dawud asked.

"You know that beer is against our religion," Naji replied.

"Yes, but we are in America now. And we are doing Allah's work. I think Allah will turn a blind eye to a few sins," Dawud said with a broad smile.

"I will go see what is keeping Osman," Naji said. "You check on our prisoner," he ordered. "It is even more critical that we keep him now."

They were keeping Art in a bedroom of the two-bedroom apartment. His arms were behind him, and his wrists were manacled to the back of a ladder chair. When Dawud went into the room where they were keeping him, he was surprised to see that the American was sitting in the chair with his head drooped forward.

"Are you awake, Jensen?" Dawud asked.

Art didn't answer.

"Jensen, wake up," Dawud said, moving closer to him.

Art still made no response.

"Do not die on us, American dog," Dawud said. He chuckled. "It seems now that you will serve us better alive than dead. Your countrymen think you are a traitor and a coward. They believe that you are running away."

Art still didn't answer.

Dawud began to get concerned. Prince Azeer had specifically ordered that the prisoner be kept alive. What would happen to him if the prisoner died?

They had not fed Jensen, nor supplied him with water, since they captured him. He knew a person could go without food for several days, but he wasn't sure how long one could go without water.

The prisoner had been complaining of thirst. Had he died of dehydration?

"Open your eyes, Jensen," Dawud ordered. "Open your eyes and I will bring you water."

When Jensen still failed to open his eyes, Dawud grew even more concerned and he walked over to stand very close to him.

"Jensen," he called sternly. "Jensen, wake up!"

Dawud leaned over so that his head was but an inch from Jensen's head. "Are you alive, you American dog?"

Suddenly, and totally unexpectedly, Art Jensen snapped his head up, then forward, butting heads with the terrorist. When Dawud went down, Art, who had broken the ladder rail around which his hands were manacled, leaped up from the chair, then threw himself upon Dawud's prostrate body.

"Here! What are you—?" Dawud started, but that was as far as he got with words. What followed next was a scream.

Art opened his mouth and bit Dawud on the neck. Dawud's scream turned quickly into a gurgling sound as Art bit deeply into the flesh. He found the jugular, feeling the warm gush of blood as he did so. With a mighty jerk of his head, Art ripped the jugular and the windpipe from Dawud's throat.

Dawud, his eyes opened in shock, tried, desperately, to breathe. His efforts were futile and within seconds he was dead.

Art raised himself up with a large piece of bloody flesh hanging from his mouth. Satisfying himself that Dawud was dead, Art spat the flesh out, then lay down beside him, with his back next to the body. Feeling about with his manacled hands, he located the key to his handcuffs. Finding it, he unlocked the cuffs and was just reaching for Dawud's gun when Naji and Osman came into the room. Osman was carrying a couple of boxes of pizza.

"Dawud, I hope you like—" Osman started. Then, like Naji, he stopped in his tracks and looked on in shocked horror at the scene displayed before them. Dawud was lying motionless on the floor with his eyes open and unseeing, and a huge, gaping, bloody hole where his throat should have been. The prisoner was standing before them with his mouth and chin covered with blood.

"Allah's beard!" Osman shouted in alarm, dropping the two pizzas and pointing at the bloody apparition. "It is Satan himself!"

Both men stared at Art in horror for a brief moment, trying to comprehend what they were seeing. That moment was all the time Art needed to react, and he grabbed Dawud's gun.

Naji, who was carrying a weapon, realized quickly what was happening, and he tried to bring his gun up, but it was too late. Art pulled the trigger twice, sending two bullets into Naji's heart. He fell back, dead before he hit the floor.

Art turned his pistol toward Osman then, pulling the trigger twice more. In less time than it would take to describe it, he had killed both men.

Holding the still smoking gun, Art went into the bathroom and washed the blood away from his face and hands. Then he put his mouth under the faucet and drank deeply.

CHAPTER
THIRTEEN

Grabbing one of the cell phones, Art called Kinnamon, then remained in the apartment with the three men he had just killed. He was eating pizza when both the military and civilian police arrived. He gave his statement as to what happened, even describing how he had killed Dawud.

One of the younger policemen, watching Art eat pizza as he calmly recited how he killed a man by ripping open his throat with his mouth, grew sick and threw up. A few of the others blanched.

Once all the reports were taken, Art accompanied the MPs back to the base, where he learned he was being put into "protective" custody.

Although a few of the initial news reports reported Art's escape in a favorable light, as more exact details began to surface as to how he killed Dawud, he became less a hero and more a psychopathic killer.

Within a couple of days after the event, the *World Enquirer*, a supermarket tabloid, had a full front-page artist's conception of Colonel Jensen's escape. The artist depicted him with glaring, wild eyes, flared nostrils, and a bloody backbone hanging from his mouth. The headline read: VAMPIRES IN THE AMERICAN ARMY!!!

World Cable News Studios, Atlanta, Georgia

"We're coming live in five seconds," the floor manager said.

Bill Jacoby, the host of *World Cable News Sunday*, made a last-minute primp of his hair, then stared into the camera. The floor manager held up his hand with five fingers extended, then brought them down one finger at a time. When the last finger came down, the red light on the camera came on. The monitor showed a tight one-shot.

"Good morning and welcome to *World Cable News Sunday*. I'm Bill Jacoby, and our guest today is John Williams."

The camera pulled back for a two-shot to include John Williams in the picture.

"The entire nation, indeed the world, is following the trial of Colonel Art Jensen. And, of course, it took on a rather bizarre twist recently, when Colonel Jensen, evidently taken hostage by terrorists, affected his own escape in a bloody killing spree of all three of his captors. Our guest today knows Colonel Jensen better than just about anyone, having seen him up close and personal. John was embedded with Colonel Jensen during some of the fiercest fighting in Iraq.

"In fact, it is with some justifiable pride, I think, that we here at WCN can say that it was our correspondent John Williams's reporting of the killing in the mosque that has brought about the trial we are following today. John, as I said in the introduction, you know Colonel Jensen as well as just about anyone. What can you tell us about him?"

"I believe we could say that Colonel Jensen is a trained, and very efficient, killing machine," Williams replied. "He is a man with a total disdain for human life. We saw this in the way he shot and killed the Iraqi prisoner."

"But to be fair, John, he hasn't been found guilty of that yet," Jacoby said.

"He hasn't been found guilty of the charge of murder, or manslaughter," Williams corrected. "But there is no doubt that he did shoot the prisoner. The video clearly shows that."

"Allow me to play the devil's advocate here, John. I would suggest that shooting an enemy soldier in time of war does not mean that he has a total disdain for human life," Jacoby said.

"Yes, but there is a difference between soldiers who kill because they are forced to, and someone like Colonel Jensen, who enjoys it."

"How do you know that he enjoys killing?"

"Because he has made a point, in fact, I believe he takes pride, in being expert at it. He has turned murder into an art form. He knows a hundred ways to kill a man without using a weapon, and he can do it without blinking an eye."

The interviewer nodded attentively. "But isn't this exactly the kind of soldier we want on our side?"

"Perhaps, during an all-out war," Williams agreed. "But I would like to remind you, as well as all our viewers, that our government insists that the war is over. That means we are now trying to win the peace. You don't win the peace by using your teeth to rip out the throats of your fellow human being."

"And yet, it was a daring escape, was it not?" Jacoby asked. "In fact, one might even call it a courageous and heroic act."

"Courageous, perhaps, but certainly not heroic. Heroism denotes a degree of nobility. It is a manifestation of righteousness. But, with Jensen, I think his escape speaks more to his evil than to his gallantry," Williams replied.

"Necessity," the host added.

"I beg your pardon?"

"It was an act of necessity."

Williams nodded, then added, "Evil necessity."

"I take it, John, that you would not count yourself as one of Colonel Jensen's supporters."

"I do not. I believe that when Mary Shelley wrote about the Frankenstein monster, she was writing about the result of our military system that trains, promotes, and indeed lauds people like Art Jensen. He has truly become a Frankenstein monster, and it is people like him who have generated a climate for the anti-American sentiment that is so prevalent in the world today."

JAG Court Building, Fort Leslie J. McNair, D.C.

It was six more days before court reconvened. By now the entire world knew of Art's capture and subsequent escape, and Colonel Brisbane addressed that very issue with his opening remarks.

"Colonel Jensen, this court hereby issues an apology for declaring you absent without authorization. All such warrants as were pertaining to you on those charges have been rescinded."

"Thank you, Colonel," Art replied.

"But the initial charge, and the charge for which you are being tried, remains in effect." Brisbane looked at Nighthorse and Kinnamon. "Do either of you have just cause for further delay?"

"I am ready to resume trial, Your Honor," Kinnamon said.

"As am I, sir," Nighthorse added. "But, if it pleases the court, I would like to make a statement with regard to the DVD that prosecution has entered as evidence."

"What is your statement?" Colonel Brisbane asked.

"Given the question raised by witnesses as to exactly when the statement 'shit, the son of a bitch isn't armed' was made, I have had my video expert look into it."

"And?" Brisbane said.

"As it turns out, the original tape has been destroyed. Therefore there is no way to determine whether or not that line of dialogue may have been inadvertently transposed during the dubbing and editing process. Therefore, I ask that the court disregard any testimony or statements that may have been made pertaining to the exact timing of that comment."

"So ordered," Brisbane said. "Now let us proceed."

"Damn," Asa said under his breath. "There's not one in a

hundred prosecutors who would do what Nighthorse just did. Art, my friend, we are facing a man of honor and integrity."

The trial by court-martial lasted for two more days before both Nighthorse and Kinnamon delivered their closing arguments.

"It has been said," Nighthorse began, "that Colonel Jensen isn't really on trial here. Newspaper and television pundits have pointed out that we are trying the American antiterrorist campaign. These same commentators say that we must find Colonel Jensen guilty, in order to show that we are willing to punish our own in any violation of Islamic law.

"Nothing can be further from the truth. We are trying Colonel Jensen for murder and manslaughter under Articles 118 and 119 of the Uniform Code of Military Justice. This is the same code under which we have been trying American military personnel since 1950. It has everything to do with whether or not an American soldier has violated American laws, and it has nothing to do with making a statement, or a showing, to the Arab world.

"I ask that you consider his guilt or innocence based entirely upon the evidence and testimony that has been presented in this court-martial. If you do that, I think you will find that Lieutenant Colonel Jensen violated his oath as an officer, his conduct as an American, and his dignity as a human being."

Nighthorse sat down then, and all eyes turned toward Kinnamon. He remained oblivious of their stares for a long moment as he finished a couple of notes, and then he stood to give his closing argument.

"Four of you, I see, are wearing the Combat Infantry Badge. A great writer, James Jones, who wrote *From Here to Eternity* among other books, once stated that, of all the awards and medals given by the U.S. Army, the CIB is the most prestigious. It denotes that the wearer has been tried in combat, and has succeeded.

"I am proud to say that I, too, earned the CIB for my tour of duty in Vietnam. All of you are wearing ribbons that denote your service in a combat zone. I see among your decorations a Silver Star, a Distinguished Flying Cross, all of you are wearing a Bronze Star, and four are wearing Purple Hearts.

"I am glad that my client, Lieutenant Colonel Art Jensen, is having his case tried before a jury of his peers, men and women who understand the hazards of combat, who understand the instant decisions that must be made under harrowing circumstances.

"Despite the fact that it was not shown on the video, there can be no doubt that there were two insurgents who stole their way into a room that had been set aside for respect of the dead, respect, I might add, for the enemy dead. Lying down with the bodies, they awaited their opportunity and when that opportunity presented itself, they acted. The first terrorist killed Sergeant Baker, but before the second terrorist could act, Colonel Jensen killed him.

"Would you have done the same thing? You heard Captain Chambers testify that he was about to do it, didn't do it only because Colonel Jensen reacted faster than he did. I think, if you examine your heart, and recall your own days in combat, you will come to the conclusion that Colonel Jensen's reaction was not only justified, it was heroic."

Finished with his presentation, Kinnamon took his seat, as Colonel Brisbane released the board for deliberation.

Art and Kinnamon were waiting in a small anteroom in the same building in which the court-martial was being held.

"Coffee, Asa?" Art asked, as he stepped over to draw a cup for himself.

"No, thanks," Kinnamon said. He looked at his watch. "It's been two and a half hours." He drummed his fingers on the table.

"What are you so nervous about?" Art asked, as he returned to the table.

"I let you down. I blew the case," Kinnamon said.

"No, you didn't. I thought your closing presentation was brilliant."

Kinnamon shook his head. "I'm not sure," he said. "I may have overplayed the 'they are all heroes' a bit. It almost came across as pandering."

Art smiled. "Well, it would've worked for me," he said. "Of course, I do confess to being a little prejudiced."

"Art, I have to tell you, I don't have a very good feeling about this one," Kinnamon said. "I wish there were some things I could do over."

"Don't worry about it."

"What do you mean, don't worry about it? You do understand the ramifications of a guilty verdict, don't you? If you are found guilty of Article 118, you could be executed."

"They won't find me guilty of 118," Art said.

"No, to be honest, I don't think they will either," Kinnamon said. "I would have felt better if they had tried you only for murder. It would have been a lot easier to defend you against a charge of premeditated murder. But I'm afraid they might find you guilty of Article 119, manslaughter."

Art took a swallow of his coffee. "There's no 'might' to it," he said. "They will find me guilty."

"They *will* find you guilty? That sounds like an absolute."

"It is an absolute," Art said.

Kinnamon laughed nervously. "Well, there's nothing like having no confidence in my legal skills," he said.

Art reached across the table and put his hand on Kinnamon's arm.

"It has nothing to do with your legal skills, or even the merits of this case," he said. "It has everything to do with geopolitics. The United States government cannot afford to find me not guilty. Why, that would smack of protectionism, and it would reverberate throughout the Arab world. I know that, the judge knows that, and in his closing argument, Nighthorse reminded the jury of it, albeit he told them that wasn't a consideration."

"What are you saying?" Kinnamon asked.

"I'm saying I'm a pawn."

"The fix is in?"

Art shook his head. "No, it isn't a fix exactly. At least, not to the degree that the board has been instructed as to how they will vote. But every officer on that board knows what is at stake here, and they will find me guilty of manslaughter."

"Mr. Kinnamon, Colonel Jensen, the board has returned," Lieutenant Colonel Barnes said, sticking his head into the room at that moment.

Art took a last swallow of his coffee, then stood up. "Into the breach," he said under his breath.

"Art, I'm sorry," Kinnamon said.

Again, Art reached across the table and squeezed Kinnamon's hand.

"It's all right," he said. "I could not have asked for a better defense than the one you gave me."

Not one member of the board of officers looked at Art when he returned. Art sat down, then stood, along with the others, when the law officer came into the room.

"Please be seated," Colonel Brisbane said.

When all were seated, Brisbane looked toward the major general who was acting as president of the board.

"General Borders, has the board reached a conclusion?"

"Yes," General Borders replied.

"Then if you would, sir, please tell the court what the verdict is."

"Of the charge of murder, under Article 118 of the Uniform Code of Military Justice, the board has found the defendant not guilty."

General Borders paused and looked over at Art. Art returned his gaze, not challengingly, but not weakly.

"Of the charge of manslaughter, under Article 119 of the Universal Code of Military Justice, the board has found the defendant guilty."

Art let out a long sigh. This did not come as a surprise to him, but he was almost relieved that this part of his ordeal was over, even though it had resulted in a guilty verdict.

"And what penalty has the board assessed?" Colonel Brisbane asked.

"It is the recommendation of this board that Lieutenant Colonel Arthur Kirby Jensen be dishonorably discharged from the United States Army, that he forfeit all medals, rights, and honors heretofore accrued, and that he be sentenced to a military prison for a term of not less than five, nor more than twenty years."

"Thank you, General," Colonel Brisbane said. "The board is dismissed. Colonel Jensen, please stand."

Art stood.

"Do you have anything to say?"

"I do not," Art replied.

"Very well, this court concurs with the recommendations made by the board. You are hereby reduced in rank, and are dishonorably discharged from the U.S. Army. All medals, decorations, and honors are revoked. I further sentence you to a prison term of ten years to be served in the United States Disciplinary Barracks, at Fort Leavenworth, Kansas. Your sentence is to start immediately."

Art nodded, but said nothing.

"Colonel Nighthorse, see to it that Mr. Jensen is taken into custody."

Brisbane emphasized the word "Mr." to show that Arthur Kirby Jensen was no longer a lieutenant colonel in the U.S. Army.

"Yes, sir," Nighthorse answered.

Nighthorse nodded at two of the MPs who were standing in the back of the courtroom. The MPs came to the front of the room and stood to either side of the defense table.

"I'm sorry," Kinnamon said.

"Don't worry about it, Asa," Art replied. "You did a good job. The deck was just stacked against you, that's all."

"Colonel, would you come with us, please?" one of the MPs said.

Art looked at the MP and smiled. "I'm not a colonel anymore, Sergeant. Didn't you hear the verdict?"

"Yes, sir, I heard it," the sergeant said. "And I think it sucks. As far as I'm concerned, you're still a colonel."

"Thank you, Sergeant, I appreciate your vote of confidence," Art said.

"Cuff him," Nighthorse said, coming over to the defense table then.

"Sir, I don't think—" the MP sergeant started to respond, but Nighthorse cut him off.

"You think I'm enjoying this, Sergeant? It is regulations. Cuff him."

"Yes, sir," the MP sergeant replied.

"I'm sorry," Nighthorse said to Art.

Art nodded. "Like you said, Colonel. It is regulations."

CHAPTER
FOURTEEN

United States Disciplinary Barracks,
Fort Leavenworth, Kansas

The prison population of the United States Disciplinary Barracks at Fort Leavenworth, Kansas, is made up of enlisted personnel who are sentenced to seven years or more, and all officers who are sentenced to incarceration, regardless of the time they are required to serve.

The military prison facility at Fort Leavenworth has been in operation since 1875, opened after the secretary of war called attention to the unethical treatment of military prisoners at stockades and state penitentiaries.

The centerpiece of the original barracks was called "the Castle" because of its imposing appearance, a massive, dome-shaped brick building. It had eight wings that could house up to fifteen hundred inmates, and it was encircled by a rock wall varying from fourteen to forty-one feet high. The Castle was quite noisy, with the sounds of inmates and guards shouting, metal doors slamming, interspersed with the occasional jangle of restraints.

In 1994, Congress authorized $68 million for the construction of a new prison, and it was to this prison that Art was sent to begin serving out his sentence.

The new prison is much quieter than the Castle. Rather than barred doors, the new facility has a solid door with a window. This blocks out most of the noise and makes the cells more comfortable for sleeping at night.

Lieutenant Colonel Peter Garth was the warden of the prison, though that wasn't his official title. His official title was Chief of Staff of the United States Disciplinary Barracks.

Garth was overweight, and had the army not been quite as stressed for people as it was now, he might have faced the possibility of being involuntarily released from service for medical reasons. For the time being, though, the doctors merely counseled him about his weight, pointing out that he was forty pounds over the upper limit, and suggesting strongly that he do something to get his weight under control.

Garth had been passed over for promotion during the last promotion zone, and he wasn't certain whether he would be able to stay on active duty long enough to retire.

He was worried about the new prisoner he would be getting. He, like the rest of the country, had followed the court-martial of Arthur Kirby Jensen. He had mixed emotions about Jensen coming here.

On the one hand, Garth didn't like Jensen. It wasn't that Jensen had ever done anything to him, it was just that things seemed to come so easy for Jensen. Garth remembered him from West Point. Garth had been two classes ahead of Jensen, struggling to make his grades, meet the PT requirement, and stay in school. Jensen, even then, was playing varsity football, breezed through all the PT tests, maintained a near 4.0 average, and had no trouble with the discipline. It didn't seem fair that there were people like that, to whom everything came so easily.

But now, Mr. Jensen had his ass in a crack. He was coming to Fort Leavenworth, not as a highly decorated overachiever, but as a dishonorably discharged—which meant that all his medals and honors had been revoked—prisoner. He would be under Garth's control.

Garth wasn't sure how he felt about that part of it. On the one hand, if there was no trouble, if he handled this high-profile prisoner without difficulty, it would have to look good on his record. On the other hand, there were many people in the country, including some powerful politicians, who were displeased with the verdict.

COURT-MARTIAL VERDICT PLAYS INTO TERRORISTS' HANDS, was the way the *Kansas City Star* put it.

It could be that those who felt strongly that Jensen should not be in prison would transfer their anger toward Garth, as the chief of staff of USD. Garth knew that he would be under the microscope for some time, so he was going to have to handle this situation with kid gloves.

"Colonel?" Garth's adjutant said, interrupting his musing.

"Yes?"

"Colonel Jen . . . that is, Jensen is here."

"Have him brought in."

"Yes, sir."

A moment later, Art Jensen, wearing an unmarked uniform that resembled the army fatigue uniform of the sixties, was brought into his office. Jensen stood before his desk, neither belligerent nor subservient. Garth had to hand it to him. Even in this obviously very difficult situation, Art Jensen had control of himself.

Art had always known that the possibility existed of him being a prisoner of war. He wasn't a prisoner of war, of course, though in his mind this was no different. He knew men who had been prisoners of war, and he had talked to them at some length. The reaction from all of them was universal. The best way to handle the situation was not to look ahead to an uncertain future, but to take it one day at a time. That was a trite cliché perhaps, but one day at a time was exactly the way he was going to handle this.

And, after all, he told himself, he wasn't likely to face physical torture and starvation here. That meant he would have it easier than those who had been prisoners of war.

"I don't suppose you remember me, do you, Jensen?" Garth asked.

"I remember you, Colonel," Art said. "You were two years ahead of me at the academy."

"Two years ahead of you, yet you were promoted to lieutenant colonel ahead of me."

Art didn't know how to take the comment, so he remained quiet.

"I hope you understand, Jensen, that while you are in this facility, you are not a colonel, you are not an officer, you are not even a soldier. You are a prisoner."

"I understand," Art replied.

"Good," Garth said. "As long as you understand that, and as long as you keep your nose clean, we won't have any trouble."

"I have no intention of making trouble for you, Colonel."

"Sir," Garth said.

"Sir," Art added.

"Good. Good. The first few days will be for processing and orientation. Once that is completed, you will have all the privileges . . . such as they are . . . of any of the other prisoners."

"Thank you," Art said.

"You are dismissed."

Art came to attention, and resisted the urge to salute.

Art was in processing and orientation for three days before he was allowed to go out into the exercise yard. He was somewhat of a celebrity when he arrived, not only because he had been a colonel, which was a very high rank among the prison population, but also because many had been able to follow his trial.

The reactions to his arrival were as varied as the prison itself. Some ignored him, some were awed by him, and some resented him. Not long after he showed up in the prison yard, a very large black man confronted him.

"They tell me you was a colonel."

"Yes."

"Well, let me tell you somethin'. You ain't no colonel in here. In here, you ain't nothin' but a prisoner, same as the rest of us."

"Yes, I was told that in orientation," Art said.

"So, don't be tryin' to pull no rank on nobody."

"That wouldn't be possible," Art said. "I don't have any rank to pull."

The big black stood about six feet four inches tall and had a body that rippled with muscles from daily workouts. He pointed to himself with his thumb. "My name is Troy, and I'm the colonel in here," he said.

"Really? And here I thought you just said there was no rank in here."

Troy grinned. "Ain't no rank except for my rank," he said. "And I can back my rank up with this." He bent his arm, flexing his muscle.

"Very impressive," Art said calmly.

"So, ex-Colonel, when I say shit, you squat and ask how much."

"I don't think so," Art replied.

"Say what? What you say to me, boy?"

"Well, we have already established that there is no rank in here, haven't we? So I don't intend to recognize any rank you say you have. Go play your games with someone else."

By now several of the nearby prisoners had overheard the confrontation, and they began drifting over to see what was going to happen.

"Boy, you don't know who you're messin' with," Troy said.

"I'm not messing with anyone," Art said. "That's the whole point. You go your way and I'll go mine."

Troy opened one big palm, and began rubbing his fist.

"Maybe I better just show you who's in charge round here," he said.

"Leave him alone, Troy. He's new here. He doesn't know the ropes yet," Art heard someone say.

"Then it's up to me to teach him the ropes, ain't it?"

"Kick his ass, Troy," someone else said. He giggled. "I've always wanted to see a colonel get his ass kicked."

"Troy, looks like you and I got off on the wrong foot. Why don't we start over and be friends?" Art stuck out his hand in the offer of a handshake.

"Nah," Troy said. "I don't want to be your friend. I want to kick your ass."

"Oh, I wouldn't want you to do that," Art said. Again, his comments were cool and quiet, not at all the reaction of someone who was intimidated by Troy's obvious strength and size.

Troy chuckled. "No, I don't 'spect you would," he said.

Art sighed. "Here's the thing, Troy. I don't want to hurt you." The expression on Troy's face turned from one of almost eager anticipation to surprise. Then he laughed.

"What you say, boy? You don't want to hurt me?" Troy looked around at the other prisoners, in order for them to share his appreciation of the humor of Art's comment. "He don' want to hurt me," Troy said.

"That's what I said," Art replied. "It's not too late, you know. If you call this off now, you won't get hurt."

Several of the other prisoners laughed as well, and the confrontation was beginning to draw several more to the scene.

"Colonel, have you taken a good look at Troy? How are you going to hurt him?" one of the prisoners said.

"Guys, I'm not so sure," another prisoner said. This was the same prisoner who had asked Troy to leave Art alone. "Maybe you all didn't read how he handled those three terrorists who kidnapped him. He ripped the jugular and windpipe out of one of them, using nothing but his teeth."

"Is that right, Colonel? Is that what you done?" Troy asked.

"Yes," Art said. "Then I ate his liver with fava beans and a nice Chianti." Art made a smacking sound with his lips.

"Say what?" Troy asked, obviously confused by Art's remark.

One of the other prisoners laughed. "Troy, you mean you didn't see *Silence of the Lambs*?"

"I don' know what you talkin' about," Troy said. "But I'm

tired of talkin'. I think it's about time I did me some ass kickin'."

Troy lunged toward Art, but Art stepped adroitly to one side, kicking his foot out as he did so. His heel caught Troy's knee in the side, smashing the kneecap to pulp.

Troy let out a yell of pain and anger, then turned toward Art, but his knee didn't let him react quickly enough. Again, Art stepped easily out of his way, this time smashing Troy's other knee.

Troy went down, and Art went down with him, putting his knee on Troy's throat.

"Holy shit!" one of the other prisoners said, almost reverently. "Did you see that?" Everyone grew quiet.

"Troy," Art said. His voice was still calm and conversational. "You are about one-sixteenth of an inch from dying. I can crush your larynx quite easily, and if I do, you will die, very painfully, gasping for breath. Shall we continue this?"

"No, no," Troy said. "I've had enough. I need a doctor, man. My knees is both gone. You crippled me, man!"

"Yes, I did, didn't I?" Art said. He stood up then, taking the pressure off Troy's throat. "But you have to admit that it is better to walk with a limp for the rest of your life than it would be to die, don't you agree?"

Troy didn't say anything.

"Troy, I asked if you agree with me," Art said. Not once, during the entire confrontation, had Art raised his voice. Now the cold, calm, emotionless delivery had a chilling effect that reached everyone present.

"Yes, sir, I agree, I agree," Troy said, his voice tinged with pain and fear.

"Oh, you don't have to say sir to me," Art said. "As you pointed out, I'm not a colonel anymore."

"Oh, please, let me up. Don't kill me. Dear God, don't kill me."

Art reached his hand toward Troy. "So, what do you say, Troy? Are you and I going to put this behind us and be friends?"

"We be friends, we be friends," Troy said eagerly.

"I thought you might see things my way," Art said. He looked into the shocked faces of all who were gathered around him. "Gentlemen," he said. "Have a nice day."

For the rest of the day, wherever Art walked, prisoners parted for him like the Red Sea parting for Moses.

That night, while in his cell, Art was able to read the journal that had just been returned to him that day at the conclusion of his in-processing. It had been his first opportunity to read it since the part where Smoke had been sentenced to hang. Now Smoke was in jail, and again, Art found the coincidence striking, almost as if Smoke had anticipated Art's difficulty and was sharing his own experiences with him to make the ordeal easier to bear.

From the journal of Smoke Jensen

> *For three days, I lay on the bunk in that small, hot, and airless cell, listening to the sound of carpenters constructing a gallows. The window to my cell was so high that, in order to look through it, I had to stand on my bunk, and even then I couldn't actually see the gallows . . . though, in the late afternoon, I could see its shadow against the side wall of the apothecary.*
>
> *By that way I could measure the progress each afternoon. The first day there was just the base. The second day I could see the base and the steps, and the beginning of the gibbet. Sometime in the afternoon of the third day, the hammering and sawing stopped, and when I looked at the shadow that evening I could see the entire gallows, complete with gibbet and dangling rope, the hangman's noose already tied.*
>
> *Having faced death many times before, I was convinced that I had come to an accommodation with it. But I was about to be hanged for something I did not do, and there was something about that prospect that bothered me even more than the actual dying. It wasn't just that I*

was going to be executed, though that was bad enough, it was that those who actually were guilty were getting away with it.

Marshal Turnball had a deputy by the name of Pike, an evil-minded person who took a great deal of delight in standing just outside my cell and telling me how much he was going to enjoy watching me swing. During the night before I was due to hang, Pike was the deputy on duty. Just as the clock struck ten, he came over to the cell to tell me that I had only eight hours to live. He came back at eleven, at midnight, and again at one. Each time he counted down the hours with particular glee.

As it so happened, I had a good view of the clock from my cell, so, just before two, I climbed up to the very top of the cell, and hung on with feet and hands. As I expected, Deputy Pike came to the cell as the clock was striking two in order to give me the latest countdown. But, because I was in the shadows at the top of the cell, he didn't see me.

"Jensen?" he called. "Jensen, where are you?"

I was in an awkward and uncomfortable position and didn't know how much longer I could hold on. I watched Pike's face as he studied the inside of the cell, and I could tell that he was both worried and confused.

Pike walked back to get the key, then returned and opened the door to step inside. I'm not sure I could have held on for another moment, but I managed to hold on until he was well inside, clear of the door. Then I dropped down behind him.

"What the hell?" he shouted, turning around to face me. That was as far as he got, before I took him down with a hard blow to the chin.

Working quickly, I dragged him over to the bunk, then I pulled off his socks and stuffed them in his mouth. That was to keep him from shouting the alarm after I left. I handcuffed him to the bunk so he couldn't get rid of the socks, then I closed and locked the door.

By then, Pike was conscious, and he glared at me with hate-filled eyes. He tried to talk, but could barely manage a squeak.

"Deputy Pike, it has been fun," I said. "We'll have to do this again sometime."

No more than ten minutes later I was riding out of town, on my own horse, having found him in the stable. I have no doubt but that the marshal intended to auction Stormy off after my hanging. I also had my own pistol back, retrieving it from the bottom drawer of Marshal Turnball's desk.

I could have just kept on riding until I was well clear of the county, but I knew if I did I would have dodgers following me for the rest of my life. In order to clear myself, I would need to find the sons of bitches who set me up. (Excuse me for swearing, Art, I'm not sure if son of a bitch is a phrase you will recognize. It's a rather foul one, and I don't know if folks will still be using it in your day. But it was a very useful phrase in my time.)

Actually, I not only needed to find them, I wanted to find them. I had more than just a little score to settle with them.

CHAPTER
FIFTEEN

Memphis, Tennessee

Abdul Shareef and Mohammed Hussein were having breakfast together at the Delta Night Motel. The two men had stayed in the motel the night before, parking their rental trucks at the back of the parking lot.

They went through the breakfast buffet, then sat down at a window table that afforded them a view of the Mississippi River, and both Memphis bridges across the river.

"You have taken bacon, Abdul?" Mohammed asked, surprised to see it on Abdul's plate.

"Yes."

"But you know pork is forbidden."

Abdul smiled. "We are angels of the Prophet now," he said. "Nothing is forbidden."

"That is true, isn't it?" Mohammed said.

Abdul picked up a piece of bacon and tasted it. "Uhmm," he said. "This is very good."

Mohammed reached across to take a piece of bacon from

Adbul's plate. He took a bite, smacked his lips, then smiled broadly.

"It is good," he said. "All this time, we have not eaten pork. Why did someone not tell us it was good?"

"Because it is forbidden unless you are someone like us. Angels of the Prophet."

Mohammed returned to the buffet and filled another plate with nothing but bacon and sausage. He brought it back to the table and the two men ate all of it.

"When I get to paradise, I will have virgins feed me bacon," Mohammed said.

"And give me wine," Abdul answered.

After a few minutes, Mohammed groaned.

"What is it?" Abdul asked.

"I have a stomachache," Mohammed said.

Abdul laughed.

"What is so funny?"

"In less than one hour you will be in paradise," he said. "Why worry about a stomachache now?"

Mohammed laughed with him.

The two men paid their bill, then walked out to the back of the parking lot where the two trucks were parked, back to back, to prevent anyone from opening the doors. They put their hands on each other's shoulders.

"*Allah Akbar*," Mohammed said.

"*Allah Akbar*," Abdul replied.

Royal quarters at the Qambari Arabia consulate,
New York City

Prince Azeer checked his watch and, as he saw the appointed hour draw near, he felt a rush of adrenaline. Picking up the remote, he turned on the news.

". . . it is almost as if the stock market was bound by impassable parameters," a financial wizard was saying. "It is prevented from going too high by a volatile oil market, and from going too low by what is, in all other cases, a very robust economy. One can hardly decide what—"

The interview was suddenly interrupted by a riff of attention-getting music. The screen went blue for a moment, then was filled with the words, WORLD CABLE NEWS ALERT.

There was a voice-over.

"We interrupt this program to bring you a World Cable News alert. We take you now to Memphis, Tennessee, where there has been a very large explosion of unknown origin. Here now, our WCN field reporter, Dave Gregory. Dave, what can you tell us?"

"George, at exactly eight o'clock, local time, there was a huge explosion in the middle of the Hernando DeSoto Bridge, dropping the entire structure into the Mississippi River."

As Dave was giving his report, there was a low, booming sound and, in the middle of his report, Dave suddenly looked to his right.

"Oh my God! There has been another explosion!" Dave said. "From here I can see that it is the other bridge, the Frisco Bridge.

The camera turned toward the Frisco Bridge and recorded it, as the entire span fell into the water, dropping cars and trucks into the river as it fell.

As the scene played out on the TV screen, George, the anchor back in the Atlanta studio, began talking. "What a terrible déjà vu," he said. "Our viewers might recognize this as tragically reminiscent of that scene on nine-eleven when, even as we were watching one of the World Trade Center Towers burning, an airplane crashed into the second tower."

"Yes, George," Dave said from Memphis. "This means that both bridges across the Mississippi River have been destroyed . . . and now it is almost certain that this isn't an accident."

"Any report on casualties yet?"

"Not yet, though as it is the morning rush hour here, there are estimates that as many as one hundred cars may have been on the bridge. And of course, you can just about double that number now, with the Frisco Bridge."

"Thank you, Dave," George said. The scene returned to the studio with the anchor staring at the camera. "Here, now, with an analysis of what this might mean, is—" George started to say, but he interrupted his comment in midsentence and held his finger to his earpiece as something new was coming in.

"Wait, this just in, we have just learned that there has also been an explosion on the I-70 bridge across the Mississippi River in St. Louis."

The scene on the TV screen switched to St. Louis where a cloud of black smoke could be seen rising into the blue sky against the backdrop of the Gateway Arch. A newsman on the scene gave a breathless report, stating how a large eighteen-wheeler stopped right in the middle of the bridge, then exploded, bringing the entire bridge down.

After a few more eyewitness accounts, and some pictures of firemen and policemen rushing to the site, the scene returned to the studio.

"And now, here, with an analysis of what this might mean is WCN contributor Jason Gurney."

"George, although the loss of life from these attacks may not be as high as what we suffered on nine-eleven, the economic impact might be just as severe. What viewers may not understand is that, nearly sixty percent of all east-west traffic in the United States uses the I-70 and I-40 corridors. That means it is going to be much more difficult, and you can make that expensive, to ship freight from coast to coast. Whoever planned this attack is a genius."

"Ha!" Azeer said, laughing out loud and slapping himself on the knee. "Did you hear that, Hamdi? I am a genius!"

"A genius, blessed by Allah," Hamdi replied.

"Yes," Azeer said as he drank his bourbon and water. "Touched by Allah."

Washington, D.C., the Pentagon,
office of the secretary of the army

"Colonel Nighthorse, the secretary will see you now."

"Thank you," Nighthorse said, getting up and walking into the secretary's office. Giles met him just inside the door and escorted him over to the seating area.

"Would you like something to drink?" Giles asked. "Coffee? Coke? Sprite? Root beer?"

"A Sprite would be nice," Nighthorse said.

Giles opened the small refrigerator and pulled out a Sprite and a Coke. Handing the Sprite to Nighthorse, he popped the tab on his Coke and sat down.

"When I was in Vietnam," Giles said, "I was drinking as many as twenty of these a day." He laughed. "I got something called NSU, nonspecific urethraitis. Some of my friends laughed at me, and I didn't find out until later that it was an old army gimmick to say that officers never got the clap . . . though they did sometimes get NSU."

Nighthorse chuckled.

"Colonel, I don't know if I've told you, but you did one hell of a job in prosecuting that very difficult case."

"Thank you," Nighthorse said. "So why don't I feel good about it?"

"I know what you mean. Despite the outcome of the case, I believe Art Jensen to be a good man. And, right now, if the terrorists are going to keep hitting us in places like St. Louis and Memphis, we need someone like him, someone who will take a little initiative."

"No, Mr. Secretary," Nighthorse said. "We don't need someone like Jensen, we need Jensen."

Nighthorse said the word with such authority that Giles squinted at him.

"Colonel Nighthorse, do you have something specific in mind?"

"Yes, sir, Mr. Secretary, I do."

Nashville, Tennessee, Christ Holiness Church of Nashville

Jay Peerless Bixby had started his evangelical career as a revival preacher, taking a tent from city to city to preach the gospel. As he did so the crowds who came to hear him grew larger and larger, his fame and fortune grew until finally he built a huge church in downtown Nashville.

Although he started out as a Southern Baptist, he now considered himself an ecumenical "full gospel" preacher, and as such, he had no particular affiliation, other than, in Bixby's own words, "an affiliation with our Lord and Savior, Jesus Christ."

Christ Holiness was now the largest church in Nashville, and one of the largest in the country. And today, he was holding a meeting with his board of deacons.

"My brothers and sisters in Christ," he began, "I have had an inspiration. You might call it a divine inspiration, because I am absolutely certain this is what God wants me to do.

"You may remember that it was President Richard Nixon who went to China the first time, opening up relations between our two countries. JFK didn't go. LBJ didn't go. Neither one of them could go, and why not?" Bixby held up his finger. "They couldn't go, because people considered them soft on Communism.

"Nixon had no such baggage. Everyone knew exactly where he stood. Therefore he could take the bold step of recognizing China.

"Now, my friends, God has given me the sight to see myself in the same position. Everyone knows exactly where I stand in my love of our Lord and Savior, Jesus Christ. I am steadfast in my belief that only through him shall we find salvation.

"But the Jews and the Muslims worship the same God who gave us his only begotten Son. So, this is what I propose to do. I propose to have a service, where all of our brothers and sisters are invited, Jews, Muslims, Catholics, other Protestants, a true coming together in the worship of God. I think God wants me to do this. I think Jesus wants me to do this.

And I think, if we do this, we might just lay the first stone in building a bridge between our religions that will bring peace to the world."

United States Disciplinary Barracks,
Fort Leavenworth, Kansas

"Jensen."

Art stirred in his sleep.

"Jensen, wake up."

Art opened his eyes, then, through the window of his door, saw Cooley standing just outside his cell. Cooley was one of the guards.

"Wake up," Cooley said.

"I'm awake," Art said groggily. He sat up and rubbed his eyes. "What time is it?" he asked.

"Oh-four-hundred."

Art was confused. Wake-up call was 0530. "Why so early?"

"Colonel Garth wants to see you."

"Now?"

"Right now," Cooley said.

"All right."

"Better bring your book."

"What?"

Cooley pointed to the journal. "You set some store by that notebook you are always reading, don't you?"

Art looked at Smoke's journal. He had fallen asleep reading it last night.

"Yes, I do," he said.

"Well then, you better bring it along if you want it. The colonel said you won't be coming back."

"Am I being transferred to another prison?"

Cooley chuckled and shook his head. "Now, Jensen, you bein' a colonel once, you should know better'n to ask me a question like that. That's way above my pay grade, and you know it. I just know that I was told to tell you that you won't be coming back."

"Yes, well, thanks for the heads-up," Art said.

"Listen," Cooley said as he led Art by the dark cells toward the corridor gate. "To tell the truth, I seen on TV what you done in Iraq . . . and if it had been up to me, I'd'a given you a medal."

Art chuckled sardonically. "Too bad you weren't on my court-martial board," he said.

They reached the closed gate at the end of the corridor, and Cooley turned toward the camera. "Hold both hands in front of you," he said to Art.

Art knew the drill. When a guard was escorting a prisoner through one of the electronic doors, the prisoner was required to show both hands, to prove that he wasn't forcing the guard to open the gate.

Art stuck both hands out in front of him.

"This is Cooley. Open three," the guard said into his radio.

There was a buzz, a click, and then the barred gate slid open and Art and Cooley stepped through. Cooley escorted Art to the main office. The night duty officer was sitting at a desk, watching TV. Glancing toward the screen, Art saw a fiercely burning bridge. The Arch in the background identified the bridge as being in St. Louis.

"When did that happen?" Art asked.

"Yesterday afternoon," the duty officer replied. "They hit that one, and two in Memphis. Took all three of them out."

"They? You mean terrorists?"

"I don't mean the Boy Scouts," the duty officer replied.

"Damn," Art said.

"Colonel Garth says you are to go on in."

Cooley started toward the door.

"Not you, Cooley," the duty officer said. "Just Jensen."

"That's not policy," Cooley said.

"It's what Colonel Garth wants," the duty officer said. "And as far as I'm concerned, that makes it policy."

"Yes, sir," Cooley replied.

When Jensen stepped into the office of the chief of staff, Lieutenant Colonel Garth was standing near the window, looking out onto the well-lighted yard. Unlike the Castle, there were no towers looking down over the yard of the new facility, and there were no imposing stone walls. Instead, it was ringed by two fourteen-foot, chain-link fences, topped with razor wire. The fences were equipped with a detection system. If someone tried to climb or cut through the fence to get out, cameras would automatically begin recording that sector and guards, who were on roving patrol, would respond immediately.

Art stood quietly for a long moment. He could see his own reflection in the window, so he knew that Garth knew he was here. He knew, also, that Garth was waiting for him to give some indication of his presence, perhaps as innocuous as a discreet clearing of the throat.

Art remained silent.

"You are quite the controlled person, aren't you?" Garth said without turning around.

"I try to be," Art said.

Garth turned then. "You know that I could add three years to your sentence for what you did in the yard yesterday."

"I was attacked," Art answered.

"Don't worry. I'm overlooking it," Garth said. "You might say it's because of the West Point brotherhood."

"Thanks."

Garth sighed. "You might say that, but you would be wrong. The truth is, you are no longer my problem."

Art wanted to ask what Garth was talking about, but he said nothing.

"Aren't you the least curious?" Garth asked in exasperation.

"Yes, I'm curious," Art said. "But it is not my place to ask. I assume you will tell me when you are ready to tell me."

Garth picked up an envelope and handed it to Art. "Here," he said. "You are free to go."

This time Art couldn't keep the question in. He wasn't sure what Garth meant.

"Free to go? Free to go where?"

"Anywhere you want to go," Garth said. "The president of the United States has commuted your sentence. You are no longer a prisoner of the United States Disciplinary Barracks."

CHAPTER
SIXTEEN

Alexandria, Virginia, one month later

Art had always been frugal with his army pay. He wasn't married, and had little to spend it on except for food and quarters. As a result he had a comfortable bank account, supplemented by a good portfolio, so he wasn't in danger of becoming destitute any time soon.

But he did need to find some type of employment, not only to keep from having to dip too deeply into his savings, but also for his own sanity. Art was not the sort of man who could just sit around and do nothing.

He had been approached by a company called "Military Consultants Inc." about working for them. They were a mercenary group, headquartered in the United States, but doing business all over the world.

The pay was good, excellent, in fact, more than he had been making while he was on active duty. And the job appealed to him, consisting of training the military of small countries. What made him decide against it was the fact that Military Consultants Inc. made no distinction about whom they would do business with.

"We don't get into politics," Art was told. "We will take any job, anywhere, as long as we are paid. Believe me, it is much cleaner that way." Art didn't believe it was cleaner that way, so he declined the offer.

He had also been offered a job as a private detective, as chief of security for a large company, and even as a pitch person for the largest automobile sales company on the East Coast. None of those jobs appealed to him, so he was still waiting to see what would come along.

Opening a can of chili, Art prepared a bowl, then took it and a grilled cheese sandwich out onto the patio. There, he ate his supper and drank a beer as he looked back across the river toward Washington, D.C. As he looked at the night-lights of the city, one seemed to detach itself from the others, and begin climbing into the sky. He realized then that it was an airliner, bound for some distant destination.

His phone rang.

"Jensen," he said, answering the phone.

"Art, meet me at the Watergate," his father said.

"When?"

"Now. As soon as you can get there."

"What room?"

"There will be a message for you at the desk," Cal said mysteriously. "You remember the name of the kid who went skiing with us when you were twelve? The one who broke his arm?"

"Yes, it was—"

"Don't say the name now. When you reach the hotel, there will be a letter at the desk. Ask for it under that name."

"Dad, what's all this about?"

"You'll find out when you get here," Cal said, hanging up then to prevent any further questioning from his son.

The Watergate Hotel, Washington, D.C.

Opened in 1967, the Watergate is best known for the role it played in the downfall of President Richard Nixon. It was built on the defunct Chesapeake and Ohio Canal, and the last lock, which diverted water from the Potomac River into the Tidal Basin at flood stage, was known as the "water gate." It was from this lock that the hotel got its name.

Art crossed the wide, very plush lobby, then stepped up to the desk.

"Yes, sir, may I help you?"

"I believe you have a message for Darrel Wright," Art said.

"Let me check, sir."

The clerk checked behind the desk, then produced an envelope, which he handed to Art. Thanking him, Art opened the envelope. The only thing written on the paper inside the envelope was the room number, so Art went to the elevator, then proceeded directly to the room.

Art's father answered the knock, then stepped back to let his son in.

"An executive suite," Art said, looking around. "I'm impressed."

"You are about to be more impressed," Cal replied.

"What's going on, Pop?"

"It's not my place to say," Cal said. "You want something to drink? There's beer in the refrigerator."

Art was getting his beer when there was another knock at the door. He heard his father open it, then invite the visitor inside. Closing the door to the refrigerator, he turned to see who it was, and was surprised to see Lieutenant Colonel Temple Houston Nighthorse.

"Come in, Colonel," Cal invited.

Nighthorse, who was carrying a briefcase, came into the room, then looked over at Art. "Good evening," he said.

"What are you doing here?" Art asked.

"Easy, Son," Cal said. "You'll see everything in a few minutes."

"Yeah? Well, I'm not all that sure I want to see it," Art said.

"Aren't you going to offer our guest a beer?" Cal asked.

"He's not my guest, he's yours," Art said.

"He was just doing his job," Cal said.

Art paused for a moment, then smiled at Nighthorse and

extended his hand. "Hell, Colonel, I don't mind you doing your job," he said. "I just wish you weren't so damn good at it."

"Believe me," Nighthorse replied, shaking Art's hand. "It wasn't something I wanted to do."

Art returned to the refrigerator, opened the door, and took out a beer. "Have one," he offered, handing the beer to Nighthorse.

"Thanks," Nighthorse said.

There was another knock on the door and Art looked toward it in surprise. "What the hell, Dad, is there anyone who isn't coming here tonight?"

"This is the last one, I promise," Cal said. When Cal opened the door, Art gasped in surprise at the sight of the tall black man who was standing there.

"Mr. Secretary," Cal said. "I'm glad you could make it."

"I'm sorry if I'm a little late," Secretary of the Army Giles said. "I had to testify before a congressional hearing this afternoon, and it ran long."

"No problem. We're having a beer. Will you join us?"

"I don't mind if I do," Giles said. Looking toward Art, he smiled. "Does he know yet?"

"No, sir," Cal replied. "I figured that was for you to tell him."

"Know what?" Art asked. "Will somebody please tell me what in the Sam Hill is going on?"

"I guess there's no sense in holding it back any longer," Cal said. "You asked why Colonel Nighthorse was here. He was very instrumental in getting the president to commute your sentence."

"Really? Well, I thank you for that, Colonel," Art said.

"It wasn't only commuted," Nighthorse said. "You have been given a full pardon."

"And reinstated in the army," Cal said.

Art could scarcely believe the good news. A wide smile spread across his face as he looked at Giles. "Is this true, Mr. Secretary? I have been reinstated? At my rank?"

Giles shook his head. "Uh, no, not at your old rank, I'm afraid."

"So, what am I? A major? A captain? I don't care, I'll work hard and—"

"You are a brigadier general," Giles said, interrupting Art.

Art gasped, and felt his head spinning. "What did you say?"

"Read the orders, Colonel Nighthorse," Giles said. "Then I'll swear him in."

Nighthorse opened his briefcase and pulled out a folder. Extracting a paper from the folder, he began to read.

"Special Orders 102005, by authority of Congress, Arthur Kirby Jensen, DOB 22 November 1972, HOR Alexandria, VA, is reinstated to active duty in the U.S. Army with unbroken continuity of service, with the rank of brigadier general. DOR from date of swearing in. Signed, Jordan T. Giles, Secretary of the Army."

"Is all this real?" Art asked, scarcely able to believe what he was hearing.

"Oh, it's all real, all right," Giles said. "Assuming you agree to the terms."

"The terms?" Art asked, a look of confusion crossing his face. "What terms?"

"As far as the world is concerned, you are still a discredited civilian. Your reinstatement to the army is top secret."

"I don't understand. Why is it top secret?"

"From the moment the trial was over, Colonel Nighthorse has been pursuing this," Giles said. He chuckled. "He made himself such a pest in the offices of the secretary of defense and secretary of homeland security that they started coming down on me."

"I thank you for backing me up, Mr. Secretary," Nighthorse said.

"Yes, well, I figured if you were that dedicated, I could take a little heat for you."

"So, I not only owe my freedom to you, I owe my reinstatement as well," Art said. "It could be that I had you all wrong, Colonel."

"Could be," Nighthorse said. "But maybe you had better hear the rest of it before you get carried away with your praise."

"Yes, maybe I had better," Art said. "You can begin by explaining why my reinstatement is being kept a secret."

"It is not only your reinstatement and your rank that are secret, your mission is secret. Top secret, in fact."

"What is that mission?"

"I can't tell you that, until you are sworn in," Nighthorse said.

"You mean I'm going to have to just accept this mission at face value? I can't even evaluate whether or not I will accept it?"

"You can decline being sworn in," Nighthorse said. "But once you are sworn in, you are committed to the mission."

Art laughed nervously. "This is the damnedest thing I've ever heard of. All right, swear me in."

"Hold up your right hand," Giles said.

Art did as directed, repeating the oath after Giles.

"I, Arthur Kirby Jensen, having been appointed an officer in the army of the United States, as indicated above in the grade of brigadier general, do solemnly swear that I will support and defend the Constitution of the United States against all enemies, foreign or domestic, that I will bear true faith and allegiance to the same, that I take this obligation freely, without any mental reservations or purpose of evasion, and that I will well and faithfully discharge the duties of the office upon which I am about to enter, so help me God."

"Congratulations, General," Giles said, shaking Art's hand.

"Congratulations, General," Nighthorse said, saluting him.

"Damn," Art said, returning Nighthorse's salute. "You don't know how much I have been wanting the privilege of saluting."

"Don't get too attached to it, General," Giles said. "In your new position, you won't be doing that much of it. Especially, since nobody is to know that you are even in the army."

"So you said earlier," Art said. "So I guess now it's time to tell me just what my mission is."

"You are to continue to be regarded as a discredited former army officer," Giles said. "Continue to look for work and, from time to time, we may release some information that may help, or hurt, you in finding employment, depending upon the situation.

"Your mission—"

"Should I accept it," Art teased, mimicking the old *Mission: Impossible* TV series lead-in.

Giles laughed. "Too late for that. You have already accepted it. You are to be chief of the DOD Special Function Unit."

"Special Function Unit? I don't think I've ever heard of it."

"No, you couldn't have. It doesn't exist, and won't exist until you activate it. And just to give you an idea of how secret this unit is, only seven men know of its existence. You, your father, Colonel Nighthorse, me, the secretary of defense, the secretary of Homeland Security, and the president of the United States."

"Black Ops," Art said.

"Black Ops," Giles repeated.

"What about the other people in Black Ops? Surely, they know about me."

Nighthorse laughed.

"What's so funny?"

"I am the other people in SFU," he said.

"You?"

"Colonel Nighthorse will continue with his assignment at JAG, but that will just be a cover. In fact, he will be your go-to person when you need specific military help."

"I'm a brigadier general, but I need the authority of a lieutenant colonel to get something done?"

Giles shook his head. "You will have the authority of the president of the United States," he said. "But you are in charge of the operations. You will know what you need and when you need it."

"I'm your gopher, General," Nighthorse said. "I will do

nothing without your specific request, and I will do anything you request of me, so long as it is humanly possible."

"Within reason, you can have any asset you want, any amount of money you need, to get the job done," Giles said. "As I said, Colonel Nighthorse is your military contact. Your contact with Homeland Security will be your father."

"I thought you were retired," Art said to his father.

"Like you, I've unretired," Cal said.

"All right, it sounds . . . interesting," Art said, setting the word apart from the rest of the sentence.

"From time to time you may be contacted by others who will bring you information, but they are cellular. They won't know who you are, or what your mission is," Nighthorse explained.

"And, speaking of mission, I assume you have some immediate job for me, otherwise you would not have been able to arrange all this," Art said.

"We do," Giles said. "I'm sure you are aware of the attacks against the bridges in Memphis and St. Louis."

Art nodded. "Who isn't aware? It has dominated the news for the last month. The total killed is, what, seven hundred?"

"Seven hundred and twelve known dead, sixty-three still unaccounted for," Giles said. "And beyond that, the disruption to our transportation grid has been tremendous. Even with temporary spans in place, we are still losing millions of dollars in production every day."

"You want me to find out who did it?"

"Oh, we know who did it," Giles said.

"I beg your pardon?"

"We know who did it," Giles repeated.

"Who?"

"It was Prince Azeer Lal Qambar, a member of the royal family of the Kingdom of Qambari Arabia."

"Qambari Arabia? I thought they were friendly to the United States."

"Ostensibly they are allies of the United States, and vital to us because of their oil. But, as I'm sure you know, Qambari

Arabia is anything but friendly," Giles said. "They are ruled by a dictatorial family who controls their people by allowing, and even planting, hatred and distrust for America, all the time making public pronouncements of friendship with America."

"Where does Prince Azeer fit in to all this?"

"Azeer is a member of a Qambari Arabia Trade Council in the U.S. This gives him access to all levels of U.S. government and business, and, using his position as cover, he is secretly organizing and funding sleeper cells of terrorists, all across the country, including the suicide bombers who destroyed the bridges. The problem is, our government knows this . . . but the situation is too sensitive for us to react."

"So, what am I to do?"

"React," Giles said simply.

"Ha," Art said. "You don't want me to do that. My reaction would be to kill the son of a bitch."

Giles looked pointedly at Art, but said nothing.

"Wait a minute," Art said. "That's what you want me to do, isn't it?"

"Whatever you do is outside the chain of command, or even the awareness, of the United States government," Giles replied. "You will never receive written orders, nor will you ever receive specific verbal orders. From time to time Colonel Nighthorse will make you aware of the problems."

"And my job will be to make those problems go away," Art said. It was a statement, not a question.

Giles looked at his watch. "Well, I must be going," he said, pointedly avoiding a response to Art's comment.

"I must be going as well," Colonel Nighthorse said.

"Colonel, how will I contact you?" Art said.

Nighthorse gave Art a card. "This has my cell phone number," he said. "Call me only on that number, never through the office. And I'd feel better about it if you learn the number, rather than carry it. If anything happens to you . . . and to be honest, General, with some of the things you are going to get into, that is a distinct possibility . . . I would not want someone to find that you were carrying my phone number."

"I'll remember it," Art said.

"Good luck."

"Thanks."

After Nighthorse and the secretary of the army left, only Art and his father remained.

"Well, what do you think?" Cal asked.

"I appreciate everything you have done for me, Pop," Art said.

"Don't be silly, I didn't do anything."

"Right," Art said sarcastically. "Homeland Security just happened to get involved."

"Maybe I talked to a few people, but if Nighthorse hadn't come through for you, you'd still be on the outside, looking in."

Art laughed. "Hell, I am on the outside looking in. Here I am a general, and I can't even enjoy any of the perks."

"Maybe so, but look at the good side," Cal said.

"What good side?"

"Look how much money you are going to save on uniforms," Cal said.

Both men laughed.

"What do you say we go have dinner somewhere?" Cal asked.

Art started to say that he had eaten his dinner, then recalled that he had left half a bowl of canned chili uneaten.

"All right," he said. "I assume that I am back on the government payroll, and this time as an O-7?"

"You assume correctly."

"Then I'll buy."

CHAPTER
SEVENTEEN

From the journal of Smoke Jensen

> *Once I escaped from jail, I knew better than to go back home to Sugarloaf, or to even try to get in touch with Sally. I figured the marshal would have people there waiting for me. The only way I could avoid going back to jail, and keeping a date with the hangman, was by finding the real bank robbers and murderers.*
>
> *One of the things I had learned from my days living in the mountains with the man called Preacher was how to track. Now, most anyone can track a fresh trail, but Preacher could follow a trail that was a month old. In fact, some folks used to tease that he could track a fish through water, or a bird through the sky.*
>
> *I never was as good as Preacher, but I could follow a cold trail better than most, and after I returned to where I had encountered the bank robbers, I managed to pick up their trail.*
>
> *It was difficult, the trail being nearly two weeks old now, but I was helped by the fact that they were wanting*

to stay out of sight. Because of that, they avoided the main roads, and that made their trail stand out. The funny thing is, if they had stayed on the main roads I never would have found them because their tracks would have been covered over, or so mixed in with the other travelers' that I wouldn't be able to tell which was which.

But cutting a trail across fresh country the way they did led me just as straight as if they had left me a map. Things were going well until they separated. I flipped a coin, then chose to follow the trail that was heading south. That led me straight to the little town of Dorena.

I had never been in Dorena before, but I had been in dozens of towns just like it so there was a familiarity as I rode down the street, checking out the leather goods store, the mercantile, a gun shop, a feed store, an apothecary, and the saloon.

Stopping in front of the saloon, I reached down into the bottom of my saddlebag, moved a bit of leather, and found what I was looking for. I kept one hundred dollars there as an emergency fund, keeping it in a way that a casual examination of the pouch wouldn't find it.

Fortunately it had escaped the marshal's examination when I was arrested, and my horse and saddle were taken.

Armed with the money, which was in five twenty-dollar gold pieces, I went into the saloon, had a beer and a plate of beans, then joined a card game that was in progress.

Now you may think it strange for me to play a game of cards under the circumstances, the circumstances being that I was a man on the run. But I was also a man on the hunt, and I had learned, long ago, that the best way to get information was in casual conversation, rather than by the direct questioning of people. When you started questioning people, the natural thing for them to do was to clam up.

Interestingly, one of the other men who was playing cards that day was the deputy sheriff, a man named

Clayton. With him being there, I figured that if a telegraph message of my escape had reached the sheriff's office here, I would learn right away. But, as Deputy Clayton made no move toward me, nor gave any indication of being suspicious of me, I knew that, for now, I was safe to continue my search.

To the casual observer it might appear that I was so relaxed as to be off-guard. But that wasn't the case, as my eyes were constantly flicking about, monitoring the room, tone and tint, for any danger. And, though I was engaged in convivial conversation with the others at the table, I was listening in on snatches of dozens of other conversations.

"I believe it is your bet," Deputy Clayton said to me.

I looked at the pot, then down at his hand. I was showing one jack and two sixes. My down-card was another jack. I had hoped to fill a full house with my last card, but pulled a three instead.

"Well?" Clayton asked.

I could see why Clayton was anxious. The deputy had three queens showing.

"I fold," I said, closing my cards.

Two of the other players folded, and two stayed, but the three queens won the pot.

"Thank you, gentlemen, thank you," Clayton said, chuckling as he raked in his winnings.

"Clayton, you have been uncommonly lucky tonight," Doc McGuire said good-naturedly.

"I'll say I have," Clayton agreed. "I've won near a month's pay, just sittin' right here at this table."

"We'd better watch out, gentlemen, or Clayton will give up the deputy sheriffin' business and go into gambling, full-time," Doc said.

"Ho, wouldn't I do that in a minute if I wasn't married?" Clayton replied. "Another hand, boys?"

"Not for me," I said, pushing away from the table and standing up. "I appreciate the game, gentlemen, but the

cards haven't been that kind to me tonight. I think I'll just have a couple of drinks, then turn in."

After a few drinks, I walked next door to the hotel, checked in, then went upstairs to the room. I lit the lantern and walked over to the window to adjust it to catch the night breeze. That was when I saw a sudden flash of light in the hayloft over the livery across the street. I knew I was seeing a muzzle flash even before I heard the gun report, and I was already pulling away from the window at the precise instant a bullet crashed through the glass of the window and slammed into the wall on the opposite side of the room.

I cursed myself for the foolish way I had exposed myself at the window. I knew better, I had just let my guard down. I reached up to extinguish the lantern.

"What was that?" someone shouted from down on the street.

"Gunshots. Sounded like they came from the—"

That was as far as the disembodied voice got before another shot crashed through the window.

"Get off the street!"

I heard a voice, loud and authoritative, floating up from below. "Everyone, get inside!"

I recognized the voice. It belonged to Deputy Clayton, the man I had been playing cards with but a few minutes earlier. On my hands and knees so as not to present a target, I crept up to the open window.

"Clayton, stay away!" I shouted down. I raised myself up just far enough to look through the window and saw Clayton heading for the livery stable with his pistol in his hand. "Clayton, no! Get back!"

My warning was too late. A third volley was fired from the livery hayloft, and Clayton fell facedown in the street.

With pistol in my hand, I climbed out of the window, scrambled to the edge of the porch, and dropped down onto the street. Running to Clayton's still form, I bent down to check on him. Clayton had been hit hard, and through the open wound in his chest, I could hear the gurgling sound of his lungs sucking air and filling with blood.

"Damn it, Clayton, I told you to get down," I scolded softly.

"It was my job," Clayton replied in a pained voice.

At that moment, another rifle shot was fired from the livery. The bullet hit the ground close by, then ricocheted away with a loud whine. I fired back, shooting once into the dark maw of the hayloft. Then, leaving Clayton, I ran to the water trough nearest the livery, and dived behind it as the man in the livery fired again. I heard the bullet hit the trough with a loud popping sound. After that, I could hear the water bubbling through the bullet hole in the water trough, even as I got up and ran toward the door of the livery. I shot two more times to keep the shooter back. When I reached the big, open, double doors of the livery, I ran on through so that I was inside.

Once inside, I moved quietly through the barn itself, looking up at the hayloft just overhead. Suddenly I felt little pieces of hay-straw falling on me and I stopped, because I realized that someone had to be right over me. That's when I heard it, a quiet shuffling of feet. I fired twice, straight up, but was rewarded only with a shower of more bits and pieces of hay-straw.

"That's six shots. You're out of bullets, you son of a bitch," a calm voice said. I looked over to my left to see a man standing openly, on the edge of the loft. It was one of the bank robbers, the pockmarked, drooping-eyed son of a bitch who had set me up.

"How the hell did you get out of jail?" he asked. "I figured old Turnball would have you hanged by now. I was some surprised when I seen you come into the saloon tonight."

"Where are the other two?" I asked.

The man laughed. "You got some sand, mister," he

said. "*Worryin' about where the other two are, when I'm fixin' to shoot you dead.*"

"*Where are they?*"

"*They're in a town called Bertrand, not that it'll do you any good,*" the outlaw said as he raised his rifle to his shoulder to take aim.

I fired.

"*What?*" the outlaw gasped in shock, dropping his rifle and clutching the wound in his stomach.

"*You should have stayed in school,*" I said flatly. "*Maybe you would have learned to count.*" I watched as the man fell from the loft, flipping over so as to land on his back in the dirt below.

I didn't bother to go back to my hotel room. Instead, I saddled my horse and rode out of town that very night. If the other two were in Bertrand, I planned to get there before they left.

CHAPTER
EIGHTEEN

Chateau Spud Bar, Alexandria, Virginia

The song "Stand by Your Man" was blaring in the background as Art took a seat at the end of the bar. The mirror behind the bar was encircled with a tube of blue neon. Several bottles on a glass shelf in front of the mirror doubled their impact with the reflection.

"You're back, I see," the bartender said, picking up an empty glass from the space in front of Art and passing his towel over it. "Have any trouble?"

"No," Art said. "He came along peaceably."

The reference was to Art's current job, chasing down bail-bond jumpers. He had just brought a prisoner back from Newport News, Virginia.

"I wouldn't care much for a job like that," the bartender said. "You never know what you are going to run into."

"That's all right," a man sitting a couple of stools down from Art said. "If the colonel there runs into any trouble, he'll just shoot 'em. That's what you do, ain't it, Colonel? You just blow people away, like the prisoner you blew away in Iraq?

And if you don't have a gun, why, hell, you'll just eat 'em. You are that colonel, aren't you?"

"I am no longer a colonel," Art said.

"Oh yeah, that's right," the man said tauntingly. "You are no longer a colonel. Fact is, you ain't nothin' now, are you? What I can't figure out is why they ever let your sorry ass out of jail."

"Do you have a problem with something?" Art asked.

"No, I ain't got no problem," the belligerent man answered. "Fact is, I'm happy as a pig in shit. See, I was a lowly EM, and I like it when a high-ranking muckety-muck like you winds up getting your ass in a crack."

The music changed then, and a very pretty woman came up to Art.

"I tell you what, handsome. Why don't you dance with me before you and that unpleasant gentleman get into a fight?"

Art hesitated for just a moment.

"Unless you don't want to dance with me," the woman said.

Art smiled. "I would love to dance with you," he said.

They began dancing and halfway through the dance the woman moved very close to him and spoke quietly into his ear.

"When you leave tonight, take your napkin with you," she said.

Art didn't respond. He realized then that the belligerent man at the bar and this beautiful woman were part of a contact team. Whether they were from the military, the FBI, or the CIA, he didn't know. He just knew that, for the first time since taking his assignment, he had been contacted.

When the dance was finished, Art returned to the bar. The belligerent one was gone.

"Another drink?" the bartender asked, returning to Art's end of the bar.

"No, thanks," Art said. "I think I'll just have this one and turn in for the night. I'm beat."

"Sounds like a plan," the bartender said.

Art finished the drink, then picked up the napkin and put

it in his pocket. He didn't look at it until he was back at his apartment. *Check key in potted plant by south elevator. Go to security storage locker building. Key fits locker 5689.*

Art waited until nearly midnight before he went out into the hall at his apartment complex, then walked down to the elevators. There were two elevators serving the occupants of the seven-story building where he lived. He approached the security camera from an angle that could not be observed by the camera, then draped a towel over the lens. After that, making sure that he wasn't being observed, he went over to the potted plant, felt around until he found the key. Then, returning to the camera, he took the towel off and went back to his room.

After his run the next morning, Art drove down to the building that housed the security storage lockers and, going inside, found locker 5689. Again, waiting until he wasn't being observed, he opened the door and took out a manila folder.

Art made no attempt to look at it until he was back in his apartment where he poured himself a cup of coffee, went into his study, and settled down to see what he had. The folder contained two photographs and a single sheet of printed information.

Art studied the photographs. The first was of a man with Middle Eastern features, dark skinned, dark eyes, and with a mustache. He looked to be in his midfifties and his hair was beginning to turn white. On the back of the picture was the name Adulla Balama Shamat.

The second picture made him gasp, then feel an instant wave of pity, followed by anger. The picture was of a young blond girl, obviously taken at a crime scene, for she was nude, spread-eagled, and very dead. Her eyes were open, still imprinted with the horror of what was happening to her. There was something sticking out of her mouth and for a moment Art didn't know what it was. As he studied it more closely, though, he realized that it had to be her panties.

He turned it over to see what was on the back. The writing said *Amber Pease, age fourteen.*

Art read the report.

Information on Abdulla Balama Shamat

Shamat is a rug dealer who now lives in Dallas. Before coming to the U.S. Abdulla was an enforcer for the Jihad of Allah. One of the ways he enforced fatwahs was by raping females in the family of his target.

We now know that one of his victims was Amber Pease, the daughter of Lieutenant Colonel Anthony Pease, the marine commandant of guards at the U.S. embassy in Redha, Qambari Arabia. Eyewitnesses saw Shamat, and semen found on the young girl has positively identified Shamat as her rapist and killer. He left young Amber spread-eagled, nude, and with her panties stuffed in her mouth.

The DNA evidence, though damning, would not be considered by the government of the Kingdom of Qambari, as they consider semen "unclean." As a result, they have no interest in extraditing him. On the contrary, Prince Azeer recently arranged for Shamat's entry into the United States on a diplomatic passport.

Shamat is currently living in Dallas, Texas, doing business out of a shop on Preston.

The fact sheet on Shamat went no further than to tell who he was, where he was, and a bit of his history. It did not suggest that Art take any specific action as a result of the information provided him.

Art knew that specific orders would never be written, thus preserving the option of deniability. Anything Art did, as a result of the information given him, would have to be of his own volition.

That was fine. Art preferred to work that way. He liked the trust in him that such an arrangement implied. He also liked the freedom of operation. He knew they would never comment if his decision was correct, and they would not come to his assistance if anything he did would have a sudden, and very negative, worldwide reaction.

Art picked up the phone and dialed a number as he stared at the photo.

"Yes," he said when the phone was answered. "I would like a ticket to Dallas."

"When would you like to leave?"

"In the morning."

"And return?"

"I think Friday."

Art could hear a tapping sound as the agent at the other end of the phone was using a computer keyboard.

"All right, sir, I can put you on American Airlines flight number 1705, departing DCA at 7:06 a.m., that will put you into DFW in Dallas at 9:16 a.m."

"I'll take it."

"That will be eight hundred and thirty-two dollars. How will you be paying for that?"

"American Express," Art said. He gave the card number and expiration date.

"Very good, sir, your ticket will be at the American Airline desk. Please have a photo ID."

"Right. Thanks," Art said.

Dallas, Texas

The problem with flying into DFW, Art decided, was that when the plane touched down on the runway, you were only halfway to your destination. The terminal buildings were so far away as to be low-lying smudges on the distant horizon. The airplane had to taxi for nearly half an hour, waiting frequently as it crossed other runways, until finally reaching the arrival gate.

Art rented a car, then drove toward Dallas on the LBJ until he reached Preston, where he turned north. He found the shop just south of Campbell, tucked in between a service station and a bagel restaurant. Ali Baba's Persian Rugs.

A yellow ribbon sticker was on the front door, stating SUPPORT OUR TROOPS. A bell rang as Art stepped inside.

"Yes, can I help you?" Although he was Middle Eastern, the clerk who came to speak to him was not Shamat.

"I'd like to look at some rugs," Art said. "I'm interested in Tabriz."

"Ah yes, yes, a very nice rug. We have some back here, may I show them?"

"Just show me where they are and let me look for myself," Art said. "I might look around at some of the other rugs as well."

"Very good, sir."

"Are you the owner?" Art asked as he was led toward the section of Tabriz rugs.

"No, my name is Rafeel. The owner is Mr. Shamat. Do you wish to see him? He is in his office in the back."

"No, that isn't necessary," Art said.

The Tabriz rugs were very near the office and, through the open door, Art could see Shamat on the telephone. Shamat was speaking in Arabic.

Rafeel left Art and hurried to the front of the store to greet another customer.

Art looked through the rugs for a while, then moved to another pile. That was when he saw Rafeel summon Shamat to talk to the customer who had just come in.

Art slipped into the office when Shamat left and, very quickly, put a bug into the telephone, and another just under the shade of his desk lamp. He barely managed to get back out of the office before Shamat returned.

"Have you found something you like?" Shamat asked.

"I've found two or three that I like," Art said. "But I had better talk to my wife first. I can't make a decision like that on my own."

Shamat chuckled, and shook his head. "American men are dominated by their women. You would never hear anyone in my country say anything like that."

"Where are you from? Iraq? Iran? Saudi Arabia?"

"Qambari Arabia," Shamat said. "Our women know their place."

"Yes," Art said. "I imagine they do. Well, I'll be back."

Leaving the store, Art drove away, heading north on Preston. Turning east on Campbell, he left the road just the other side of the service station and parked in a large parking lot. There, he opened up a laptop computer, made a few adjustments, and was able to pick up conversation from within the store.

Most of the conversation was in English, and it had to do with the normal business of the store. Then he heard a voice he recognized as Rafeel's. And Rafeel was speaking in Arabic.

Art called up the voice recognition translation program and watched as the words, spoken in Arabic, were typed out onto the screen. There were a few errors on the screen, but no more so than for any other voice recognition program.

I go to eat my lynch if with you is okay. [Rafeel].

Where go you? Yesterdaxx too long you are gone. [Shamat].

To get bagels.

A Jewinx fxxd you eat?

I like bagrels. Bagels popular with Americans.

Bagels food of infidelxys. Americax are infidels.

Why do you live in America if Amergls you like not?

I have reasox to live herxg

[Rafeel laughs.] *I think your reaxsn is money.*

From where he was parked, Art was able to see the entry to the bagel restaurant, and a couple of moments later he saw Rafeel going in. Then he heard the tones of a telephone being dialed. His computer determined the number from the tones as 212-555-2740.

It then did a quick reverse-number check, identifying the recipient of the call as the Qambari consultate, New York City.

"Qambari consulate." The answer was in English.

"Shamat for Prince Azeer." The response was also in English. There was a pause, then another voice.

"This is Hamdi."

The language now switched to Arabic, and Art had to read it in translation.

This is Shamat. With Prince Azeer I wisx with sprak.

[A moment of silence.]

Azeer. [A new voice.]

You were rigxht abxt Rafeel. To the CIAXX is hx speaking. You know whxt to do.

Yex. His family I will take care of so he wilx know then I wixl of him taxk carx.

Allah Akbar.

Art turned off the laptop, then picking up the photograph of Amber, he got out of the car. Walking casually, he crossed the service-station drive, then went up the alley until he reached the back of the carpet store. The back door was secured but Art picked the lock in a matter of a few seconds, then let himself in. The door opened into a storeroom at the back of the shop. Art moved through the storeroom to the front door and looked out over the shop itself.

At the moment, the only person in the entire store appeared to be Shamat himself. Art waited a moment longer, just to be certain, then stepped out into the showroom.

"Who are you?" Shamat said, startled when he saw him. "I did not hear you come in."

"I didn't want you to hear me come in," Art said.

"What?" Shamat said, confused by the strange reply.

Art held up the picture. "Do you recognize this young girl?"

Shamat looked at the photo while Art studied his face. Art saw a very slight reaction to the picture, though he had to hand it to Shamat for being able to maintain his composure.

"You look at rugs," Shamat said as he started toward the office. "If you need me, call."

"Thanks," Art said.

Art remained where he was, knowing that Shamat could see his reflection in a mirror at the back of the store. Then, just as Shamat went through the door into his office, Art stepped behind a pile of rugs so as to be out of sight. Bending over at the waist, he moved quickly, using the long row of rugs as cover.

It was no surprise to Art when Shamat appeared a second later, bursting out of his office with a gun in his hand.

"*Allah Akbar!*" Shamat shouted.

Art waited until Shamat was even with him, then stepped out and swung the knife-edge of his hand hard, against the base of Shamat's nose. The blow broke his nose and sent splinters of bone into his brain.

Shamat died instantly.

Art moved quickly to the front of the store where he turned the OPEN sign around so that it read CLOSED. After that he positioned Shamat the way he wanted him, then let himself out the storeroom door in the back in the same way he had arrived.

When Rafeel returned to the shop a few moments later, he was surprised to see the CLOSED sign. He supposed that Shamat might be taking a noon nap, so he let himself in, using his own key.

"Shamat!" he called. "Shamat, I'm back."

Not receiving an answer, Rafeel began exploring the shop. He gasped when he found his employer.

Abdulla Balam Shamat was lying back on a pile of rugs, spread-eagled, nude, and dead. His underdrawers were stuffed into his mouth. His right hand was open, but his finger was wrapped around the trigger guard of his gun.

Lying on his forehead was a playing card, the ace of spades.

CHAPTER
NINETEEN

Two weeks after the incident in Dallas, Art received a DVD through the mail. The slipcover for the DVD read: *Fishing Opportunities in the Missouri Ozarks*. The label of the DVD showed a smiling man holding up a large crappie.

Art knew that the slipcover and label were to camouflage the actual contents, so he put it into his computer.

The picture of a Middle Eastern man came up. He had large, liquid brown eyes, a nose that had been broken, a scar on his left cheek, and a heavy mustache.

After a few seconds of silence, a voice-over began speaking.

"This is Balli Daftar Taleb," the voice-over said.

"And this is also Balli Daftar Taleb."

This time the picture showed an American prisoner, holding a sign. There were two masked men standing on either side of the American prisoner, and there was a fifth masked man standing just behind him. An arrow pointed to the man behind the prisoner.

"The prisoner is Bernie Gelb, an American citizen who was working at one of Iraq's electrical-generating stations. He was taken prisoner shortly after the fall of Saddam."

The masked man behind Gelb bagan speaking. The camera moved in close enough to be able to see his eyes and mouth, though the full hood covered the rest of his face.

"We, the Freedom Fighters of the Jihad of Allah, have tried this Jew for crimes against Islam. He has been found guilty, and the sentence is death. Let this be a lesson to all Americans, Jews, and other infidels who would come to Iraq."

The picture on the screen went into freeze-frame, and once more there was a voice-over.

"Be warned that the next scene is a very graphic and difficult one to watch."

Anticipating what was about to happen, Art braced himself for the next scene. The freeze-frame dissolved, and the man who was previously identified as Balli Daftar Taleb produced a long, curved knife. Grabbing Bernie Gelb by his hair, Taleb brought the knife across his neck. Blood began spewing immediately as Gelb cried out. His cries were soon silenced, however, as Taleb continued to carve. It took several seconds before Taleb was able to separate the head from the body. Then the men who were holding Gelb's now headless body let it go and it fell forward. Taleb held the severed head up for a close-up from the video camera.

"Death to all Americans, Jews, and infidels," Taleb said.

The grisly scene left the screen, to be replaced, once more, by a picture of Balli Daftar Taleb. This time, Taleb was speaking to a reporter. The voice-over continued.

"A voice analysis has confirmed that this man, speaking to an Al Jazira Television reporter, is the same man who appeared on the video with Bernie Gelb. In addition, we have confirmed by several other sources that Balli Daftar Taleb was not only the one wielding the knife, he was also the leader of the group of kidnappers and assassins who killed Mr. Gelb. Now it is known that Taleb is living in the United States.

"An investigation of Taleb, designed to prove his participation in the brutal murder of Mr. Gelb, was halted when the ACLU filed a protest against the Justice Department for harassment and violation of Taleb's privacy.

"Today, Balli Daftar Taleb lives in Springfield, Missouri, where he operates a tobacco shop."

That concluded the information on the DVD, and the screen went black. As before, there were no instructions, nor was there any suggestion as to what was expected of Art. There was only the clinical presentation of the facts surrounding Balli Daftar Taleb.

St. Louis, Missouri

As the airliner began making its descent into Lambert Field, Art looked through the window at the Mississippi River below. He saw the remains of the I-70 bridge, some of which had been cleared away to allow barge traffic to pass through. The barge traffic did not have an unrestricted passage though, as a pontoon roadway had been put in place as a temporary bridge, and because it was at surface level, it halted all river traffic.

The pontoon bridge was one two-lane road and could be crossed at no more than twenty miles per hour. As a result, traffic was backed up for several miles on either side of the river.

In addition, every two hours the center span of the pontoon bridge would have to be opened by tugboats to allow the river traffic through. The center span would remain open for one hour, during which time all road traffic came to a halt. As a result, much of the traffic was being diverted south to Ste. Genevieve, Missouri, and Chester, Illinois, and in some cases as far south as Cape Girardeau, Missouri, and Cairo, Illinois. And even those bridges were choke points, since all vehicles crossing had to go through a security checkpoint now.

Art had read an estimate that taking out the bridges in St. Louis and Memphis, thus interrupting the free flow of traffic along the I-40 and I-70 corridors, was costing the U.S. economy over one billion dollars per week.

Once on the ground in St. Louis, Art rented a car. He could have made a flight connection all the way to Springfield, but figured that driving from St. Louis would provide him with more cover. The drive to Springfield would be about three hours down I-44. And, again to provide himself with some cover, Art decided to go to Branson, rather than directly to Springfield.

Although he had heard of Branson, Missouri, this was the first time he had ever visited the town. The WELCOME TO BRANSON sign indicated that the population was six thousand, but when he drove down Highway 76, known locally as the Strip, he could swear that there were at least that many in the parking lot of just one of the many theaters.

Art pulled into a small and unassuming motel on Gretna Road. The lobby was little larger than a telephone booth, and nobody was behind the counter. The counter was filled with brochures of the various shows and entertainment venues. Art rang the little bell.

"Yes, sir," a man said, coming out of a little room from behind the counter. "Can I help you?"

"I'd like a room."

"Yes, sir, and for how long?"

"Oh, three days should do it," Art said. He picked up one of the brochures and started looking through it.

"Are you a country music fan?" the clerk asked.

"Yes."

"Well, you are going to love Branson then. We have the best musical shows in the country, if you ask me."

"I'm sure I will enjoy myself," Art said, as he filled out the registration form. He passed it back to the clerk and the clerk looked at it for a moment, then chuckled.

"Jensen. I'll bet you don't know that you have a very famous name," he said.

"Oh?"

"Well, maybe it's not quite so famous now. But I'm a western history buff." He pulled a book out from under the counter. The title on the cover was *Gunfighters of the Old West*.

"This is a very good book if you are into such things," he said. "It has stories of all the famous old gunfighters, men like Wild Bill Hickock, Bat Masterson, Wyatt Earp, Falcon

MacCallister, and the fella some say was the best of 'em all, Smoke Jensen."

"Is that a fact?" Art asked. "Well, sir, then I had better make sure I don't do anything to dishonor the name."

The proprietor chuckled. "I'm sure you won't," he said.

That night Art had dinner, then went to a show. The show ended with waving flags, and a salute to all veterans. For someone who had been living in the jaded society of Washington, D.C., the almost-over-the-top patriotism was refreshing.

After the show, Art drove the forty miles into Springfield. The data on Taleb indicated that he lived alone, in an apartment, over the top of the Smoke Shop.

It was after midnight when Art drove by the little shop. A sign in front advertised EXOTIC HOOKAH TOBACCO FROM THE MIDEAST.

Finding a used-car lot a block down the street, he pulled the car in and parked it with the others. That way the casual passerby would not see a car sitting alone somewhere.

Wearing dark shirt, trousers, and gloves, Art stayed in the shadows as he moved up the alley toward the Smoke Shop. Reaching the rear of the shop, he used the drainpipe as a means of climbing to the second story. There, he opened a window and let himself in. Once inside, he put on a dark hood, exactly like the hood Taleb had worn when he killed Bernie Gelb.

Stopping by the kitchen, Art looked through the cooking utensils until he found what he was looking for. The butcher knife was long, and the blade was sharp.

Moving down the hallway, Art could hear snoring coming from the bedroom. Stepping into the bedroom, he moved quietly to the side of the bed, then turned on the bedside lamp.

There was only one person in the bed and Art could easily identify him from the pictures he had seen on the DVD.

Taleb woke up, and seeing Art standing over him, wearing a hood, gasped in fear.

"Balli Daftar Taleb?" Art asked.

"Yes. Who are you? What do you want?" Taleb asked, his voice cracking with fear.

"Was it like this for Bernie Gelb? You took him from his apartment in the middle of the night, didn't you?" Art asked in a low, hissing voice.

"What?"

"You do remember Bernie Gelb, don't you?"

"The Jew, yes, I—" Taleb started, then realizing that he might not want to confess to knowing him, changed in mid-sentence. "No, I . . . I don't know who you are talking about."

"Don't lie to me, Balli Daftar Taleb. I get upset when people lie to me."

"I . . . it wasn't my fault," Taleb said. "I wanted to let him go."

Suddenly Taleb reached under his pillow and produced a pistol. Seeing that Art was armed only with a butcher knife, he smiled as he pointed the pistol at the intruder.

"There is an old Arab saying," Taleb said with an evil smile. "Never take a knife to a gunfight."

"Actually, I believe that is Irish," Art said calmly. "You did kill Gelb, didn't you?"

"Yes. And the Jordanian and the Italian and the Jewish cow."

"Well, when I kill you I will settle accounts for a lot of people, won't I?" Art said.

"How are you going to kill me, when I have the gun?" Taleb said, pointedly aiming it. Art saw his finger tightening on the trigger.

Reacting quickly, so quickly that Taleb was unable to even fathom what was happening, Art slapped the gun hand aside. The gun went off, but the bullet plunged harmlessly into the wall. At almost the same time, Art brought his right hand around quickly, the blade of the knife slicing about two inches deep into the front of Taleb's neck.

Taleb, his eyes showing shock, put his hands to his neck in an attempt to stop the bleeding. The blood poured through his fingers.

"This is for Bernie Gelb, and the others you murdered," Art said, stepping closer to the bed.

* * *

Watching the news from his hotel room the following night, Art saw the report.

"A grisly discovery was made at the Smoke Shop located in the nine hundred block of West Sunshine early today," the news anchor on KYTV said. "The Smoke Shop, which specializes in Middle Eastern tobaccos, was run by an Iraqi named Balli Daftar Taleb. KY3's Karl Anderson files this report."

"Steve, when Jerry Balder came to work today, he found the severed head of his employer, Balli Daftar Taleb."

"Robbery, Karl?" Steve asked.

Karl shook his head. "Apparently not. According to Mr. Balder, there was no sign of any rifling of the cash register, nor did anything else appear to be missing. And, even more telling, and chilling, is the condition of the head. It was found wearing a black hood, much like those worn by the terrorists who have made videos of themselves with their prisoners. Those hoods have become all too familiar to American TV viewers as we have seen men, and women, killed by their captors."

"Karl, is there any significance to the fact that Mr. Taleb was Arab, and that he was found wearing just such a hood?"

"It seems that there is," Karl replied. "For indeed, today, we have learned from our sources that the U.S. Justice Department had attempted to investigate Mr. Taleb for complicity in the beheading of Bernie Gelb a couple of years ago."

"Did they find any connection?"

"They were unable to continue the investigation," Karl explained. "The ACLU demanded that the evidence which was leading them to investigate Taleb be made public, but the Justice Department, fearing that making that information public would put into danger some of their underground contacts in the Middle East, refused to make that information available. Because of that, the federal court sided with the ACLU and issued a cease and desist order on any further investigation."

"So what you are saying is, there appears to be some linkage between that suspicion and the killing and beheading of Taleb?"

"At this point, there is no way of knowing for sure," Karl said. "But, in addition to the hood that the severed head was wearing, there was one more thing that would lead one to think this. Protruding from the mouth of the victim was a solitary playing card. The ace of spades."

"Is there any significance to that?"

"Again, it is only speculation," Karl said. "But some of our viewing audience may recall that last month, Abdulla Balama Shamat, a rug dealer in Dallas, was found dead in his shop, also with the ace of spades prominently displayed. And, like Taleb, there were very strong suspicions that Shamat had deep ties with the terrorists."

"So, we are dealing with what? Someone who is seeking revenge?"

"Of course, that is always a possibility, a relative or close friend of Bernie Gelb, perhaps, but police say that isn't likely."

"Oh? Why not?"

"Well, for one thing, whoever did this seems to be a professional. There was not one piece of evidence found at the scene. I'm told that there aren't even any fingerprints."

"What about the weapon?"

"Even the weapon that was used deepens the mystery," Karl said. "The killer used a common butcher knife, and in fact, left it at the scene. It almost certainly came from the kitchen of the victim."

"Perhaps so. But I doubt that there is going to be too many tears shed over the deaths of these two men. In fact, a great deal of fresh evidence, directly linking Shamat with the Jihad of Allah, and, more specifically, with the rape and murder of young Amber Pease, has been leaked to the press. I would not be the least bit surprised if the same thing doesn't happen with Taleb. Now that the constraints are off, I'm certain that the investigation will be continued, this time without ACLU interference. And I wouldn't be surprised if we found Mr.

Taleb very much involved in some of the more heinous crimes perpetrated by the terrorists."

"It sounds as if there is some personal vigilante out there, doing his best to make things right," Steve said.

"That is so, Steve," Karl answered. "And indeed, some of the policemen who are working the case are already comparing the 'Ace of Spades,' as they are now calling him, with the vigilante portrayed by Charles Bronson, in the *Death Wish* movies. And, like his character, this vigilante, I feel, will garner some public support."

"Thanks, Karl, good work. In Jefferson City yesterday, a spokesman for the governor's office said that he would—"

The report ended in midsentence when Art picked up the remote and clicked the TV off. He had left the ace of spades with Shamat, and now with Taleb, not to garner any public support for what he was doing, but to send a message. He wanted whoever was the head of the group that called itself the Jihad of Allah to know that someone was on their trail.

Art put on his jacket and went out to the parking lot to get to his car. He had another show to see tonight.

The Potomac Mall parking garage, Alexandria, Virginia

When Nighthorse stepped out of the elevator on the fourth level of the parking garage, he saw the lights flash one time in the Lincoln Navigator. He walked across the garage and got into the car.

Giles was behind the steering wheel, and he chuckled. "I feel like a character in a Tom Clancy novel," he said. "Arranging secret meetings in secret places."

"I know," Nighthorse said. "At least we know that there is no likelihood of our conversation being overheard here."

"You saw the news coming out of Springfield, Missouri?" Giles asked.

"I saw it."

"What do you think?"

"I think our . . . operative . . . is doing exactly what we intended him to do."

"Yes," Giles said. "The only thing is, I wish—" He stopped in midsentence.

"You wish what?"

"I wish he weren't so damn flamboyant about it. Shamat found spread-eagled with his pants in his mouth. Taleb beheaded."

"Sort of poetic justice, though, don't you think? Duplicating the crimes they committed?"

"That's not what we set out to do," Giles said.

"Oh? What did we set out to do? If we had been able to bring them to trial, we would have called for the death penalty, would we not?"

"Yes, but they would have been executed in a structured way."

"Right. And everyone would have known about it, and would have drawn from it the inference that if you commit a capital crime against an American citizen, you are going to pay for it," Nighthorse said.

"Yes."

"Don't you see, that's exactly what Jensen is doing. He is showing the terrorists that if they commit a capital crime against the U.S., they will pay for it. And since he doesn't have the structure of a public trial to do the job for him . . . he has to find some other way."

"I suppose you are right," Giles said. He sighed. "I just hope this doesn't all blow back in our faces."

"Mr. Secretary, let's remember who is taking the real risk here. It could be our careers, it could be Art Jensen's life."

"You're right," Giles said. "You are absolutely right. You have my word, Nighthorse, you will never hear another peep of indecision from me. You and General Jensen will have my one hundred percent support."

"Thank you, Mr. Secretary. That's all either of us can ask for."

CHAPTER TWENTY

Prince Azeer Lal Qambar stood at the window of his forty-second-floor apartment, and looked out over the skyscrapers and commerce of Midtown Manhattan.

"The ace of spades?" he said.

"Yes, *Al Sayyid*," Hamdi replied. "It was found with both martyrs."

"This is not good, Hamdi. It means that someone has penetrated our network. Someone is providing the Americans with information."

"Surely, Prince Qambar, you do not believe that the American government killed Shamat and Taleb?"

"Do you think they did not?"

Hamdi shook his head. "I think it is against the American law to do such a thing. And I do not think the Americans have the courage to do such a thing. You have seen how slowly they react to everything. We attacked and killed them with impunity until nine-eleven, and not once did the Americans strike back."

"If it was not the American government who killed Shamat and Taleb, who was it?"

Hamdi shook his head. "This, I do not know," he replied. "But I think perhaps it is the act of one man, and he is working outside the government."

"Why would one man do such a thing?"

"He may be what the Americans call a hot dog," Hamdi said.

"A hot dog?" Qambar asked, clearly puzzled by the term. He shook his head. "I don't understand."

"A hot dog is someone who does something in order to be noticed," Hamdi said. "It is someone who seeks attention."

"He seeks attention?"

"Yes."

Qambar was silent for a moment, then nodded his head. "Good, good. Let him seek attention. In that way, we will learn who he is. And when we do learn, we will give him the attention he seeks."

The Watergate Hotel, Washington, D.C.

When Art let himself into the room it was empty. He waited for half an hour, but no one showed up. Then, just as he turned on the television and settled back to watch a TV show, the phone rang.

"Yes?"

"This is the dining room, sir. Your order will be right up."

Art started to say that he had made no order, but held back. "Thanks," he said.

Earlier today, Art had discovered an envelope under the potted plant just outside the door to his apartment. Inside the envelope was an electronic door key, of the type issued by hotels. It was wrapped by a single sheet of paper, and the only thing on the paper were the words *Watergate—412*.

Less than five minutes after the telephone call, there was a light knock on his door.

"Room service." The voice was muffled.

Art started toward the door, then thought better of it.

Instead, he picked up his pistol and covered it with a towel as if he had just come from washing his hands.

"Come in," he called.

The door opened and a cart was pushed in. At first, Art did not see the bellhop who was pushing the cart, because his back was turned as the door was being shut. But when the bellhop turned, Art gasped in surprise, then laughed.

"Colonel Nighthorse!" he said. "Doing a little moonlighting, are you?"

"One can always use a few extra dollars," Nighthorse replied with a chuckle. "By the way, my friends call me Temple, and I hope you like lamb."

"I love lamb."

"Good," Nighthorse said. "Because that's what we are having for dinner."

Nighthorse was wearing a long white jacket, but he removed it to show that, beneath it, he was wearing the army green summer uniform. The summer uniform looked like the winter uniform, except it was made of lighter material, and in this case he was wearing a light green short-sleeve shirt instead of the full blouse.

"Do you always bring your own meals when you call on someone?"

"Only if I don't trust them to serve lamb," Nighthorse said. He put the two dishes on a table, then lifted the silver tray covers, revealing the thickly cut lamb chops, roasted potatoes, and green peas.

"Looks good," Art said.

"Looks good? That's like saying Niagara Falls looks like a leak," Nighthorse said as he sat down to the meal. Looking up, he saw that Art was still standing there, still holding a towel over his hands.

"Are you going to stand there holding that gun all night? Or are you going to join me?" Nighthorse asked.

"Oh," Art said, looking down at his hands. "I'd almost forgotten I was carrying this."

He put the pistol down on the bedside table, then joined

Nighthorse, who had already taken his first bite. Nighthorse closed his eyes and puckered up in an expression of pure joy.

"Oh," Nighthorse said. "I haven't had lamb this good since my grandmother made it, back on the reservation."

"The reservation?"

"The Rosebud," Nighthorse said. "I am Oglala. Or at least, my father is. My mother is Irish."

"Funny, you don't look Irish," Art said.

Nighthorse looked up in surprise, then laughed. "No, I don't suppose I do," he said.

"Sioux, huh?" Art asked. He too took a bite of the lamb chop. "Oh, you are right, this is good," he said.

"Yes, I'm Sioux."

"My great-great-grandfather—" Art started, but Nighthorse interrupted him.

"Was inducted into the Warrior Society," Nighthorse continued.

"Yes. How did you know that?"

"Because my great-great-grandfather, Stone Eagle, was his sponsor and blood brother."

Art looked at Nighthorse in surprise. "Well, I'll be damned," he said.

"In a way," Nighthorse said. "I suppose that makes us brothers."

"Yeah? Well, some brother you are, the way you prosecuted me."

"Let's just say that was in lieu of making you undergo the ritual of the sun dance."

"Wait, the sun dance. Isn't that where hooks are stuck through your chest and you hang by your skin?" Art asked.

"Yes."

Art chuckled. "I guess I did come out ahead of the game at that," he said. He stuck his hand across the table. "Brother."

"Are you getting all the information you need?" Nighthorse asked.

"Yes."

"And equipment?"

"Yes."

Those were the only two questions Nighthorse asked that were anywhere remotely connected to Art's situation and position. The rest of the evening the two men just exchanged pleasantries. As it turned out, both were historians, and they spoke of such diverse things as the Civil War, the Indian campaigns, and Vietnam. Both had close relatives who had fought in Vietnam, Art's father, and Nighthorse's older brother.

When Nighthorse left that evening, he left the long white jacket he had worn hanging on the hat rack just inside the door. At first, Art nearly called out to him, but then he realized that the jacket had just been a ruse to allow him to come up to the room without being noticed.

That was when Art saw an envelope sticking out of the pocket of the white jacket. He retrieved the envelope, opened it, and pulled out a photograph, and a rather lengthy, typewritten page.

Azoon Jabri Shadloo is employed by the Baldwin County School District, Baldwin County, Alabama. He works in the school bus maintenance department. It is not the first time Shadloo ever had anything to do with a school bus.

Two months ago in Redha, Qambari Arabia, a school bus carrying American dependent children was destroyed by a remotely detonated bomb. Seven children were killed and four were badly wounded. The driver and the marine guard were also wounded.

Our investigation has uncovered an overwhelming preponderance of evidence, as well as numerous eyewitness accounts, establishing that the operation was planned, the bomb was placed, and the explosion was detonated by Azoon Jabri Shadloo.

Despite our presentation of the evidence to the authorities in Qambari Arabia, no action was taken. We then learned that Shadloo was sent to the United States on a diplomatic visa through the Qambari embassy as part of the Trade Council. We lost track of him for a while, but have since located him at the school bus maintenance facility in Bay Minnette, Alabama.

Art examined the photographs that were included with the report. As usual, there was no mention, anywhere, of what disposition Art was to make of the information he had been provided.

Bay Minette, Alabama

It was within a few minutes of quitting time when Art reached the Baldwin County Board of Education transportation facility just off Highway 59. A fenced-in area contained two dozen busses, while half a dozen more buses were inside a large, barnlike building. These were the buses that were undergoing maintenance of some sort.

The building was noisy with the sound of mechanics at work: hammers striking wheel rims, air-powered wrenches, and idling engines. At least three radios were playing, all on different stations. A couple of the men were carrying on a conversation, but as each was working on his own bus, their dialogue was quite loud. Art heard enough of it to realize they were talking about fishing.

"Can I help you, sir?" someone asked. Unlike the mechanics, all of whom were wearing coveralls, this man was wearing street clothes.

"And you are?" Art replied.

"Tim Moser."

"Are you the supervisor, Mr. Moser?"

"No, I'm the parts clerk. Ed Tracey is the supervisor."

"I wonder if I could speak to Mr. Tracey."

"Concerning?"

"My name is Phil Wyman," Art said, handing Moser one of his cards. "I am with the U.S. Department of Education."

"Oh yes, sir. Well, Mr. Tracey isn't here right now, but if you would care to wait over there, I'll call him."

"Thank you," Art said.

As Moser stepped into the office, Art began wandering around the building. He found who he was looking for at the far corner of the building. Shadloo was working under a bus that had been elevated on a lift.

Looking around, Art saw a door that led out of the building. The door was located behind a shelf of tires, and a network of spiderwebs indicated that it was rarely opened. Taking care not to be seen, Art unlocked it, then opened it to make certain that it could be opened. He closed it, then stepped back out into the building, just as Moser and another man were coming toward him.

"Oh, here you are," Moser said. "I thought you were going to wait."

Art smiled. "I thought I would get a better look at your facility if I moved around on my own," he said. He stuck his hand out. "Mr. Tracey, you are to be congratulated. From all that I can see, your maintenance facility is a model for others to follow. It will reflect on my report."

"Your report?"

"Yes. I'm on an inspection tour just to see how many bus maintenance operations are meeting the federal code."

"I didn't know there was a federal code."

"Oh yes, there is a code, and you would be amazed at how many facilities are not up to par. From my preliminary inspection, though, yours appears to be just fine. But, just so that you know, I plan to hang around for about three days in order to put together a full report."

"Oh, Mr. Wyman, I hope you don't need me to be with you during that time, I've got—"

"No, no, no, not at all," Art said, holding up his hand. "As a matter of fact, I prefer to be alone. Don't worry, I'll be as unobtrusive as a mouse. I don't want to do anything that will interfere with your routine. In fact, it won't even be necessary for me to talk to any of your employees."

"Good."

* * *

Art had no idea what his plan was from this point on. He was just going to play it by ear until something developed. As it happened, something developed the very next day, when Shadloo asked Tracey for some overtime.

Tracey sighed. "You are always trying to get overtime, Shadloo," he said. "Trust me, the budget isn't large enough to handle too many overtimes."

"You want the bus tomorrow?"

"Yes, I want the bus tomorrow," Tracey said. "I have three more coming in for scheduled maintenance."

"Three hours," Shadloo said. "I need only three hours."

Tracey sighed. "Take all the time you need, Shadloo. But you are only going to get paid for two hours."

"That will do," Shadloo said.

That night, after supper, Art returned to the maintenance facility, but this time he parked a couple of blocks away. Walking back, he let himself in through the back door.

The garage was dark, except for a few lights that shone dimly from high overhead, and did little to push away the gloom. The one exception was the corner where Shadloo was working. His area was very brightly lit.

Art stepped up behind the tire rack where, shielded from Shadloo's view, he could observe the mechanic working.

At first, Art wasn't sure what Shadloo was doing. Then he realized that he was strapping two large propane tanks to the underside of the bus. For a moment he considered the possibility that there might be an innocent explanation to that, such as an alternate fuel source, but he abandoned that line of reasoning when he saw what happened next.

Shadloo pulled a small fuse from his pocket and connected it to a cell phone. He put the cell phone and fuse on a workbench, then, with a second cell phone, dialed the first. Art watched, as the cell phone on the bench responded to the call, first with a ring, then a flash, as the igniter fuse detonated.

Smiling at the success of his test, Shadloo put his phone

down and picked up the trigger phone. Connecting it to a second fuse, he went back under the bus to arm the propane bomb he had just constructed.

As soon as Shadloo was out of sight, Art moved quickly out from behind the tire rack. He picked up the telephone Shadloo had left lying on the table, and left the ace of spades in its place. Then he hurried outside. He waited until he was a block away before he punched the redial on Shadloo's phone.

There was something satisfying about the sound of the explosion.

CHAPTER
TWENTY-ONE

Washington, D.C.

"Prince Azeer," Senator Harriet Clayton said, greeting the Qambari prince in her office. "How nice to see you."

"It is always my pleasure to call upon such a beautiful woman," Azeer replied graciously. "Especially someone like you, who understands the delicate dynamics between my people and a superpower like the United States."

"You mean a bully like the United States," Harriet replied. "Don't be frightened to say it. Lord knows, I have made a number of speeches, trying to hold this administration to count. Please, come into my office where we will be more comfortable. Jeanie, you will bring coffee and snacks?" she said to one of her interns.

"Yes, ma'am," the young girl replied.

Once inside the office, Harriet showed the prince around, pointing out photographs on the wall.

"As you know, I was the nation's second lady for eight years, while my husband was vice president," she said. "And during that time I got to travel rather extensively. Here is a picture of me with your father, I believe."

"Yes, my father spoke of that visit fondly," Azeer said.

Jeanie brought the coffee and a tray of pastries, set them on the table, and withdrew.

"How do you like your coffee?" Harriet asked, as she poured.

"Without cream or sugar, thank you."

With filled coffee cups in hand, the two moved to a seating area. Azeer sat on a sofa, Harriet sat in a chair at right angles to the sofa.

"Now, Prince Azeer, what can I do for you?"

"Senator, I'm sure you remember the unpleasant incident a few years ago, when you were held hostage by a terrorist named Mehdi Jahm Shidi?"

"How can I forget? It was a terrifying experience," Harriet replied.

"You do remember, as well, that my government provided assistance to your government in bringing about your release?"

"Yes, I am very grateful."

"I remind you of this, because I want a favor from you."

"From the United States?"

"No, Senator, from you, personally."

Harriet hesitated for a moment; then she cleared her throat. "Well, of course I will do all that I can," she said. "What do you need?"

"Perhaps an investigation," Azeer suggested. "One that, as chairman of the Senate Human Rights Committee, you would be able to hold."

"Prince Azeer, if this is about the terrorist prison camps, I think you will find that there are many of us who are—"

"Forgive me for interrupting you, Senator," Azeer said. "But it is not about the prison camps. It is about a string of murders that are taking place right here in the United States, sanctioned, I believe, by the United States government."

"Oh, I'm sure you must be wrong," Harriet replied. "As

you know, I am one of the biggest opponents of this administration, but not even I believe it would sanction murders."

"Nor would I want to believe it," Azeer said. "But consider these facts. Three men have been killed. And not just killed, Senator. In every case, the method of their death has been brutal and bizarre."

"Who are these three men, and why do you have a particular interest in them?"

"The three are Abdulla Balama Shamat, Balli Daftar Taleb, and Azoon Jabri Shadloo. All three were my countrymen, working in America. They were all good men, from fine families. Now I am ashamed to face their families, because I, personally, arranged for the visas that allowed them to come to America. They thought they were coming to improve themselves, instead they came here to be murdered."

"What makes you think that the U.S. had anything to do with their murders?" Harriet asked.

"You will recall that I said the method of their death was bizarre. In the case of Shamat, he was found nude, his body displayed in a shameful manner, with his, uh . . ." Azeer paused for a moment. "You will excuse me, Senator, for being indelicate, but his underwear were stuffed into his mouth. Taleb was beheaded, his head found in a tobacco humidor, and Shadloo was killed in a school bus explosion."

"Yes," Harriet said. "I do recall reading about those cases. The press is referring to them as the 'Ace of Spades' murders, I believe, because in every case the killer left an ace of spades as his calling card."

"That is correct."

"But why does that lead you to believe that our government is involved?"

"In each case, Senator, the method of death has duplicated, or nearly so, the method of death of a victim in the Middle East. And in each case, the United States government has made the claim that these were the men responsible. For example, Shamat was accused of the rape and murder of young Amber Pease, who was the daughter of Colonel Pease, the commandant of the marine guards at the American embassy in Redha. Taleb was accused of being the one who beheaded the American oil worker, the Jew, Bernie Gelb. And your government claimed that Shadloo was guilty of bombing the school bus that killed several American schoolchildren. In fact, the U.S. government has even gone so far as to offer to waive extradition and send the three men back to Qambari Arabia so they could stand trial."

"You do not think these three were guilty?"

"No, Senator. We have conducted our own investigation, a much more thorough investigation than that conducted by the U.S., I must say."

"What makes you believe your investigation was more thorough?"

"Well, as I'm sure you can understand, we have resources that are unavailable to the U.S. There were witnesses who would talk to us, who would not talk to the U.S. investigators. And, if I must say, our interrogation methods are a bit more severe. We are able to elicit confessions from the guilty when the American way of interrogation would leave them sticking by their lies."

Azeer sighed. "No, Senator, we are perfectly satisfied that those three men were innocent of the charges that were leveled against them. And yet, despite the fact that they were innocent, they were murdered in a duplication of the original crime."

"Very well, Prince Azeer, I will look into it for you," Harriet said.

"Thank you."

Washington, D.C., Senate Committee Room

The meeting room was filled with spectators, reporters, and cameras. Senator Paul Harris banged his gavel several times until the room grew relatively quiet.

"This Senate Subcommittee on Contract Services will come to order," he said. "The committee calls Bert Mossenberg."

A tall, thin, gray-haired man stepped up to the witness table.

"Mr. Mossenberg, you were sworn in yesterday, and I remind you, sir, that you are still under oath," Senator Harris said.

"Yes, sir."

"Please be seated. I believe Senator Clayton has the microphone."

Harriet Clayton leaned into the microphone. "Thank you, Senator Harris," she said. "And I also want to thank the senators on my side of the aisle who have relinquished their time to me. Mr. Mossenberg, your company, Transworld Oil, is engaged in contract services in Iraq, is it not?"

"It is, Senator."

"And how much is that contract?"

"It depends upon how much work is done," Mossenberg replied.

"But it does have a rather generous cap, does it not?"

"I am satisfied with the cap," Mossenberg said.

"In fact, Mr. Mossenberg, isn't the cap for two billion dollars?"

"We have not billed that much," Mossenberg said.

"But you have been paid a great deal of money, have you not, Mr. Mossenberg? A great deal of American taxpayers' money?"

"We have been paid more by the Iraqi oil industry than we have received from the U.S. government," Mossenberg said.

"Still, your compensation is very high."

"Our risks are high," Mossenberg said. "I would remind you that Bernie Gelb worked for us. We have also had six other employees killed."

"The other six were not Americans, were they?"

"One of them was an American, one was German, and four were Iraqi. But they were all employees of Transworld Oil, and we felt their loss keenly."

"And you would like revenge for their deaths, would
you not?"

"I'm not sure what you mean, Senator. If you are asking i
I would like to see their killers brought to justice, the answe
is yes."

"Have you done anything to bring them to justice?"

"I don't understand."

"I'm sure you are aware, Mr. Mossenberg, that three citi
zens of Qambari, who were in the United States, were foun
murdered."

"I've read about it."

"I am told that we have very strong reason to believe tha
these Qambaris were guilty of murder of American citizens
One, a Mr. Shamat, is suspected of being the killer of you
employee, Bernie Gelb."

"Yes, I'm aware of that."

"Did you have anything to do with the death of these thre
men?" Harriet asked.

"I did not."

"Are you aware of, and do you have any knowledge of, a
secret organization of the U.S. government that might have
something to do with the killings?"

"I have no such knowledge, Senator."

"Thank you, no further questions."

Harriet smiled. She had gotten the question of a government star-chamber before the Senate. That was exactly wha
she set out to do.

WCN Studios, Atlanta, Georgia

Bill Jacoby, host of *World Cable News Sunday,* stared int
the monitor, using it as a mirror while he combed his hair.

"Coming up in five, Bill," a voice in his earpiece said.

Jacoby looked into the monitor, checked his image, then
changed the expression to one he considered to be more ap-
propriate. The red light came on.

"Is there a sanctioned star-chamber at work in the halls of our own government?" he asked, beginning this segment. "Is our State Department, or perhaps our Department of Defense, killing suspected terrorists, without so much as a trial? Our next guest, Senator Harriet Clayton, is looking into just such a charge."

The screen split, with Bill Jacoby on the left, and Senator Harriet Clayton on the right.

"Senator Clayton, thank you for taking time out of your busy schedule to visit with us tonight."

"Thank you for the opportunity," Harriet replied.

"I should tell our viewers that you are in Washington now, and you have been looking into this charge of government involvement in a string of bizarre killings, have you not?"

"I have, Bill, and in fact, I put the question in the record while I was questioning Bert Mossenberg."

"Do you really believe that Mossenberg may have something to do with it?"

"It is not beyond the realm of possibility," Harriet replied. "And I must say that some of the preliminary results of my investigation have been quite disturbing."

"Disturbing in what way, Senator?"

"Disturbing in the way the murders have been planned, co-ordinated, and executed. Although a playing card, the ace of spades, has been left at the scene of each crime, I believe that is a ruse."

"A ruse in what way?"

"Well, consider this," Harriet said. "Suppose there are several 'hit teams' carrying out these atrocious events, but they wanted to make it appear as if only one person is doing it. What better way than to find some 'signature' that all could leave behind at the scene of the crime?"

"Yes," Jacoby said. "Yes, I can see your point. But wouldn't such an activity be a violation of the law?"

"Oh, indeed it would be," Harriet replied. "Not only U.S. law but international law as well."

"What is your purpose for investigating it?" Jacoby asked.

"Look, we have had enough difficulty maintaining our image in light of the . . . what some are calling an unnecessary war in which we are engaged. We have also had to deal with the atrocities against the Muslim prisoners, carried on in our prisons. Someone has got to put a check on this administration."

"And so you have taken on that responsibility?"

"Indeed I have, Bill. And I am always reminded by the mantra of the conscientious when called upon to perform an unpleasant and often difficult task. If not now, when? And if not my committee, which has watchdog responsibility over such things, then by who?"

"You raise a good point, Senator. An excellent point," Jacoby said.

Secretary of the Army Jordon Giles's home,
Washington, D.C.

At the end of the show, Giles turned off the TV and glanced over at Colonel Nighthorse. When, earlier today, the two men had learned that Harriet Clayton was to be a guest on *World Cable News Sunday*, they agreed to meet at the secretary's house in order to watch it together, and to discuss any specific ramifications.

"What do you think," Giles asked, "did she hurt us?"

"No," Nighthorse said. "She didn't say one thing that would make me believe she was anywhere close."

"Yes, I think you are right. Still, all the digging around does make me nervous. How strong is our disconnect?"

"I beg your pardon, Mr. Secretary?"

"I mean how hard is it going to be to keep the government clear of any responsibility for what is going on?"

"I think General Jensen has already helped us there," Nighthorse said. "It was his idea to leave an ace of spades behind each event. That tends to point to a private individual . . . a crazed vigilante."

"Good for Jensen," Giles said.

"Mr. Secretary, I do hope you aren't suggesting that we would ever abandon General Jensen," Nighthorse said.

"No, no, I have no intention of throwing General Jensen to the wolves. I told you before, and I tell you again. I will not abandon General Jensen. You can rest easy on that score," Giles said.

"We all knew this would be a difficult and trying operation when we went into it," Nighthorse said. "My recommendation is that we stay the course until everything is taken care of."

"Then what?"

"Then we promote General Jensen to Major General, let him move back into the public, and give him a command somewhere that would be befitting his rank and ability."

Giles shook his head. "We don't have a command commensurate with his ability. He is practically a regiment, all by himself."

CHAPTER
TWENTY-TWO

Nashville International Airport, Nashville, Tennessee

Bert Mossenberg was riding in the back of his limo, heading for the executive aviation terminal. He had just returned from the Senate Committee Hearings two days earlier, had a brief visit with his family, and was now heading for Los Angeles to meet with some people from Pacific Coast Recording. In the strange world of diversified businesses, Transworld Oil owned Pacific Coast Recording.

Billy Jay Packer was with him. Billy Jay, who was Pacific Coast Recording's number-one star, was one of the hottest singers in country music, with his latest song, "Lovin' You Has Made Me a Better Man," currently sitting at number two on the charts.

"I watched some of the Senate Hearings on TV," Billy Jay said. "And I'll tell you the truth, Mr. Mossenberg, I don't know why you didn't just crawl over that table and kick Harriet Clayton in her skanky ass."

Mossenberg laughed. "I did think about it," he said.

The car drove through the gate, and right out to the executive tarmac. The airplane, a Gulfstream IV, sat waiting for them. The plane was white, but with an anodized gold band framing the windows, and running the length of the plane. The gold swept up to the tail, rising high above the cluster of four engines. The name TRANSWORLD OIL was in green script, just above the windows, and the logo of an oil derrick, in green, was displayed on the high-sweeping, gold tail.

The crew of the Gulfstream, pilot, copilot, and flight attendant, were standing just at the foot of the air-stair as the limo arrived. They waited as the driver got out, came around, and opened the door.

"Mr. Packer," the flight attendant said, holding forth a CD album. "My name's Heather Thorndike. Would you autograph this for me?"

"Why, yes, ma'am, I'd be glad to," Billy Jay said, smiling broadly and taking the album.

Mossenberg was on his cell phone as he slid out of the backseat.

"No, no, no," he said, speaking animatedly into the telephone. "We need those drill bits yesterday. Do you understand that? Yesterday! Look, getting those drill bits is the difference between having the Iraq fields at sixty percent and ninety percent. You have all the money you need to get them there, and all the authority that is necessary to get the job done. I want results, not excuses."

Mossenberg closed his phone, then smiled at the flight crew. "I'm sorry about that, folks, just a little disagreement with someone who seems bound and determined to make my life a bit more complicated than it needs to be. How about getting me up there where there is some peace and quiet? Tell me, Karl, what's the weather look like?" he asked the pilot.

"Weather looks good, Mr. Mossenberg. We should have a very smooth flight to Los Angeles, Mr. Mossenberg," Karl answered.

"Good, good," Mossenberg said.

"Heather?" Karl said, looking around. "Did you put my brain bucket on board?"

"Brain bucket?" Billy Jay asked as he handed the CD album back to the flight attendant.

"No, Karl, I didn't," Heather replied. Then to Billy Jay, she explained, "Brain bucket is what the pilots call their briefcases, because they have all the files, manuals, and directives they need."

"Are you sure? I know I left it right here," Karl said, as he continued to look around.

"I haven't seen it," Heather insisted.

"Damn," Karl replied. "That's got my approach plates and—"

"Wait a minute, is that it?" Heather asked, smiling as she pointed to a briefcase sitting about ten yards away from the aircraft.

"Yeah," Karl said. "Yeah, it is. How did it get over there?"

"The caterers probably moved it when they were putting the meal aboard," Heather said. "They do things like that all the time. I'll get it for you."

"Thanks."

Inside the airplane, Mossenberg and Billy Jay settled down for the three-hour flight to LAX. The inside of the plane was paneled in gleaming oak, while the sofa and chairs were in white and gold leather, embossed with the same logo that appeared on the tail.

"Heather, do we have anything to drink?" Mossenberg asked.

"We're fully stocked, sir," the beautiful young attendant said. "What would you like?"

"How about a root beer with a scoop of vanilla ice cream?" he asked.

Heather smiled broadly. "I figured you would want that," she said. "Coming right up."

"Uh, darlin', you wouldn't have a beer, would you?" Billy Jay asked.

"I do indeed."

"Oh, that would be wonderful," Billy Jay said as he settled into an overstuffed leather chair.

In the front of the airplane the copilot made an adjustment to the radio.

"Karl, we're on Nashville ground, 121.9," he said.

"Thanks, Al," Karl replied. "Nashville ground, GS Four, Transworld, request permission for taxi and takeoff," he said into the microphone.

"GS Four, clear to taxi to runway two-zero right, cross three-one at pilot's discretion. Altimeter two-niner-niner-seven. Winds two-one degrees at ten knots. Change to tower frequency, 118.6."

"Roger, 118.6," Karl replied, then nodded to Al to make the frequency change.

Karl picked up the phone and pressed a button. Back in the cabin the phone next to Mossenberg's seat buzzed, and he picked it up.

"Yes, Karl," Mossenberg said.

"We have clearance for immediate taxi and takeoff, Mr. Mossenberg, if you are ready."

"Ready back here," he said.

The four engines spooled up, and the airplane moved away from its parking place. Mossenberg picked up the evening newspaper and began to look through it. As was so often the case since his company took on the contract of refurbishing Iraqi oil fields, he found his name with very little difficulty.

MORE TROUBLES FOR TRANSWORLD OIL

In a recent appearance before the Senate Subcommittee on Contract Services, Senator Harriet Clayton questioned Bert Mossenberg about any possible involvement he, or his company, might have with the recent deaths of two Qambaris, living in the United States. Senator Paul Harris, chairman of the committee, accused Senator Clayton of engaging in a witch-hunt, stating that she had absolutely no justification for accusing Mossenberg.

However, regardless of the outcome of Senator Clayton's investigation, the troubles for Mossenberg, and Transworld Oil, continue to mount.

The group calling itself Americans for Sane Policy has now asked the ACLU to look into the possibility that Transworld Oil is stealing from the people of Iraq.

Dean Kerry, a spokesperson for ASP, said, "We believe that, under the guise of returning Iraq's oil production to its prewar levels, Bert Mossenberg of Transworld Oil is siphoning millions of barrels of oil for the private coffers of Transworld. We have asked the United Nations to look into this scandal, which reaches into the innermost circles of the current administration."

Kerry went on to point out that the war in Iraq is unjustified and that it is now becoming increasingly more obvious that it is a "payoff" to the oil cronies who helped the president get elected.

When the Gulfstream reached the end of runway 2-0 right, Karl called the tower.

"Nashville Tower, GS Four ready for takeoff."

"GS Four, cleared for immediate takeoff," the Nashville tower told Mossenberg's pilot. "Change to departure frequency 119.35, and report fifteen thousand."

"Roger, 119.35, report fifteen thousand," Karl repeated.

Karl then activated the cabin intercom.

"Uh, we're at the end of the active with immediate clearance. Heather, please be sure you are seated. We're rolling," he added as he moved the thrust levers forward to full takeoff power.

Heather sat in an aft-facing seat against the forward firewall, and fastened her belt and harness, just as the engines went to full power.

In another part of the airport, the part used by commercial aviation, two baggage handlers managed to take their break at the same time. The men, Hohsen bin Hassan, and Soofah Aziz Labib, were citizens of the Kingdom of Qambari Arabia, but both were working in the United States on permanent visas.

As the two men were in highly sensitive jobs, it had been necessary to vet them, then vet them again, in order to get them the security clearances they needed. The Qambari embassy had been most helpful in facilitating all of the paperwork.

"Where is he now?" Hassan asked, speaking of the Gulfstream IV.

"He is over there," Labib said, pointing to the very expensive business jet that was just now beginning its takeoff run.

From various points around the airport, people turned to watch the beautiful airplane as it gathered speed, rotated, then, tucking away its landing gear, took up a sixty-degree climb to get itself cleared, quickly, from terminal airspace traffic.

Hassan and Labib stepped out to the edge of the luggage area apron to watch the airplane climbing beautifully against the backdrop of a large, billowing white cloud. Labib turned on a small pocket radio, then tuned it in to the frequency of departure control so they could listen in to the pilot's conversation with various control agencies.

"You are sure it is aboard?" Hassan asked.

"Yes. When they were not looking, I put it in the pilot's briefcase."

"What altitude is it set for?" Hassan asked.

"Eighteen thousand," Labib replied.

"Nashville Departure, this is GS Four, reporting fifteen thousand, request altitude and route clearance IFR to LAX," the radio said.

"Climb to three-zero-thousand feet, take up a heading of two-seven-zero until clear of Nashville airspace."

"Roger, climbing to three-zero-thousand."

Moments after the last radio transmission there was a flash, high in the air. The flash was followed by a puff of smoke, and bits and pieces of wreckage coming down. It took almost fifteen seconds for the sound of the explosion to reach the ground.

Hassan and Labib saw the explosion, then, silently shook hands.

"Allah will be pleased," Labib said.

"And so will Prince Azeer," Hassan replied. Hassan pulled out his cell phone and made a call.

"The Satan of the oil fields is no more," Hassan said when Azeer answered.

"Good. It is time for the next step."

CHAPTER
TWENTY-THREE

Office of the secretary of the army, Washington, D.C.

"You are sure they said the Satan of the oil fields is no more?" Giles asked.

Nighthorse nodded. "Yes. Of course, at the time, our monitors didn't know what they were talking about, but later realized that the conversation had taken place within moments of the crash that killed Bert Mossenberg."

"And you are certain that he was talking to Azeer?"

"Absolutely certain," Nighthorse replied.

"Damn. If there was ever any doubt about that son of a bitch, there is no doubt now."

"They are planning something else," Nighthorse said.

"What?"

Nighthorse shook his head. "We don't know yet, but it is something big."

"All right, stay on it. And get Art in on this now. I don't want to react after the event, I want to prevent it if we can."

"Yes, sir, will do," Nighthorse said.

CHAPTER
TWENTY-FOUR

Chateau Spud Bar, Alexandria, Virginia

"You've been a busy man," the bartender said as he set a frosted mug of beer in front of Art.

"What?"

"Well, you haven't been in here in a while," he said. "I figure you must've been chasing down bail jumpers."

"Oh yes, I have," Art said.

"I figured there must be some reason why you haven't been around for a while."

"You plan to drink alone? Or would you like some company?" a woman's voice asked.

Turning, Art saw the same beautiful woman who had connected with him on one of his previous visits to Chateau Spud.

"The company of a beautiful woman is always appreciated," Art replied.

"Aren't you the flatterer though?" she asked.

"Johnny, give the lady whatever she wants."

"I'll have what he's having," she said.

"Coming right up."

"I didn't get your name before," Art said.

"Tiffany," the woman said.

Art chuckled. "It would be."

Tiffany smiled. "Yes, I thought you might appreciate that."

Johnny brought Tiffany her beer, Tiffany smiled her thanks, then took a drink. She spoke as she held the glass to her lips, thus concealing the fact that she was speaking, and speaking only loudly enough for Art to hear.

"You have a tee-off time reserved for you at Hilltop tomorrow afternoon at two," she said.

Returning to his apartment that evening, Art turned on his TV, but finding nothing to watch that interested him, he looked over at his great-great-grandfather's journal.

"Well, Grandpa Smoke," he said quietly, "we seem to be running parallel paths here, taking care of the bad guys. How did it work out for you?"

From the journal of Smoke Jensen

The sign I was looking at said "Welcome to Bertrand, population 312." Behind it, another sign said "A vibrant city of the future! Come grow with us!"

I wasn't at all sure if the fella who wrote that sign was talking about the same town I was riding into about then. I didn't see much vibrant about the little town. It had two dirt roads that formed a cross in the middle of the high desert country, a handful of small, shotgun houses on the outskirts, and a line of business buildings, all false-fronted, none painted. The saloon was partially painted, though, with its name, "Lucky Nugget," painted in red, high on its own false-front.

I started toward the saloon, as much to slake my thirst as to find information. I tied my horse off in front and then looked around before I stepped inside.

I didn't see anything to alarm me . . . but I was alarmed, nevertheless. Art, I don't think this is something you can teach a person, and I know I can't explain it to you. You will either understand what I am about to tell you . . . or you won't, and there's nothing more to be said about it. But I felt something, a tingling of the hair on the back of my head, a prickling of the skin . . . call it what you will, but I knew that there was danger close by.

I pulled my pistol from its holster, spun the cylinder to check the loads, then replaced the pistol loosely, and went inside. I had long had a way of entering a saloon, stepping in through the door, then moving quickly to one side to put my back against the wall as I studied all the patrons. Over the years I had made a number of friends, but it seems that for every friend I made, I made an enemy as well. And a lot of those enemies would like nothing better than to kill me, if they could. I didn't figure on making it easy for them.

As I stood there in the saloon with my eyes adjusting to the shadows, I saw him. I may not even have noticed him had he not been wearing my shirt, the very shirt my Sally had mended when I tore it on a nail in the barn. As I thought about it, I began to get angrier and angrier. I was not only angry with him for being one of the men who framed me, I was angry because he was wearing a shirt that Sally's own hands had mended and washed.

What right did that son of a bitch have to be wearing, next to his foul body, something that Sally had touched!

The man was talking to a bar girl and, so engaged was he that he noticed neither my entrance nor my crossing the open floor to step up next to him.

"That's my shirt you are wearing, you son of a bitch," I said.

"What?" the man replied, turning toward me. For a moment he was confused, then, perhaps because I was wearing the very shirt he had been wearing, he realized who I was.

"Where's your friend?" I asked.

"What friend? What are you talking about?"

"You know what I'm talking about," I said. "You and two other men set me up to take the blame for a bank you robbed in Etna. I've already taken care of one of your friends. I've got you and one more to go."

The man's eyes widened. "You got Dooley?"

"Was that his name? I didn't catch it."

The man laughed nervously. "I . . . I don't know what you are talking about."

"You asked if I got Dooley."

"Yes, well, I . . . I mean you come in here tellin' me you got one of my friends. He was just the first name that come to mind, that's all."

"Mister, are you saying this man robbed a bank?" the bartender asked.

I nodded. "Robbed a bank and killed a man. I didn't know anything about that when I run across them on the road outside Etna. They attacked me and left me for dead, after changing shirts with me so that the people in town would think I was one of them."

"You're crazy."

"I don't know that he is so crazy," the bartender said to the man wearing my shirt. "I've wondered where you and your friend got all the money you two been throwing around ever since you come here. Besides which, he's wearing a shirt just like the shirt your brother is wearing."

"We . . . we sold some cows, that's where we got the money. And the shirt's just a coincidence."

"So, the other fella is your brother, is he? I'm only going to ask you this one more time. Where is he?" I asked.

Suddenly the man went for his pistol. I drew mine as well, but rather than shooting him, I brought it down hard on the top of his head. He went down like a sack of feed.

"Who are you?" the bartender asked nervously.

"Jensen," I replied. "Kirby Jensen."

"Jensen? Say, you wouldn't be the one they call Smoke Jensen, would you?" the bartender asked.

"That's me," I said, a little wary of answering because of fear that word might have gotten here that I was an escaped prisoner.

Happily, the bartender stuck his hand across the bar. "Well, it is an honor to meet you, Mr. Jensen," he said.

"Thanks." I stared at the man on the floor. "Do you have any idea where his brother is?"

"Oh yes. He's upstairs," the bartender said.

"Which room?"

"First room on your right when you reach the head of the stairs. He's in there with Becky."

"Thanks."

The altercation at the bar had caught the attention of all the others in the saloon, and now all conversation stopped as they watched me walk up the stairs to the second floor.

When I reached the room at the top of the stairs I stopped in front of the door, then raised my foot and kicked it open.

The woman inside screamed, and the man shouted out in anger and alarm.

"What the hell do you mean, barging in here?" he shouted.

"Get up and get your clothes on," I said. "I'm taking you back to Etna."

"The hell you are."

From nowhere, it seemed, a pistol appeared in his hand. I should have been more observant. If I had been, I would have noticed that he had a gun in the bed with him.

He got off the first shot and I could almost feel the wind as the bullet buzzed by me and slammed into the door frame. I returned fire and saw a black hole suddenly appear in his throat, followed by a gushing of blood. His eyes went wide and he dropped the gun and grabbed his throat as if he could stop the bleeding. He fell back against the headboard as his eyes grew dim.

The woman had not stopped screaming from the moment I kicked open the door. I started toward her, intended to calm her down, but she was convinced that I was going to kill her as well, and her screaming grew even louder.

Because of the screaming, I didn't realize that someone was behind me. I heard the gunshot and saw his bullet hit the iron headboard of the bed.

Whirling around, I saw that the man I had encountered downstairs was awake and tending to business. Before he could shoot me, I fired back and saw my bullet hit him in the middle of his chest. He backed out of the room, partly under his own power, and partly from the impact of the bullet. He hit the railing then, and was carried over by his own momentum.

I hurried to the railing and looked down. He had fallen on one of the tables, crashed through it, and was lying on the floor below me.

When I ran downstairs to him he was laughing, or at least trying to laugh. About as much wheezing and blood as laughter was coming from his lips.

"What are you finding so funny?" I asked.

"We recognized you right off," the man said. "We figured it would be a pretty good joke to play on the great Smoke Jensen if we could get him hanged. Almost worked, too."

After that, there were a few more coughs and wheezes, and then he died. I looked around at some of the others who had come close.

"Did any of you hear that?" I asked.

"I heard it, Mr. Jensen," one of the others said.

"I heard it too," another admitted.

"Don't worry, Smoke, we'll tell the sheriff what happened here."

"And what you just heard," I told them. "I'm a wanted man because of them, and I'd like to get it all cleared up."

The sheriff in Bertrand sent a telegram back to Marshal Turnball, explaining the entire situation, and stating that he had a prisoner who had confessed to everything, while at the same time the judge at Bertrand, who just happened to be an appellate judge, issued a letter overturning the result of my trial. I was a free man once more.

By the way, Art, I never did lease out Sugarloaf. I figured if I could come through what I had just come through, Sugarloaf could weather a little storm. And, I'm proud to say, it did.

CHAPTER
TWENTY-FIVE

"Here it is, Reverend Bixby," Deacon Norton said, holding up the newspaper. What he was pointing to was a full-page advertisement.

"It's beautiful, isn't it?" Norton asked.

"It is indeed," Bixby said. "And I believe God will reward us for reaching out to all his children." Bixby spread the page out on his desk so he could get the full impact as he read it.

TO ALL PEOPLE OF FAITH

CHRISTIANS, JEWS, AND MUSLIMS
We, the Christ Holiness Church of Nashville,
a full gospel, nondenominational church,
plan to have a

CELEBRATION OF FAITH

We all worship the same God, let us join together
to celebrate his Glory.
The Reverend J. Peerless Bixby

The Shabihul Mosque in Nashville, Tennessee

Sheikh Muhammad Kamal Mustafa poured heavy cream into his coffee, then sweetened it with three teaspoons of sugar. He swirled the spoon around in the beige-colored liquid as he talked to Hassan and Labib.

"You have brought honor on yourselves by your action in killing Mossenberg," Kamal said.

"We did not do it to honor ourselves, but for the glory of Allah," Labib said.

"Yes, and that is as it should be," Mustafa said, taking a drink of his coffee. Lowering his cup, he used his forefinger to wipe a bit of the liquid from his mustache.

"Suppose you were called upon to perform a deed of even greater importance, would you do so?"

"Yes," Labib said.

"And you, Hassan?" Mustafa asked.

"I will do whatever is asked of me," Hassan said.

"You do understand that those who serve Allah best, those who will be with him in paradise, are sometimes asked to give much."

"Yes," Labib answered.

"Hassan?"

"Yes."

"You do understand what I am saying, don't you?"

"You are asking us to die for you," Labib said.

Mustafa held up his finger and shook his head. "Listen to this quote from the Noble Quran, 3:169–171," he said. Clearing his throat, he quoted the verses from memory.

"Think not of those who are slain in Allah's way as dead. Nay, they live, finding their sustenance in the presence of their Lord. They rejoice in the Bounty provided by Allah. And with regard to those left behind, who have not yet joined them in their bliss, the Martyrs glory in the fact that on them is no fear, nor have they cause to grieve. They glory in the Grace and Bounty from Allah, and in the fact that Allah suffereth not the reward of the faithful to be lost."

"What would you have us do?" Labib asked.

"Do you know of the Coliseum?"

Hassan looked confused. "The Roman Coliseum?"

Mustafa shook his head. "No, I am speaking of the Coliseum here, in Nashville. It is where the Tennessee Titans play their games."

Hassan was still confused.

"It is American football," Labib said. "He is speaking of the sports arena."

Smiling, Hassan nodded. "Oh yes, I know of the sport arena."

"There will be a football game two weeks from now," Mustafa said. "It is said that sixty-five thousand people will be there. More could be killed there than were killed when the holy one, the sainted martyr, Mohammed Atta al Sayed, crashed his airplane into the World Trade Center Towers."

"More would be killed?" Labib asked.

"Many more," Mustafa said. "And all would be infidels, even from their own religion, for the games are played on Sunday, which is supposed to be a holy day for Christians. Surely, their sins should not go unpunished."

"But how could this be done?"

"It would take the action of a martyr," Mustafa said.

"A martyr?" Hassan replied. He looked nervous. "Where will you find such a martyr?"

"I think we could find someone," Mustafa said. "As an iman, I say to anyone who would martry himself in such a way, he will become an even greater prophet to Islam than Mohammed Atta al Sayed."

"Martyr," Hassan said, barely able to mouth the word.

"Think of it, Hassan," Mustafa said. "A moment of fear perhaps, an instant of pain, then all earthly trials will be over, and you will be in paradise, to live at the highest level for eternity—"

"I will do it," Labib said, interrupting Mustafa. "I will do it," he repeated, almost giddy with excitement.

Hassan paused for a moment, then nodded. "Yes," he said. "Yes, I will do it as well."

"Good. Your reward in paradise will be great. But if you are to do this, it must be done by plan," Mustafa said.

"What sort of plan? All we need to do is hijack an airliner and crash it into the stadium," Labib said. "Remember, I took flying lessons with Atta. I can steer the plane into the target."

"There is more to it than that. If you take the airplane too early, word will be out that a plane has been hijacked and the Americans will have time to react. If you are too late, you will miss the opportunity."

"When should we act?"

"There is a flight leaving at two p.m. for Los Angeles," Mustafa said. "I have booked the two of you on that flight."

Again, Hassan looked confused. "But how did you know we would do this?"

Mustafa smiled benevolently. "I knew that if you were called upon by Allah, you could not refuse."

"*Allah Akbar!*" Hassan shouted enthusiastically.

"*Allah Akbar!*" Labib repeated.

Alexandria, Virginia

Art teed off on the fourth hole of the Hilltop Golf Course. He hit the ball well, and it flew straight down the center, never rising higher than ten feet, but landing far down on the fairway, then rolling almost to the edge of the green.

When he returned to his golf cart, Nighthorse was sitting in it. He had not been there when Art stepped up to the tee a moment earlier.

"Damn, Temple, you do have a way of appearing out of the blue," Art said.

"That was a good tee-shot," Nighthorse replied. "You think you'll make par?"

"I generally do make par on this hole," Art said. He started forward with the cart. "What do you have for me?"

"Yesterday, a couple of people that we have been watching booked a flight from Nashville to Los Angeles, leaving at two-fourteen p.m. next Sunday."

"How do we know this?"

Nighthorse shook his head. "It is best that we do not get into each other's territory," he said. "That way we can maintain a separation between us."

"I understand. It makes it easier for the Pentagon to cut me loose. Rather like a quick disconnect."

"Something like that," Nighthorse agreed.

"Is there something significant about two 'people of interest' booking a flight to Los Angeles?"

"Yes. First of all, we have reason to suspect these two of having something to do with the explosion on board Bert Mossenberg's private jet."

"The FBI hasn't arrested them?"

"We have no evidence of any kind, just a strong suspicion," Nighthorse said. "But we have been bugging their telephone calls, and that's how we learned that they are planning to fly to Los Angeles."

"Do we have any idea why they would be going to Los Angeles?"

"No. But here is the interesting thing about their booking a flight to Los Angeles. They could have saved two hundred dollars by leaving an hour earlier, and three hundred dollars by going two hours later. That was pointed out to them by the travel agent, but they insisted on leaving at two-fourteen."

"Does anyone have any idea why they insisted on leaving at two-fourteen?"

"Not really," Nighthorse replied. "But monitored calls have suggested that something 'big' is going to happen in Nashville."

"Why Nashville?"

"Why not? It is the center of country music, and country music performers and fans are the very core of support for the war on terror. I'm sure that the terrorists believe that striking a blow there would have as big an impact as nine-eleven did.

And, after nine-eleven, we don't intend to let the slightest clue get by us."

"All right," Art said, getting out of the cart to go to his ball. "I'll leave this afternoon." He hit the ball up onto the green, then was rewarded with a long roll toward the cup. The ball dropped in.

"How about that? An eagle!" Art called out jubilantly, turning toward the golf cart.

Nighthorse was gone, but there was an envelope on the seat.

"Damn, Nighthorse," Art said with a chuckle. "I think you are really beginning to enjoy this spook business."

When he opened the envelope, Art found photos of Hohsen bin Hassan, and Soofah Aziz Labib, along with a brief bio of each of them. He also found a photo and bio of Sheikh Muhammad Kamal Mustafa, who was identified as the imam of the Shabihul Mosque in Nashville.

> *Although he was born in Qambari Arabia, Mustafa became a nationalized citizen ten years ago. We have no evidence that he has ever, personally, committed a criminal act against the U.S., but he remains a person of interest because of his contacts. He has met, frequently, with Hassan and Labib, and, immediately prior to the bomb that destroyed Mossenberg's airplane, the meetings were intensified.*

Art examined Mustafa's photograph. The picture reminded Art somewhat of the Ayatollah Khomeini.

Looking back in the envelope, he found electronic airline tickets for a flight leaving Ronald Reagan International Airport at seven o'clock this evening.

"Thoughtful of you, Temple, to give me time to finish my game," he said, as he started driving toward the fifth hole.

CHAPTER
TWENTY-SIX

The Shabihul Mosque in Nashville, Tennessee

Sheikh Muhammad Kamal Mustafa took the telephone call in his office. The caller was Prince Azeer Lal Qambar.

"I hope I am not disturbing you," Azeer said.

"Disturbing me? No, not at all. I am honored that you would call."

"Your American citizenship, coupled with your deep faith and commitment to convert all to Islam, makes you a valuable asset to anyone who seeks only to serve Allah."

"I am pleased that you would think so," Mustafa said.

"How are you coming along with the big operation?"

"Excuse me, *Al Sayyid*, but do you think it is wise to discuss such a thing over the telephone?"

Azeer chuckled. "You need not worry. The Americans would not dare to bug a telephone in a consulate office."

"Perhaps so," Mustafa agreed. "But, rather than go into details, I will just tell you that the plan has been put into operation, and there are two warriors for Allah who are ready to carry them out."

"That is good, that is good," Azeer said. "And it is also good that you are being careful. Especially now."

"Why especially now?"

"I believe there is a rogue element within the American government, and it might cause us trouble. Go online to the site of the *New York Chronicle*. You will find an article about the star-chamber."

"I beg your pardon?"

"The star-chamber," Azeer repeated. "It is a term that refers to vigilante justice. Read it, consider all the possibilities, and then get back to me."

"Do you believe it will require a cancelation of our plans?" Mustafa asked.

"Not a cancelation," Azeer said. "But it may well require a change. I will let you decide that."

From the New York Chronicle

THE STAR-CHAMBER IS BACK

Ever since Congress passed the U.S.A. Patriot Act, Americans have remained confused and troubled by just what laxity the law allows.

A recent poll suggests that most Americans back the idea behind the Patriot Act, which gives federal agents more latitude to spy on U.S. citizens and noncitizens while hunting terrorists. But does it go too far? Does it take away some of the freedoms it purports to defend?

The Patriot Act significantly expanded the power of the federal government by allowing the FBI and CIA to share evidence and by giving terrorism investigators access to evidence-gathering tools that agents in criminal probes have used for years. But for many people, the Patriot Act has expanded into areas never intended by the framers of the legislation. For example, does the Pentagon have the authority to seek out, identify, and then pass summary judgment on people it considers "undesirable"?

Although this is not spelled out in the Patriot Act, there is some suspicion that the Pentagon is doing just that. Senator Harriet Clayton is investigating allegations that the current administration, along with the Pentagon and Homeland Security, has resurrected the star-chamber, made infamous by the Stuart kings in the seventeenth century for arbitrary, secret proceedings with no right of appeal.

A movie, filmed in 1983, used the principle of the star-chamber to develop its plot. In the movie, a judge, disgusted with criminals escaping the judicial system via technicalities, instituted alternative methods for punishing the guilty.

That was fine as far a movie was concerned. But now there is a growing body of evidence to suggest that a star-chamber is being used to combat terrorists, or, more frighteningly, suspected terrorists. For the victims of this crusade have not had their day in court, and thus have not been able to deny their involvement. Mere accusation seems to be enough, as three suspects in recent terrorist events have turned up dead.

The body of Abdulla Balama Shamat, a rug dealer in Dallas, Texas, was discovered by one of his employees. Shamat was found nude and spread-eagled on top of a stack of rugs. His underwear was stuffed into his mouth, and a playing card, the ace of spades, was found lying on his forehead.

Last year, the young daughter of an American colonel who was serving in Qambari Arabia on the U.S. embassy staff, was raped, murdered, and found in a similar condition. It is significant that Shamat had been accused by the United States of committing the murder. However, the Qambari government insisted, after a thorough investigation, that Shamat was innocent.

The other two victims, Balli Daftar Taleb, and Azoon Jabri Shadloo, had also been accused by the U.S. government of murdering American citizens. Taleb was said to be the man who beheaded Bernie Gelb. Chillingly, Talib's decapitated body was found in his tobacco shop in Springfield, Missouri, again, in duplication of his alleged victim.

Shadloo was said to have been responsible for the bombing death of seven American children, students in the American Dependent School in Redha, Qambari Arabia. Again, in a bizarre duplication of the crime for which he was charged, Shadloo was killed in a bus bomb explosion in Alabama. In the case of Taleb and Shadloo, as was with Shamat, a playing card, the ace of spades, was found, indicating that the same person, acting as a vigilante, had killed all three.

Is the vigilante working alone, a misguided superpatriot who has it in mind to seek revenge for these crimes? Or, is he working in conjunction with the U.S. government? There are some who insist that he must be, for no single individual would have the investigative resourses to be able to locate the three men.

Some may say "good riddance" with regard to the men who were killed, despite the fact that, without trial and due process, they were found guilty and executed. But the Qambari government insists that it had investigated Shamat, Taleb, and Shadloo and found no evidence to support the charge that any of them were responsible for the deaths with which they were charged. And there are those who say that the Qambaris with their unique perspective on their own society, as well as a more liberal interrogation policy, are better able to conduct an investigation than any that could be conducted by the U.S.

Mustafa exited the Web site, then sat there for a moment drumming his fingers on the desk alongside the computer as he contemplated the article he had just read. He was convinced that the vigilante, whoever he was, was not working alone. There was no way one man could do all that, without the aid of some government agency, and if that was the case, they might well be aware of the operation he had planned.

With a sigh of resignation, Mustafa called Hassan and Labib and asked them to come see him.

"I believe we are going to have to change our plans," he said when the two men arrived.

"Why?"

Mustafa showed them the "star-chamber" article.

"Do you think this vigilante knows that we are the ones who killed Mossenberg?" Hassan asked.

"I don't know," Mustafa admitted. "But if he does know, then there is a possibility he will also know about our plans to hijack an airliner and crash it into the stadium during a football game."

"So what if he does know?" Talib asked. "How is he going to stop us?"

Mustaffa shook his head. "I don't know, but he has proven to be pretty resourceful. That is why I think we should change our plans."

"But where else can we do something that will have the same impact?"

"Don't worry about that. I have an idea," Mustafa said.

CHAPTER
TWENTY-SEVEN

Nashville International Airport, Nashville, Tennessee

Armed with a Homeland Security pass that allowed him access to every concourse and boarding gate, Art wandered around the airport. He had just bought an ice-cream cone and was eating it when his cell phone rang.

"Jensen," he said.

"It's Temple," Nighthorse said. "Are you on station?"

"Yes."

"Well, you might want to give this a listen, we just picked it up."

"All right."

There were a couple of clicks, and then Art heard a voice.

"This is Azeer."

"Begin your prayers for our martyrs at twelve noon, your time. That is the moment we will separate the infidels from the true believers."

"For the glory of Allah," Azeer said.

There was another click, and then Nighthorse came back on.

"Did you hear that?" he asked.

"Yes. Who was the person talking to Azeer?"

"That was Mustafa."

"I'm confused by the reference to twelve noon," Art said. "I thought Hassan and Labib had booked a flight for two-fourteen."

"They have. But that may have been to throw us off the path."

"That is a possibility," Art agreed. "Or, they may have changed their plans for some reason."

"Changed them, but not canceled them," Nighthorse said. "Don't forget, there is still that reference to twelve noon, and separating the infidels from the true believers."

"Twelve noon, eastern," Art said. "That's eleven o'clock here."

"Yes, well, what is happening there at eleven?"

"Nothing," Art said. "It's Sunday morning. About the only thing going on is . . ." He paused in midsentence for a moment, then said, "Church. I'll be damned. When he is talking about separating the infidels from the true believers, he has to be referring to Christians or Jews. And since today is Sunday, he's talking about Christians. They are going to bomb a church."

"What would that accomplish for them?" Nighthorse asked. "I mean, how big of an impact could that possibly have? Unless you've got a church with a couple thousand people."

"Don't forget, you are talking Nashville, Tennessee," Art said.

"You are saying there is a church that big in Nashville?"

"Oh yeah," Art replied. "The problem now is to determine which one is the biggest."

"Yes," Nighthorse answered. "And you better find out by twelve."

"By eleven, here," Art corrected. "I'd better get going." He punched off the phone before Nighthorse could even respond.

Finding a telephone bank, Art started searching through the

yellow pages for churches. He groaned when he saw that there were 460 Baptist churches alone.

Deciding that he needed help, he went to the office of the airport manager. The manager wasn't in, but his assistant was. Art showed him his Homeland Security identification.

"You don't mind if I verify that, do you, sir?" the assistant asked.

"Verify it?" Art had never had any of his special passes questioned before. "Uh, no, go ahead."

Art began thinking up excuses he could use when the pass turned out to be a fake. But, to his surprise, after tapping a few keys on his computer, the assistant looked up at him with a smile.

"It checks out fine. Mr. Jensen, my name is Travis DuPree. How may I help you?"

Art breathed a sigh of relief, and made a personal reminder to himself to thank Nighthorse for his thoroughness, next time he saw him.

"Are you a churchgoing man, Mr. Dupree?"

"What?" Dupree asked, surprised by the question.

"Church," Art repeated. "Are you a churchgoing man?"

"Well, uh, no," he said. "That is, not as often as I should. May I ask what this is all about? What does it matter whether or not I attend church?"

"That part doesn't matter," Art said. "But what does matter is whether or not you know which church is the biggest one in town."

"Oh. Well, I'm not sure," Dupree started, then stopped. "Wait, I think I know who can tell us though. I have a friend who is very active in his church."

Picking up the phone on his desk, Dupree made a telephone call.

"Stan, oh, good, you haven't left for church yet. Listen, what is the largest church in Nashville?" There was a pause, and then Dupree nodded. "Thanks, I thought it might be, that's why I called you. What? No, no particular reason. I'm just talking to a fellow here about churches, that's all. Thanks."

Hanging up the phone, Dupree looked up at Art. "The biggest church in Nashville is Christ Holiness Church of Nashville, a huge, full gospel, nondenominational Christian church. You'll find it on Church Street, fittingly enough."

"Do you know the specific address?" Art said.

"I can look it up for you," Dupree said, opening a telephone book. He looked through it for a moment, then wrote the address on a piece of paper and gave it to Art. "Do you need directions?"

"No, I'll just put this into the GPS."

"Good enough. Oh, and uh, if you don't mind my asking, why do you need to locate the largest church in Nashville?"

"No, I don't mind your asking at all," Art replied. "Thanks for you help," he added.

Dupree looked on in surprise as Art left without answering his question.

At the car rental agency, Art rented a car that had a GPS, then, getting the car, punched in the address and left the airport. According to the GPS, he had only 8.3 miles to go, and most of it would be on I-40.

Art accelerated to ninety miles per hour once he was on I-40, moving in and out of the flow of traffic, thankful that it was a Sunday and not a normal day. He almost missed exit 210-C, skidding past it, and having to back up on the shoulder. Several cars honked at him as they passed by, the horns expressing the anger of the drivers.

Art roared down the exit onto Second Avenue. This was downtown so he had to slow down considerably. Nevertheless, he covered the last mile in just over a minute, then turned onto Church Street, where he saw the church in front of him.

Christ Holiness Church was a huge church, and the traffic that had been relatively light on the interstate, and on Second Avenue, was so heavy with arriving cars that police were in front, directing traffic. Art parked in a no-parking fire zone, just across the street from the church.

One of the policemen, seeing where Art parked, blew his whistle and waved for him to move.

Art remained in place.

The policeman blew his whistle again, and waved, more urgently this time.

Art still didn't move.

The policeman came toward him, the expression on his face reflecting his anger.

"What's the matter with you, mister? Are you blind?" the officer asked. "You can't park here."

Art showed the officer his FBI ID card, confident that it, like his Homeland Security ID card, was the real thing.

The policeman looked at it, and some of his anger dissipated.

"What's going on?" he asked, handing the card back.

"We have word that one of our most-wanted may show up at this church today," Art said. "I don't want to disturb all these good folks at their worship, but I'm going to have to go in there and have a look around, and when I come back, I may need to get to the car right away."

"I don't know," the policeman said. "This is a fire safety zone."

"I'll tell you what. I'll leave a key with you. If there is a fire and you have to move the car, go ahead and do it."

The policeman thought about it for a moment, then shook his head. "No need to do that," he said. "I'm glad to work with the FBI. Go ahead."

"Thanks," Art replied.

Art crossed the street and joined the crowd. Just inside the doors were several ushers greeting the arrivals, handing out pew sheets and directing them to specific aisles.

"Damn," Art said under his breath. "How am I going to find them?"

Art's confusion stemmed from the fact that there were many Muslims in the arriving crowd of worshipers. They were wearing traditional Islamic dress, blending in with the Jews, some of whom were in traditional dress, and the Christians. In front of the church, and in the foyer, all were greeting each other.

"Welcome! Welcome! Welcome!" Bixby was calling to the arrivals. "All men and women of faith are welcome here, in this, our celebration of the universal worship of God."

Standing with the Reverend Jay Bixby were a Roman Catholic priest, a rabbi, and an iman, and they joined Bixby in extending greetings to all who came by them on their way into the church.

Art started toward the balcony.

"Here, no need to go up there," one of the ushers called. "There are still plenty of seats downstairs."

"I prefer the balcony," Art said.

The usher shrugged his shoulders. "Have it your way," he said. He held out a church bulletin. "First time here?"

"Yes."

"We'll have a reception after the service for our first-time visitors. It'll be in the Esther Room," he said, pointing. "I do hope you can come."

"Thanks," Art said, taking the bulletin and starting up the stairs to the balcony.

Art took a seat in the very front row of the balcony. From here he had a panoramic view of the entire congregation. The congregation was huge, at least four thousand or more.

Art watched as the churchgoers found seats and greeted each other. He saw children moving up and down the aisles to visit with other children, but always under the watchful eye of their parents.

For a moment Art detached himself from who and what he was. He wished, with all his being, that he could trade places with one of the people down there. How different his life would be if he could be a doctor, real estate agent, broker, automobile dealer, bank clerk, anything that approached normalcy. What a wonderful thing it would be to come to church on a Sunday, visit with your friends, go out for lunch afterward, then go home to watch a football game on television.

But that notion only lasted for a moment or two. After all, part of his job was to see to it that people like that could be people like that.

Then Art saw the two men acting suspiciously. Although they had clearly come into the church together, they spoke animatedly for a moment, pointing to various parts of the church, and then they separated, one walking up the aisle on the extreme left-hand side of the church, and the other on the right. And though there were scores, perhaps as many as one hundred, Muslims present for this ecumenical service, Art was certain, by their behavior, that this was Hohsen bin Hassan and Soofah Aziz Labib.

He watched them as the two men took their seats, each of them sitting in an aisle seat. He was even more certain he was right, when he saw the two men exchange one long glance before they sat down.

Art continued to watch them closely. When the huge choir, accompanied by an orchestra, began singing the opening hymn, the music had the effect of settling the congregation down. As the choir began singing, everyone returned to their seats, and the church grew quiet, except for the music.

The song ended, and J. Peerless Bixby stepped up to the pulpit.

"Good morning, my friends, and welcome, on this beautiful day of worship, to the Christ Holiness Church.

"My friends, if you will look around you, you will see that this auditorium is filled with people of all faiths. I urge you now, if you are a Christian, reach out to a Jew, if you are a Jew, reach out to a Muslim, if you are a Muslim, reach out to a Christian. Do this, in the sure and certain knowledge that we are all God's children.

"All around the world today there is hate and distrust. Men and women, who are God's children, are killing each other in God's name. This must stop, and, friends, let us take the first step, here, today, in Nashville, Tennessee. One hundred years, nay, one thousand years from now, let it be said that God's children united on this day in Nashville, Tennessee."

Suddenly the two men Art had been watching moved to put their plan into operation. Hassan on the left, and Labib on the right, leaped up from their seats and stood out in the aisles. Both threw off their jackets, showing that both were wearing bombs. Art recognized the bombs as the kind that he had seen in Iraq, explosives packed behind rows of nails and ball bearings. They were designed to send out hundreds of lethal pellets in order to kill as many as possible.

"*Allah Akbar!*" Hassan shouted.

"*Allah Akbar!*" Labib echoed. Labib held up a radio-controlled triggering device. Hassan had no such device, and Art realized that was by design, for the same radio wave would set off both bombs simultaneously.

Labib pushed the button on his trigger, and closed his eyes in anticipation.

"Labib! The bomb! Do it! Do it!" Hassan shouted.

By now the congregation was in a panic. Women were screaming, men were shouting, and children were crying.

Labib pushed the button on his trigger one more time, but the bombs still didn't go off. When it didn't go off this time Labib, and then Hassan, dashed up the aisle to the back of the church.

"Praise be to God!" the preacher shouted. "The bombs didn't go off!"

Breathing a sigh of relief, Art put a small electronic device back into his pocket. The bombs had not gone off because he had jammed Labib's radio, thus preventing the signal from reaching the bomb's trigger.

By now the people of the church were in a frenzied babble of shock, relief, and prayerful thankfulness. Leaving the church, Art crossed the street and got into his car, just as he saw a car peel out of one of the four large parking lots that surrounded the church. As the car pulled out into the street, he saw the driver look back toward the traffic.

The driver was Hassan.

CHAPTER
TWENTY-EIGHT

As Art followed the car through the streets of Nashville, he turned on the special scanner that was tuned to cell phone frequency. After picking up a few routine telephone calls—"Pick up a gallon of milk on your way home," and "I've got an eleven o'clock tee time"—he heard what he was listening for.

"The bombs did not go off!" Labib was saying, his voice on the edge of panic.

"Are you sure you were using the right frequency?" Art recognized this as the voice he had heard on the taped recording. This was the voice of Mustafa.

"Yes, I am sure. We tested the trigger last night, many times."

"What about batteries?" Mustafa asked. "Perhaps you need new batteries."

"No," Labib answered. "I just put new batteries in."

"You must've done something wrong," Mustafa said.

"We did nothing wrong."

"If you did nothing wrong, you would both be in paradise now," Mustafa said angrily.

"What do we do now?" Labib asked.

"It is not too late to return to our original plan," Mustafa said. "Go to the airport and take the flight as we arranged."

"I want to come there first," Labib said.

"No! Why do you wish to come here?"

"We want your blessing."

"You have my blessing."

"We want your blessing, in person. I think if we had had your blessing, we would not have failed this morning."

There was a beat of silence from Mustafa's end of the conversation.

"Very well," he said. "But come quickly. I do not want you to fail a second time."

The conversation ended, and Art continued to follow Hassan and Labib through the city. So agitated were the two men that neither of them noticed the car that was behind them.

Hassan and Labib stopped in front of a domed building. The sign in front of the building identified it as the Shabihul Mosque. Art drove on by, did a U-turn in the middle of the street, then came back and parked across the street, just as Hassan and Labib were met by a third man. Art recognized the third man as Sheikh Muhammad Kamal Mustafa. The three men went inside the mosque.

Art got out of the car, walked across the street, then stuck a playing card onto a light pole that stood at the corner of the street, just in front of the mosque. The playing card was an ace of spades.

Satisfied that the card was there to stay, Art returned to his car, started the engine, then held up the device he had used to jam the triggering signal when Labib had tried to set off the bombs.

Art made a frequency adjustment, then pressed a button.

He heard a low, but loud, thumping sound. Then he saw a flash of light, followed by a huge, billowing cloud of smoke. The front third of the mosque collapsed in on itself.

New York City

Prince Azeer Lal Qambar would be returning to Qambari Arabia a complete failure. Although he had promised to strike a blow against the Americans that would make nine-eleven pale into insignificance, he had not done so.

Azeer had also hoped to demoralize the American people. He knew what everyone in the Middle East knew, that the only hope of defeating America would come from within America itself. And he was counting on a hostile press, and a large body of American citizens who hated the current administration more than they loved their country, to form his cadre.

He had planned on Senator Harriet Clayton to carry his flag for him, and indeed, she had led the battle in the Senate, accusing the administration and the Pentagon of conducting unauthorized operations. Senator Clayton had managed to rally a lot of the press to her side, but that had not stopped the man they were now calling the Ace of Spades.

Not only was Azeer unsuccessful in further demoralizing Americans, he had to face the fact that the Ace of Spades was rallying the spirit of the entire nation. And what Azeer knew, and nobody else knew, was that the Ace of Spades, whoever he was, was dead-on with his targets. Azeer didn't know where he was getting his information, but so effective had he been that Azeer's entire cadre had been wiped out. He had not one man remaining in the team he had planned to use in carrying out his operations against America.

Now Azeer had no choice but to return home, and return home in disgrace.

"Will you be going to prayers before you return home?" Hamdi asked.

"What?" Azeer replied, jerked out of his reverie by Hamdi's question.

"Prayers, *Al Sayyid*. Will you be going to prayers before you board the plane?"

"Oh, uh, yes," Azeer said. "Yes, of course."

Although Azeer justified everything he did by attributing it to the glory of Allah, he actually had no piety in him whatever. Allah was a rallying cry, a means of convincing others to do his will. He marveled at the malleability of someone who was so weak-minded as to allow himself to be talked into committing suicide.

The funny thing was that even the most cursory reading of the Quran would show that the suicide operations being carried on by the volunteers did not actually qualify them for martyrdom. But as long as there were people who were willing to kill themselves under such false hopes, then he, and people like him, would be able to maintain power.

"Lucky for me they don't understand the Quran," Azeer said under his breath.

"I beg your pardon, Prince?" Hamdi asked.

"I was quoting the Quran, 14:1," Azeer said. "The Quran, a book which we have revealed to you so that you may lead the people from out of the darkness into the light by their Lord's leave to the path of the All-Mighty, the Praiseworthy."

"Praise be to Allah," Hamdi said.

Masjid Al-Fatiha Muhammad Mosque, New York City

Prince Azeer Lal Qambar was one of five hundred men who knelt on their prayer rugs to pray to Allah. When the prayers were over, 499 men left the mosque, while one remained behind, prostrate on his rug.

It wasn't until several minutes later that one of the clerics, noticing him, went over for a closer examination.

"Shanawani, come quickly!" the cleric called to one of the others.

"What is it, Nagib?"

"Come quickly," Nagib said, as he continued to examine the prostrate form.

Shanawani, also a cleric, joined Nagib.

"He is dead," Nagib said.

"Who is it?"

Nagib turned the body over and gasped.

"It is Prince Azeer Lal Qambar!" he said.

"What is that in his mouth?" Shanawani asked.

Nagib reached down to remove it. "It is a playing card," he said. "The ace of spades."

The home of the secretary of the army, Washington, D.C.

Secretary Giles was drinking a cup of coffee as he watched the news report on TV.

"Prince Azeer Lal Qambar was forty-three years old, the fifth son of King Jmal Naib Qambar. There were no outside marking on the body . . . but it is interesting to note that the ace of spades was sticking out of his mouth."

Giles picked up the remote and turned the TV off. In another room, he heard his wife answer the phone.

"Yes," she said. "Yes, he is here." His wife came into the den. "It's for you," she said.

"Giles."

"Did you see the news, Jordan?" a familiar voice asked.

"Yes, sir, I saw it."

"Tell me this, Jordan. Do we have an asset here? Or do we have a tiger by the tail?"

"I don't know, sir. God help me, I don't know," Jordan Giles answered.